Beneath These Ruined Walls

WHISPERS IN THE HIGHLANDS

LACI MAE WYLD

WITH

SARAH JANE KIDDELL

For My Special Scottish Lass Sarah,

You hold the kind of heart that inspired this love story, a heart that holds so much love and the fiercest kind. Love that could survive through time, through pain, through loss, and still fill those around you with warmth. I love you forever X

Contents

1610

The storm had been building all night, pressing against the stone walls like a living creature, rattling the shutters with impatient hands. The torches along the corridor guttered in the restless wind, casting wild shadows that leapt and twisted across the ancient stones of Sutherland Castle.

Isla sensed the storm long before it arrived.

She stood beside the narrow window, fingers curled against the cold sill, her breath forming faint clouds in the air. Her reflection stared back at her, pale, trembling, eyes filled with secrets.

Below, the courtyard roiled with torchlight and activity. Messengers rode hard through the gates; servants hurried to secure anything the winds might steal, and above it all, the banners of Clan Sutherland whipped like dying birds against the black sky.

But none of that was why her heart raced.

No, her pulse quickened for only one reason.

He was coming.

She felt him before she heard the distant echo of boots on stone, a thrum beneath her skin, warmth spreading through her chest, the unmistakable pull of him. The bond between them was something she could never name aloud, not in a world that would burn them both for it.

The door opened silently.

Lachlan stepped into the room as if a storm had shaped itself into a man, tall, broad-shouldered, dark hair pulled back in a leather cord, gray eyes storm-bright and fixed on her as if she were the only point of light left in the world.

His presence filled the chamber, filled her, spreading through every breath she took.

"Isla," His voice was low, roughened by urgency and something deeper, something that made her knees weaken.

She turned to him slowly, though her heart had leapt toward him the moment he entered. "You cannae be here."

"Aye, I ken," he murmured, closing the door behind him. "But I'll no' leave ye alone tonight."

He crossed the room in three strides, the scent of horses and rain clinging to him, the heat of his body reaching her before he touched her. But even without contact, she felt him, felt his longing, his restraint stretched thin, his fear hidden beneath the fierceness of his gaze.

"Yer trembling," he said softly.

"I'm not." The denial shook. She hated that he noticed everything. Hated, and needed it more than breath.

Lachlan lifted a hand, stopping just short of touching her cheek. His fingers hovered in the space between them, as if the air itself resisted their separation.

"Ye been crying," he said.

She swallowed. "Ye still cannae be here. If ma Da...if Hamish..."

His jaw tightened at the name. "If Hamish comes within ten steps of this room, the storm outside will seem gentle beside what I'll do."

Her breath hitched. Lachlan rarely spoke with such cold certainty. He was gentle with her, always, but the warrior in him was never far away.

"Isla, dinna fash," he said, voice dropping lower. "They can lock me in the cellar, send me to war, bind me in chains...but I will always find ma way back to ye."

Her composure cracked she looked away, blinking rapidly. "I wish ye hadn't come tonight."

"That's no' what yer heart's saying."

Thunder rolled across the sky, shaking the very stones she leaned on. Her breath trembled as he finally touched her, his fingertips brushing her jaw, tilting her face toward him. The storm outside was nothing compared to the one inside her.

His forehead touched hers, a single intimate point of connection that set her trembling all the way down to her fingertips.

"Tell me," he whispered, "and I'll leave. One word. Tell me you dinna want me, Isla."

Her lips parted. No sound came.

He exhaled like a man who had just found treasure, his thumb brushing her cheekbone. "I thought so."

Her hands rose without her meaning them to, gathering in the fabric of his shirt, pulling him closer until her body found the familiar shape of his. The warmth of him poured into her like fire. He bowed his head, lips grazing her temple.

"Lachlan..."Her voice broke on his name.

"Ayre, mo chridhe?"

Before she could answer, another thunderclap shook the room, but this one came from inside the castle.

A door slamming.

Boots pounding.

Raised voices.

Lachlan stiffened, instinct sharpening his features, the warrior flaring fully to life. His hand went to the knife at his belt, while his other arm tightened around her.

"They're coming," she whispered, dread coiling tight in her stomach.

His eyes darkened, fierce and unyielding. "Let them. I'll no' surrender ye to anyone...not even fate itself."

The shouts grew louder. Someone yelled Lachlan's name with fury.

Isla clutched him, terror rising. "Ye must go. Please."

But he didn't move.

He pressed a kiss to her forehead, slow, reverent, full of love that spanned far beyond their lifetimes.

“Remember this,” he said fiercely. “No matter what comes. Even if they tear ma from yer side…even if death stands between us…”

He lifted her chin, and for a moment, the storm went silent.

“I will find ye again.”

The door shuddered as someone slammed against it from the other side.

Isla’s breath caught.

Lachlan’s last whisper brushed her lips, a promise bound in blood and eternity. She pulled him closer; their lips crashed together with need and desire.

“Across every lifetime, Isla. Yer mo chriḍe, and I am yers,” he said between kisses.

“Aye, always my love.” she promised him back.

The door burst open.

And the world fell apart.

CHAPTER 1

The Castle That Remembers

The radiator hisses, a dying snake in the corner of the room. It offers no heat, only noise. I press my palm against the peeling wallpaper, half expecting the dampness to seep through my skin and into my marrow. Dornoch is grayer than the postcards promised. It is a gray that eats light, swallowing the afternoon sun until only a bruised twilight remains.

I unzip my suitcase. My clothes smell like Boston. Like stale coffee and the detergent Murray liked, the cheap stuff that made my skin itch. I shove a sweater to the bottom of the drawer, burying the scent. I am here to forget him. I am here to forget the way he looked at her, his colleague, with eyes that had once promised me the world.

My hands shake. Just a tremor, barely visible, but I feel it in the tendons. I reach for the guidebook on the bedside table. Sutherland Castle: A History of Blood and Stone. The cover is glossy, mocking the ruin it depicts with saturated colors that don't exist in this landscape. My fingers brush the title. A static shock snaps against my thumb. I recoil, dropping the book. It lands face up. The stone tower on the cover seems to lean forward, looming.

There is something wrong with me. I have felt it since the plane touched down in Inverness. A vibrating frequency in my teeth. A tightening behind my eyes. I blame the jet lag. I blame the gin I drank at the airport bar to numb the voice in my head that sounds suspiciously like my mother, telling me I run away from everything hard.

I move to the window. The glass is cold, weeping condensation. I wipe a circle clear with my sleeve.

There it is.

Sutherland Castle. It sits on the jagged ridge like a broken tooth. Even from this distance, through the veils of drifting mist, it commands the valley. It is ugly. It is beautiful. It is a scar on the landscape that refuses to heal.

I stare, and the room behind me ceases to exist. My doctoral research, the dissertation on Celtic migration patterns, the academic rationalizations for this trip—they all dissolve. There is only the ruin.

It pulls at me. Not a gentle tug, but a hook in the gut. A physical demand. 'Come.'

"Stop it," I whisper. My breath fogs the glass, obscuring the castle. I wait for the fog to fade. When the stone shape re-emerges, the pull snaps tight again.

I shouldn't go yet. I should sleep. My eyes feel packed with sand, and my body aches from twelve hours in economy class. But the idea of lying in that narrow bed, staring at the water-stained ceiling, makes my chest constrict. If I sleep, I will dream. And lately, the dreams are teeth and blood and falling.

I grab my jacket. It's my father's leather one, oversized and smelling of old tobacco. I wrap it around me like armor. I need to be near the stones. I need to touch them. It is an itch I cannot scratch, a thirst that water won't quench.

The air outside is aggressive. It slaps my cheeks, wet and biting. I bury my chin in my scarf and start walking. Dornoch is quiet. The town seems to be holding its breath, huddled against the encroaching dark. The few locals I pass—a man loading crates into a van, a woman walking a terrier—watch me. Their eyes are sharp, measuring. They know I don't belong. I am too loud in my silence, too bright in my muted clothes.

I keep my head down, following the road as it twists upward. The wind picks up, howling through the glen. It sounds like a voice. A lament. 'Isla... Isla... '

My name is Fiona. I tell myself this. 'Fiona. Fi.'

But the wind doesn't care.

The road turns to gravel, then to beaten earth. The incline steepens. My boots slip on the wet grass, but I push harder, my lungs burning with the intake of cold oxygen. The rhythm of my steps beats a cadence against the ground. Thud, thud, thud. Closer.

I round the final bend, and the ground levels out.

The castle rises before me. It is immense. Photographs lied about the scale of it. The walls are not just stone; they are a geology of grief. Moss clings to the granite like velvet bruises. The main keep is shattered, the roof long gone, leaving the interior exposed to the weeping sky.

I stop. The wind whips my hair across my face, blinding me for a second. I brush the strands away.

A sign near the rusted iron gate reads: Guided Tours: 3 PM.

I check my watch. Three minutes to the hour. Fate, or something darker.

I am trembling again. not from cold. It feels like standing next to a high-voltage line. The air hums. The silence here is not empty; it is full. It is waiting.

I walk toward the small huddle of people near the gatehouse. They look trivial against the backdrop of the ruin. Bright synthetic jackets. Cameras. Safety. I am not safe. I step into the shadow of the archway, and the temperature drops ten degrees.

I am here. And God help me, it feels like coming home to a house that burned down with me inside it.

"Welcome to the seat of the Sutherland clan."

The guide's voice is a practiced instrument, projecting over the wind without strain. She introduces herself as Mrs. Moira MacPherson. No relation to me, likely, though the name is common enough in these parts. She wears a quilted vest and sensible shoes, and she looks at the ruins the way a mother looks at a delinquent child—with affection and exasperation.

"The structure ye see today dates largely from the fifteenth century," Moira says, gesturing with a hand that has seen hard work. "Though foundations from the twelve hundreds lie beneath us."

The group shuffles forward. There are six of them. A couple in matching yellow raincoats, holding hands. A man with a camera lens long enough to be a weapon. Two women who look cold and bored. And me.

I trail at the back. I don't want to hear about dates. I don't care about architectural periods or the defensive capabilities of the curtain wall. I care about the stone.

I reach out and press my fingertips to the rough masonry of the gatehouse tunnel. It is slick with damp, freezing against my skin. But beneath the cold, there is a pulse. A low thrum, like a heartbeat slowed to a geological pace.

Thump... thump...

"Careful on the flagstones," Moira calls out, her voice echoing. "They've shifted over the centuries. We've had ankles turned before."

We emerge into the inner courtyard. It is a graveyard of a room, the ceiling the gray belly of the clouds. Grass grows between the pavers. To my left, the remains of the Great Hall stand like ribs of a skeleton picked clean.

Moira launches into a story about a royal visit in 1508. I stop listening. My feet move on their own accord. They know where to go. The group moves toward the kitchens, but I drift toward the shadows of the Great Hall.

The light is different here. It struggles to penetrate the gloom, filtered through narrow arrow loops and crumbling arches. The air smells of wet earth and iron. It smells like blood that has dried and turned to dust centuries ago.

I walk deeper into the hall. The sounds of the tour—the shutter clicks, Moira's rhythmic patter—begin to fade. They sound muffled, as if I am underwater. The world narrows down to the sound of my boots on the stone and the roar of blood in my ears.

My hand trails along the wall. I find a groove in the stone, a scar from a blade or a musket ball. My finger fits into it perfectly.

A chill washes over me. Not the wind. This is a stillness. A vacuum. The birds have stopped singing. The wind has stopped howling. The silence presses against my eardrums, heavy and absolute.

I stop. The hair on my arms stands up. I am being watched.

I turn slowly, my heart hammering against my ribs.

Across the expanse of the ruined hall, under the shadow of a broken archway, a man stands.

He is not a tourist. He is not a reenactor. He is too still. He leans against the stone as if he supports the weight of the ruin himself.

He is tall, broad-shouldered, a silhouette cut from the darkness. He wears the belted plaid, the heavy wool gathering at his shoulder, darker than the stone. The fabric is rough, stained with mud and age. A wide leather belt cinches his waist, and the hilt of a dirk glints dully in the low light.

He does not move. He does not breathe. He is like a statue carved from granite and regret.

My breath catches in my throat, a sharp intake that tastes of rain.

He looks up.

The distance between us collapses. His eyes find mine instantly, as if he has been waiting for me to turn around. Even from here, I can see they are blue—a piercing, impossible blue, like glacial ice.

He does not blink. He does not smile. He studies me with a terrifying intensity. It is a gaze that strips away my leather jacket, my jeans, my skin. He looks at me and sees the marrow. He sees the nightmares. He sees the girl who ran away from Boston.

I cannot look away. I am pinned by his stare, a butterfly on a board.

My rational mind, the part of me that holds a master's degree and corrects people's grammar, screams that this is impossible. He is a hallucination. A trick of the light and stress.

But my blood knows better. My blood sings a recognition that terrified me.

Him.

The word rises from the depths of my subconscious, unbidden. *Him.*

He is the reason the wind called. He is the reason the book burned my hand.

He pushes off the wall. The movement is fluid, predatory. The silence in the hall stretches, pulling tight until it is ready to snap.

Time bends. It warps around us, pulling the gray afternoon into a tight, suffocating knot. There is only the man in the archway and the space between us—a chasm filled with centuries of dead air.

My heart strikes my ribs, a frantic bird trapped in a cage. Thud-thud. Thud-thud. It is the only sound in the universe.

He straightens. The casual lean vanishes, replaced by a tension that coils through his frame. He squares his shoulders. It is a warrior's stance. Alert. Ready. He looks at me not as a stranger, but as a problem he has been trying to solve for a lifetime. There is anger in the set of his jaw, but beneath it, something more devastating. Hunger.

He knows me. The realization hits me like a physical blow. He knows me. Not Fi MacPherson from Boston. Not the tourist. He knows the thing inside me that I can’t name.

Heat floods my skin. It starts at my toes and races upward, a flush of fever that mocks the damp chill of the castle. My hands hang useless at my sides. I should run. I should turn and scream for Ms. MacPherson.

I don't. I take a step toward him.

His eyes widen slightly. A flicker of shock, or perhaps pain. The blue of his iris burns, bright and cold. He shifts his weight, his hand drifting instinctively to the hilt of the weapon at his waist.

"Isla?"

The whisper does not come from his lips. It echoes inside my skull, a thought that isn't mine. It tastes like ash.

I open my mouth. To say what? Who are you? Why do you hurt to look at?

Something hard slams into my shoulder.

"Oh! Sorry, love! Didn't see you standing there."

The world crashes back in. The silence shatters like glass. The wind howls. The chatter of the tourists rushes into my ears.

I stumble sideways, catching my balance on a slick flagstone. It's the woman in the yellow raincoat. She is smiling apologetically, adjusting her hood. "Terrible footing in here, isn't it? Nearly twisted my ankle."

I blink, disoriented. The heat in my blood turns to ice water. "I... it's fine."

I turn back to the archway.

Empty.

The space where he stood is vacant. Just gray stone and shadow.

"No." The word scrapes my throat.

I push past the woman, stumbling over the uneven ground. I run to the arch. I have to verify it. I have to know.

I reach the spot where he was. The stone is rough under my palm. It should be cold. It should be freezing like the rest of the castle.

It is warm.

A faint, residual heat radiates from the granite, as if a body had been pressed against it moments ago. The air still holds a scent—sharp and metallic and old leather.

I spin in a circle, scanning the ruins. "Where did he go?"

The woman in yellow stares at me. "Who, dear?"

"The man. The man in the plaid. He was just here." My voice rises, shrill and frantic. I sound crazy. I know I sound crazy.

She frowns, exchanging a look with her husband. "We're the only ones here, love. Just the group."

I look at the wall again. The warmth is fading, leeched away by the biting wind.

He is gone. Vanished into the masonry, into the mist.

"Folks? If we could move along to the solar!" Moira's voice drifts from the next chamber, cheerful and oblivious.

The tourists shuffle away, casting wary glances at me. The crazy American girl talking to walls.

I stand there for a heartbeat longer. My skin still prickles, sensing him. He is not gone. He is simply... elsewhere. Watching. Waiting.

I hug my father's jacket tighter around my chest. The pull is stronger now. It is no longer just an attraction; it is a tether.

I turn and follow the group, but I look back over my shoulder. The empty archway yawns like a mouth, dark and hungry.

I saw you, I think, casting the words into the shadows.

And the shadows, I am certain, smile back.

CHAPTER 2
Night Visions

I could barely recall the walk back to the bed-and-breakfast. My mind was fixated on the ruined archway I'd left behind, on the thick blackness pooling just beyond its stones, an absence of light that felt like a living thing, heavy and patient. Though my boots sloshed with wet muck and each step left a smear on the flagstones, I have no memory of opening the B&B's heavy wooden door or climbing the narrow stairs to my room. All I remember is standing before a lock, my fingers trembling as I fitted the key, then collapsing onto the edge of the bed, still dressed in coat and boots. My heart hammered so fiercely I thought it might tear free from my ribs.

The house was quiet, as though it had been emptied of inhabitants and left to endure only its own old bones creaking in the draft. I lay on top of the covers, boots kicked off somewhere among the folds of the quilt, and stared at the wallpapered ceiling. My skin felt two degrees colder than it ought to be, yet despite the chill a strange heat glowed in my cheeks, like I'd stepped straight into bright sunlight. I closed my eyes and suddenly saw him again: that man's brutal stare, the fierce curve of his mouth, the chill blue of a Highlander's gaze. My body floated above the mattress, detached and light, and I had no idea how long I remained like that, suspended between consciousness and something else. Eventually, the western windows slid into night, and the room's hush deepened. All I could think of were those impossible eyes.

When my stomach grumbled in protest, I rose and went downstairs to dinner. I found a solitary table in a corner of the dining room, sat in its high-backed chair, and ate mechanically. The beef stew was warm and savory, but each bite tasted flat, as though a piece of me lingered back in that ruined arch, unreachable and unmoved by gravy or crusty bread. I felt hollow—a vast emptiness yawning in my chest, like the night sky between the stars. I recognized that feeling, or thought I did: the ache that had hollowed me out the day I caught Murray in the arms of that undergraduate, the sick panic of realizing someone I loved could betray me so casually. But this emptiness felt older, stranger. I finished my meal, paid without thought, then trudged back up the creaking stairs to my room.

Sleep was elusive. I lay wide-eyed beneath the covers, listening to the settling house: floorboards whispering, wind rattling the window panes, the boiler ticking through the thin walls. When sleep finally came, it betrayed me in fits and starts. I would drift off only to jolt awake, drenched in sweat, heart pounding so hard I suspected the neighbors must hear it. I lost track of how many times I counted the hours until, at last, the fragmented night fractured completely. I slipped between slumber and something else, and then the bed, the ceiling, and the wallpaper dissolved into a new reality.

The rain pelts my skin through the thin fabric of my gown, each drop a cold shock against flushed skin. I stand beneath a gnarled oak, its branches offering scant shelter as rivulets stream down my face and neck. He materializes from the mist-shrouded field, his approach deliberate, eyes never leaving mine. "Isla," he murmurs, his voice rough with tenderness, "look at ye, yer drookit lassie." The words roll from his tongue like music. His calloused hands find my waist, drawing me against the solid heat of him. "Gie's a bosie," he whispers, and I melt into his embrace, the rain forgotten as his finger tilts my chin upward, his mouth hovering a breath away from mine.

And then the dream changes.

I stood in a corridor—no longer a ruin of crumbling stones, but a polished passage in some ancient keep. Torch sconces cast wavering amber light on flagstone floors covered with fresh-cut rushes, their damp, sweet fragrance heavy in the air. The ceiling arched gracefully overhead, beams of pine oozing sticky resin. Smoke curled around the torches, so thick it burned the back of my throat. I looked down and saw I wore a gown of deep blue wool, the bodice structured like a snug vest, sleeves of starched white linen tightening at my wrists. My hands were small and pale, ringless. I felt a heartbeat thudding inside my chest that was not mine, a frantic, rabbit-caught-in-a-snare rhythm.

A cold draft rushed past me from behind, carrying a sharp tang of rain and the musty scent of animal hides. I knew I was not alone. Somewhere ahead, footsteps thudded against the stone floor—silent, predatory. I did not feel fear; instead, something ancient and familiar stirred within me, urging me forward, pulling me toward that footstep-marked warning.

I turned a corner, breath stuttering, and there he stood. The Highlander blocked the corridor with a single confident step. Torchlight danced across his face, softening the cruelty I'd glimpsed earlier. His jawline was firm, lips pressed into a line of both steel and longing, his eyes—no longer the stark, icy blue I'd seen that morning at the archway—now bore a stormy slate hue that promised drowning. My heart lurched violently. I tried to retreat, but his long, strong arm shot out and spun me toward the wall. I crashed against cold, limewashed stone, and the icy damp seeped through my dress.

He was taller than I remembered. His dark hair fell wild around his shoulders, every strand catching glints of firelight. A tartan plaid, unmistakably Sutherland blue and green, was draped over his broad frame. A battered leather belt cinched a kilt low on his hips, the sheath of a dirk dangling at his side. I wanted to study every thread of his plaid, every scar etched into his skin, but his body pinned mine against the wall, and all coherent thought dissolved beneath the press of him.

His breath, hot with peat smoke and sweat, ghosted across my cheek. My senses snapped to attention: earth and heather, raw animal heat, the faintest tang of iron. One callused hand circled my waist, digging into the thin wool of my gown, pressing me flat. His skin should have been cold against stone, but it was scorchingly warm, alive. I parted my lips, tried to say his name, but no sound came. Then I realized: I didn't know his name. The realization jolted me from within, this could be a dream, but why did it feel so real?

His lips brushed the shell of my ear, voice like gravel and silk. "Do ye remember me?" he murmured.

I wanted to answer yes, to claim him as memory, but also no, to deny this impossible meeting. The truth lay tangled between then and now: I remembered him from the tour, but my soul stirred with echoes of a love that outlived centuries. I remembered how he fit around me, the fierce claiming of our bodies pressed tight in corridors exactly like this one. But I remembered too the ache that followed, a pain I could not name, a wound that never fully healed.

Instinctively, I pressed my hands to his chest. The linen of his shirt was damp with sweat, and beneath it I felt a heart pounding, thundering in exact harmony with mine. The certainty of our shared pulse anchored me, and I clung to him—half to steady myself, half in defiance of the storm that threatened to claim me whole. His mouth found mine, first demanding, then slow and tentative, as though he weighed every touch against a sorrow too vast for one night's longing.

When he finally broke the kiss, his forehead rested against mine. "Ye said ye'd come back to me," he whispered, voice thick with longing and something darker.

I tasted salt—my tears or his, I couldn't tell. My mouth moved, shaping an answer that sounded like both a confession and a question. But before words could form, a heavy boot sounded on the stairwell, keys jangling. The Highlander's head snapped up. He caught me by the shoulders and steered me into the nearest alcove. We pressed chest to chest in the dim recess, hidden behind shadows. Footsteps passed by—indifferent to our stolen moment. I could feel his pulse beneath my palm, strong and fierce.

He bent to me again, sealing his need to my mouth in a kiss that burned hotter than any torch flame. This time, I did not resist. I gave in to the fall and the landing, all at once. His hand slid up to the hollow of my throat, thumb grazing skin so bare I shivered. I gasped, hips shifting with unbidden desire, as his body answered mine, crouching between urgent need and the gravity of what we once were.

He spoke my name then, not a pet form or an echo, but the one true name woven into my soul: "Isla," he breathed, each syllable cutting through me bright and cruel. In those syllables lay an entire past, every stolen moment, every tear cried in the dark.

The corridor's stones fractured and melted away. White light flooded me, and I found myself falling—hands flailing—until I landed, mattress-first, in a crushing gasp. I woke as though thrown ashore by a violent tide, body convulsing, arms clutching the bedding. My throat ached from holding a scream that never escaped; my limbs trembled so that my joints felt ready to snap.

Darkness swarmed around me. The room was silent except for the incessant pounding in my ears. I lay there, breath coming in ragged gasps, the memory of his hands and voice reverberating through my veins stronger than my own heartbeat. I needed an anchor, something tangible to prove I was in this room and not that corridor. My eyes strained to adjust. The only light came from the red digits of the clock on the nightstand: 3:17 AM. Its glow painted bruised red patches on the floral wallpaper.

I lay still, willing my mind to steady, but the warmth of him—his chest under my palms, the press of his mouth—lingered as real as the quilt beneath me. My body felt as though it was still pressed against cold stone, and the scratch of wool brushed my neck even though I lay tangled in cotton sheets.

Summoning courage, I tried to sit up. The room tipped sharply, then righted itself, as if protesting the motion. The corridor echoed in my mind, damp and musty, so vivid I could almost taste the smoke. I blinked hard, trying to dispel the mist of sleep. And then I saw him.

He stood in the far corner, by the curtained window, not a wisp of shadow nor a trick of streetlight, but a figure solid as carved wood. He was there, kilt pleats heavy around his legs, shoulders squared, arms folded—watching. Every angle of his face was etched in my memory: the hooked nose, the slash of a healed cut along his cheekbone, the set of his mouth in that infuriating line of longing and reproach. But his eyes—those storm-slate eyes—burned colorless in the gloom, drilling into me with a heat that had no place in this ordinary room at this late hour.

I froze. A tremor started deep in my belly and rose until it rattled my bones. I wanted to speak, to demand why he was there, but my tongue lay paralyzed. We regarded each other across the distance of a few feet, and the stillness felt thicker than the corridor's smoke. Time stretched; the clock ticked over to 3:18 in absolute silence, yet I felt each second pulse through me.

The air warped around him, shimmering like a heat mirage. He tilted his head, a small motion that sent a wave of longing through me so fierce my lungs constricted. I fumbled with my nightstand, fingertips grazing the lamp's base, searching for something, anything to prove he wasn't real. The lamp switch clicked, and incandescent light exploded, drilling into my corneas. I squinted, arms raised in instinctive defense.

And then—nothing. The corner was empty.

My heart slammed against my ribs so hard I thought I might collapse. I scanned the room under brutal lamplight: the drab wallpaper, the floral patterns washed out; the dresser mirror reflecting only me, wide-eyed and pale; the window, locked tight. The door behind me remained chained. No sign of him: no footprints in the threadbare rug, no displaced dust, no echoes of boot leather on the linoleum.

I pressed my palm to the door, leaning back, breath shallow. The room still quivered with residue—some electrical charge that hummed against my skin. The clock glared 3:18, unflinching. My legs trembled so heavily I slid down until I sat on the floor, back against the wood panel. My head lolled to one side, and I stared at the door frame, panting.

I had to tell myself it was a nightmare, a dream-scar born of exhaustion and the dark anxiety that had followed me all day. But nightmares ended with relief at waking. This left me hollow and wanting—and worse, convinced that I had not been dreaming.

Gently, I pressed my fingertips to the side of my neck, expecting to feel his pulse still pounding there. Nothing but my own rapid heartbeat, wild and uneven. My entire body tingled, as if I lay atop a web of electricity that he'd spun. The memory of his hands, his breath, the way he had said "Isla"—they pressed around me so tightly I feared I might suffocate beneath their weight.

I curled into myself on the cold linoleum, eyes fixed on the corner where he'd stood. The lamp flickered once, then burned steady. The house was quiet again, but my nerve endings remained ablaze. Why did his absence hurt so much? Why did it feel as though a part of me had been taken, a fissure ripped open in the night air?

Outside, a train whistle called from somewhere distant. The sound resonated through the walls, and I thought I heard, beneath its mournful wail, a faint echo of his voice: "Do ye remember me?"

I shut my eyes tightly, pressing my palms over them as if to hold back ghosts. The night stretched on, and I sat unmoving until the first pale glow of dawn crept between the curtains. Even then, I could not rouse myself from that curdled space between remembering and forgetting. My body remained slumped against the door, the quilt's warmth forgotten on the bed, as I waited for the world to make sense again. But it never would—not entirely—because I knew now that some things refuse to be left behind in the dark.

CHAPTER 3
The Past Reaches Me

The bell above the door jingles, a cheerful, artificial sound that grates against my nerves. I step into The Highland Heart, a gift shop that smells aggressively of lavender sachets and synthetic wool. The warmth inside is stifling. It presses against my face, trying to suffocate the cold that has settled in my marrow since yesterday.

I move through the aisles like a ghost. My fingers brush against stacks of mass-produced tartan scarves—reds and greens too bright to be natural. They feel scratchy, cheap. Not like the heavy, rough wool of the plaid I saw in the ruin. Not like the fabric that smelled of peat and rain.

A woman near the counter holds up a silver brooch. "Look, Donald," she says. "It's a Celtic knot. For protection."

I turn away. The silver is shiny, untarnished. It has no history. It has no teeth.

I am looking for him.

I hate myself for it, but my eyes are constantly trawling the space, dissecting the crowd. A tall man in a dark coat enters. My heart lurches, slamming against my ribs. I hold my breath, waiting for the turn of his head, the flash of those impossible blue eyes.

He turns. He is forty, perhaps, with soft features and glasses that fog up in the warmth. He looks nothing like the warrior.

The disappointment is a physical ache, a hollow scoop in my gut. I let my breath go and force my feet to move.

I leave the shop. The street outside is gray, the stone buildings of Dornoch huddling together against the wind. I walk without destination. I find myself in the local museum, a small building that was once a schoolhouse. The floorboards creak under my boots. It is quiet here, save for the rhythmic dripping of a radiator.

Glass cases line the walls, filled with the detritus of lives long ended. Rusted farming tools. A cracked tea set. A pair of child's leather shoes, worn at the toes.

I stop in front of a display of weaponry. A basket-hilted broadsword hangs suspended by fishing line. It is pitted with rust, dead metal. I stare at it, trying to imagine it in a hand. His hand.

"Are ye finding everything alright?"

I jump. An elderly volunteer sits in the corner, knitting a shapeless gray square. Her eyes are watery and kind.

"Yes," I say. My voice sounds brittle. "Do you have anything on the Sutherland clan? Specifically... early seventeenth century?"

She shakes her head, clicking her needles. "Not much from that time, dear. The fire in the castle record room took most of the papers in eighteen-hundred. We have some Victorian sketches in the back."

"No. Thank you."

I walk out before she can ask me why I am trembling.

The afternoon drags its belly across the sky. I retreat to a tea shop near the square to escape the biting wind. The place is cluttered with mismatched china and smells of yeast. I order tea and a scone because that is what tourists do.

The scone sits on the plate, a lump of dough and raisins. I pick at it, reducing it to crumbs without bringing a single piece to my lips. My reflection in the dark window is pale, my eyes too wide, underlined by bruises of exhaustion. I look like I am recovering from a fever. Perhaps I am.

I pull my phone from my pocket. The screen glows, a harsh blue light that hurts my eyes. I type 'Sutherland Castle history' for the hundredth time.

...built in the 14th century... stronghold of the Earls of Sutherland... ghost stories...

I scroll past the dry facts. I need a name. I need a face. I need confirmation that I am not losing my mind.

...local legends speak of a curse involving two brothers...

My thumb hovers. The signal is weak, the loading circle spinning endlessly.

A man walks past the window outside. Broad shoulders. Dark hair tied back.

I drop the phone. It clatters onto the saucer, splashing tea onto the tablecloth. I scramble out of my chair, ignoring the waitress's startled look, and rush to the door. I push out into the street, the cold air slapping me awake.

I look left, then right.

The street is empty. Just a cat sitting on a doorstep, washing its paw.

I stand there, gripping the door handle, feeling foolish and desperate. The wind tugs at my hair, whispering things I can't quite catch. I am chasing shadows. I am haunting a town that doesn't want me, looking for a man who died four hundred years ago.

Slowly, I go back inside. The waitress is wiping up the spilled tea.

"Sorry," I whisper.

I sit down and stare at the crumbs on my plate. My hand shakes as I reach for the cup. The ceramic rattles against the saucer. I am not hungry. I am starving, but not for food.

The sun dies behind the hills, leaving a stain of purple bruised across the horizon. I return to the B&B. The hallway smells of floor wax and old dust. My key turns in the lock with a rusty complaint, and I push the door open.

The room is exactly as I left it. The bed is made, the pillows fluffed, the curtains drawn.

But it is not empty.

I stand on the threshold, my hand gripping the frame. The air inside is still, suspended. It feels charged, like the moments before a thunderstorm breaks, when the ozone is sharp enough to taste.

I step inside and close the door. I turn the deadbolt. Then I slide the chain across. The metal rattle sounds loud in the quiet. It is a useless gesture. Chains keep out thieves. They do not keep out memories. They do not keep out ghosts.

I move through the room, avoiding the corner near the window. I can feel it, though. A cold spot. A void where the light bends wrong. I strip off my layers—the leather jacket, the scarf, the sweater that smells of the gift shop's lavender.

The shower is hot. I scrub my skin until it turns pink, trying to wash away the day's frustration, trying to warm the cold that lives under my ribs. The water pounds against the tiles, a steady drumbeat. I close my eyes, and for a second, I smell heather and woodsmoke.

I snap my eyes open. Just steam. Just soap.

I dry off and pull on a t-shirt and cotton shorts. The fabric feels abrasive. My skin is overly sensitive, every nerve ending exposed and vibrating.

I stand before the mirror. The glass is fogged. I wipe a circle clear, just as I did with the window yesterday. My face stares back—eyes dilated, lips pale. I look like prey.

I turn off the bathroom light and step back into the bedroom.

The lamp on the nightstand casts a yellow pool of light that barely reaches the corners. I stand by the bed, my gaze dragged inevitably to the window. To the spot.

There is nothing there. Just the peeling wallpaper and the shadows cast by the wardrobe.

"Show yourself," I whisper.

The silence answers. The radiator clanks once, then falls quiet.

I climb into bed. The sheets are stiff, starched too heavily. They rustle as I pull them up to my chin. I reach out and click off the lamp.

Darkness rushes in, immediate and total.

I lie on my back, rigid as a corpse. My eyes strain against the black, waiting for them to adjust. Waiting for the gray outline of a shoulder, the glint of a dirk.

My heart beats a frantic rhythm against the mattress. *Come back. Stay away. Come back.*

I don't know which I mean.

I close my eyes. Sleep is a dangerous country tonight. I know he is waiting there. I know that if I drift off, I will not be alone. The fear should keep me awake, but the exhaustion is a tide I cannot swim against. It pulls at my ankles. It drags me down.

The room settles. The house breathes around me, timber settling, pipes groaning.

I wait. My body is a bowstring, pulled tight, ready to snap.

The darkness does not lift; it changes texture. The starch of the B&B sheets dissolves into the rough bite of stone against my spine. The air drops twenty degrees. It smells of damp earth and iron.

I am not in bed. I am standing in a narrow passage, pressed into the shadows.

He is here.

He does not approach; he is simply there, filling the space, a wall of heat and hardness in the gloom. The moonlight slicing through the arrow loop catches the angle of his jaw, the savage line of his throat.

Lachlan.

The name rises in my throat, a bubble of blood and breath. I do not speak it. I cannot.

He moves with terrifying speed. One moment he is watching me, the next his body slams into mine, pinning me against the rough masonry. The impact drives the air from my lungs in a sharp gasp.

"Isla."

His voice is a growl, vibrating through his chest and into mine. It is not a question this time. It is a claim.

His hands are on me. They are huge, rough with calluses, desperate. One tangles in my hair, tilting my head back, exposing the arch of my throat. The other slides down my waist, gripping my hip with bruising force. The layers of my dream-clothing—linen, wool—mean nothing to him. He bunches the fabric in his fist, hiking it up, seeking skin.

I should be afraid. This is violence. This is a ghost assaulting me in the dark.

But my body does not know fear. It knows him.

I arch into him. My hands fly to his shoulders, gripping the heavy plaid, digging my fingers into the muscle beneath. A whimper tears itself from my throat—half sob, half plea.

He buries his face in the crook of my neck. His stubble grazes my skin, raw friction that sends fire racing through my veins. He bites down, gently, then harder, on the sensitive cord of muscle.

"Mine," he breathes against my skin. The word is hot, wet. "Always mine."

His hand slides higher, sliding beneath the hem of my shift. His fingers are calloused, rough as sandstone, but his touch is reverent. He maps the curve of my thigh, the dip of my hip. Every inch of skin he grazes ignites. It is a remembering. My body recalls the weight of his hand here.

He finds the center of me.

I gasp, my head falling back against the stone wall. The sensation is blinding. It is white light in a dark room. He is relentless, his fingers moving with a warrior's precision and a lover's knowledge. He knows exactly how I break.

"Lachlan," I moan. The sound echoes in the stone corridor, scandalous and loud.

He swallows the sound with his mouth. His lips crush mine, tasting of desperation. He kisses me like he is drowning, like I am the only air left in the world. I taste salt. I taste metal.

I wrap my legs around his waist, pulling him closer, needing to eliminate the space between us. I need to be ruined by him. I need to be consumed.

The stone bites into my back. The cold drafts swirl around my bare legs. But the heat between us is a furnace. He presses his hips against mine, the ridge of his desire hard and demanding against my belly. The friction is maddening.

"I have waited," he murmurs against my mouth, his breath mingling with mine. "God, Isla, I have waited so long."

He shifts, his hand working between us, guiding, preparing.

I am open. I am unguarded. I am his. The boundaries of who I am—Fi MacPherson, doctoral student, Bostonian—dissolve. I am only flesh and need and an ancient, aching love.

When he pushes inside, the world fractures. It is not pain, but a fullness so absolute it feels like dying. We move together, a frantic, ancient rhythm. Stone and skin. Ice and fire.

I am falling. I am flying.

"Look at me," he commands.

I force my eyes open. His gaze burns into mine, blue fire in the darkness. He sees me. He sees all of me.

"Stay," he whispers.

The climax hits me like a physical blow, shattering me against the stone wall, scattering my pieces across the centuries.

I come back to the world with a gasp that shreds my throat.

I sit bolt upright. The room spins, a carousel of gray shadows and recriminations. The air in my lungs is too thin. My heart is a frantic hammer, bruising the inside of my ribs.

Thump. Thump. Thump.

I am alone.

The realization is a physical sickness. I scramble backward, pressing my spine against the headboard, pulling my knees to my chest. The sheets are tangled around my legs, damp with sweat, clinging like a second skin.

My body is humming. It is a high-wire vibration that sings in my blood. I am burning. The heat is pooled low in my belly, heavy and molten, a throb that pulses in time with my heartbeat.

I look down at myself. My t-shirt is twisted, riding up my ribs. My skin is flushed a chaotic red.

Trembling, I lift a hand. My fingers hover over my collarbone, tracing the line where his teeth grazed. The skin feels tender, sensitized. I slide my hand down, over the curve of my breast, to my stomach. My muscles clench at the contact.

It wasn't a dream. It couldn't have been.

"Lachlan?" My voice is a broken whisper, rasping in the quiet room.

The corners are empty. The chair with my clothes is just a chair. The window shows the first bruised light of dawn, gray and indifferent.

I slide my hand lower, between my thighs. I am wet. Slick. My body is ready for him, aching for a ghost who dissolved the moment I opened my eyes. A sob catches in my chest—shame and desire tangling into a knot I cannot untie.

I scramble out of bed. The floor is freezing, but I don't feel it. I stumble into the bathroom and flick on the light.

The glare is merciless.

I grip the edges of the sink, leaning in until my nose almost touches the glass.

The woman staring back is a stranger.

Her hair is a wild tangle, damp at the temples. Her lips are swollen, bitten red. But it is the eyes that terrify me. The green irises are blown wide, the pupils black holes swallowing the light. They look haunted. They look hungry.

They look like hers.

I run the tap, splashing ice-cold water onto my face, gasping as the shock hits. I scrub at my skin, trying to erase the phantom touch of calloused fingers, the ghost of his scent that clings to me—leather and musk.

I dry my face with a towel, pressing the fabric hard against my eyes until stars burst behind my lids.

When I lower the towel, the reflection remains. She is still there.

I touch the silver pendant at my throat, my grandmother's knot. The metal is warm, absorbing the fever of my skin.

"Who are you?" I whisper to the mirror.

The stranger doesn't answer. But deep in the back of my mind, beneath the panic and the logic, I hear the wind howling through a ruined archway.

Isla.

I grip the sink until my knuckles turn white. I am not leaving. I cannot leave. He is here, in the stone and the wind and the blood, and now, he is in me.

CHAPTER 4

The Library of Shadows

I woke shivering, still reeling from the night's activities in my dreams. I could still feel his hands, his breath, and even his seed inside me. It was like I had stepped into some strange movie where I was the obsessed fan of some random guy, and part of me also felt like I was a victim of some weird prank. Maybe someone is drugging my food, and I am being abused in the night with only scattered memories. I paused, then laughed out loud— even I knew how desperate and ridiculous that sounded.

I rolled over and looked at the clock, 5:01AM. There would be no more sleep, not with the phantom of the Highlander lurking under my skin. I got up, moving carefully and slowly, my muscles aching in ways that told me what I experienced was real. I showered with the lights off, letting the water run hot, scrubbing myself until I felt human again. My bruises, neck, ribs, and the crescent at my inner arm were clear and visible. I studied them in the mirror, unsure if they were new or old, if they belonged to me or to some other version of myself from centuries ago.

I needed to know more, I needed to know about the Sutherlands, I needed to find out why this was happening.

Dornoch at dawn was a ghost town. I walked the main road alone, the only sound the slop of my boots in puddles and the mewling of a feral cat somewhere out of sight. The air was a living thing: wet, uncooperative, eager to force its way beneath every seam of clothing. By the time I reached the municipal library, my hands were raw and my mood brittle with lack of sleep.

The library was a squat brick block, its entrance flanked by concrete planters still full of last autumn's rot. A handwritten sign on the door said "OPEN 9-5 (ring for entry before 9)." She rang. The buzzer made a sound like a dying animal. Several minutes passed before the door jerked inward, revealing a man in his late sixties, lean and flinty, with a beard like lichen and glasses that magnified his eyes to a watery blue.

"Help ye?" he asked, not moving aside. His cardigan was buttoned wrong, the bottom edge flaring like a flag.

I adopted my best neutral-academic smile. "I'm here for the archives. Doctoral research, Boston University." I flashed my student ID, which no one ever cared about, but I thought it might make me seem less like a crazy person.

The man stared at the ID, then at me. "Yankee, is it?"

"Guilty." I smiled

He grunted. “Nobody in town reads the archive less’n they have to. What’s it you’re looking for?”

“Sutherland Castle,” I replied, and watched his eyebrows rise, just a millimeter. “Specifically, the family records. And anything about the legends.”

He shrugged, as if nothing surprised him anymore, then stepped back and let me in. “Alasdair Fraser,” he said, over his shoulder. “Mind you don’t move the stacks about, and don’t eat in the reading room.”

“Thank you, Mr. Fraser.”

“Doctor,” he corrected, with the sharpness of a man who’d had to repeat it for decades. He led me through a corridor of low shelves, the lights overhead flickering in an unbroken chain of institutional fluorescence. At the back, behind a battered fire door, was the archive: four rows of battered metal cabinets, two scarred reading tables, and a wall lined floor-to-ceiling with binders and ledgers that looked older than the state of Massachusetts.

“Registers by year, genealogies in blue, council business in red. Castle papers are up top, in the gray. If you need council minutes, ask.” He hovered a moment longer, then left, muttering something about the wisdom of Americans before breakfast.

I set up at the nearest table, stacking my notebook and laptop with the precise, defensive neatness of the lifelong researcher. I started with the gray binders, pulling the earliest volumes first. The records were meticulous, if unloving: land grants, tax rolls, lists of tenants and livestock. The

Sutherlands had left their mark not only in the ruin on the hill but in every ledger, every signature inked and duplicated.

I found the brothers fairly quickly. Hamish, the eldest, known as "the Builder," appeared first—his name prominently noted in the decades following the castle's expansion. Every record hinted at a man who preferred writing to fighting, who mapped the world through titles and deeds. But there was also a suggestion that he was ruthless; those who stood in his way often disappeared. It was the younger brother, Lachlan, who showed up in the margins: fines for fighting, citations for "unruly conduct," and a rare mention in a 1603 registry for "disturbance at kirk, resolved by father's order." Even centuries later, it was clear which one had cast the other's shadow.

I flipped through years at a time, hands smudged with dust, the chill in the archive slowly eating through my gloves. The narrative pieced together like bones from a disarticulated skeleton. Hamish inherited, then died abruptly, some fever or perhaps drink; the record was careful not to specify. By the time the land and title reverted to a distant cousin, Lachlan was gone from the rolls.

I hunted for traces of the curse, of the legend Ms McPherson recited for tourists. There were no outright admissions, no scandalous revelations. But now and again, the brothers' names appeared in proximity to a woman, sometimes a servant, sometimes a tenant's daughter. None lingered more than a page or two. Then, in a parish death record, I found a fragment:

"Isla, daughter of H.C. and M. (nee Grant), deceased at 22, cause unknown"

No surname. No gravestone, just a half-inch of faded script and a gap in the official story.

I copied the line into my notebook, underlining the name. Isla. It felt important, though I couldn't say why; I heard the name in the dream, but what was its significance? I paged forward searching for more, but the record did not indulge her. In the decades that followed, the name did not repeat.

It was only when I pulled the later council records, a battered blue volume marked "Incident & Law, 1607 - 1634," that I found it again.

Entry: "Summons issued for L. Sutherland on suspicion of violence toward tenant girl (I. Grant). Complainant H. Sutherland, dismissed for lack of evidence. Girl and L. Sutherland missing: presumed eloped."

And then, in the following spring: "Tenant family vacated, no forward address. Property ceded to laird, no contest."

I stared at the entries, reading them over and over, trying to scrape meaning from the silence between words. I felt an irrational surge of anger at the neat, bureaucratic cruelty of it. A girl vanished, a family erased, and the only evidence a few lines in a musty ledger.

I copied the notes, hands trembling with a cold that was now more than just temperature. Above, the lights flickered, settling into a rhythm that seemed deliberate, like code. The air in the archive felt suddenly thick, as if someone had turned off the oxygen. My neck prickled.

Then I was somewhere else entirely....and someone else.

"Isla, straichten yer shooders, lass," my father said as we waited for the door to open.

I didn't want to be here; my father had promised me to the laird of this castle to save his wee farm. I knew it was my duty.

The door opened, and a servant bowed and gestured for us to enter. We followed her into a grand hall. The Laird of the castle, Hamish, came down with false smiles and too many teeth showing. He was a handsome man but known for his cruelty; he often took girls from our village, and they never returned.

"Isla, lass, it's a pleasure tae meet ye. Let me hae a look at ye," he said, circling me like a predatory bird preparing to land on a fallen sheep.

"Aye, m'laird," I said softly with a small curtsy.

The Laird and my father began discussing terms, and I let their voices fade into the air. I wouldn't have any say in any of this anyway, so why listen?

Just as I thought I was going to fall asleep upright, the door burst open with the sound of laughter and sharp verbal banter. Hamish looked up, his expression darkening.

"Brother, we've guests. Keep yer horseplay outside," Hamish growled.

"Och, Brother, ye need tae learn tae hae a bit o' fun," the new man jeered, poking Hamish in the ribs playfully.

Then he looked at me — and the world stopped for us both.

And just like that, I was back in the stacks, glanced up, and saw the shelves were empty. The corridor beyond was lit but still. My laptop's screen reflected my face, pale and drawn in the flat light, but behind me, there was a shape. Not a person, not exactly, but the unmistakable silhouette of a man—tall and broad-shouldered, head bowed as if in thought.

I whipped around, pulse thundering. Nothing. The air hung heavy and undisturbed.

My eyes scanned every aisle, every possible place a person could stand. Silence. What the hell was that? What was happening to me? I could still smell the grass and the smoke of the wood burning in the castle's hearth. I listened for footsteps, for breathing, for the faint whiff of someone else's presence, but all I could hear was the echo of my own heart.

I turned back to the screen. The reflection was gone now.

My hands hovered above the keyboard, uncertain. I typed the name Isla Grant into the digital index's search field, half-expecting the system to spit it back at me with a smirk. Instead, the machine whirred, loading as slowly as molasses. After a minute, it returned a single, fragmentary hit: an unsigned letter, folded into the council papers, dated in the 1600s, though the exact date is hard to make out.

I pulled up the scan. The text was blurred, the script slanted with haste, I couldn't understand the words, but a translation was written by it.

"To whom it may concern, know this: she did not flee. She was taken. If you hold any care for the quiet of her soul, let her rest, and trouble not her shade. For what has been done, there is no justice left—only silence."

There was no signature. The clerk had underlined "taken" twice and noted: "Hand unknown. Destroy after reading." But it had survived.

I stared at the letter, my own breath fogging the air in front of me. "Let her rest," the letter said, but the itch at my neck and the cold in my bones told me rest was never on the table.

A shadow drifted across the frosted glass of the fire door, the outline of a man, moving slowly. For a split second, the memory of the Highlander's hands gripped my shoulders from behind. I turned so fast I knocked my coffee to the floor. The puddle spread, black and glossy, seeping into the cracks of the tile.

This time, there was a voice, faint but real.

"You all right in there?" Alasdair's voice, muffled by the door.

I cleared my throat, "Fine," I said, my voice coming out more hoarsely than I intended. "Just...dropped something."

"Close up when you're done. I'm for the post."

The shadow moved on.

I slumped in my chair, adrenaline leaking out of me in slow pulses. My hands still trembled from the flashback, memory, or whatever the hell it was that saw me smashed back in time for a minute. I did my best to clean up the spill while not making a bigger mess. When I sat back down, I scrolled through the digital letter, rereading it until the words seemed to burrow down into me.

Taken. Let her rest.

I closed the browser. I shut the ledger. I looked over my shoulder one last time, found nothing but old air and shelves that did not creak.

On the way out, I left the lights on, even though the sign clearly stated not to. I needed the brightness. The darkness seemed too sinister right now.

I carried the evidence back to the B&B in a plastic shopping bag, handles stretched to transparency by the weight of the photocopies, notebooks, and borrowed hardback. I was halfway up the lane to the B&B before I realized how tightly I was gripping it; my knuckles burned, and my fingernails left crescents in my palms.

The house was empty, though someone had left the TV on in the parlor, muffled, unintelligible voices leaking through the wall. I climbed to my room and locked the door behind me, then dumped the bag's contents across the bed in a riot of disorder. I sat in the center of it all, knees up, laptop balanced on the windowsill, surrounded by the silent chorus of the dead.

I took a deep breath and set to work.

First, I lined up the names from the parish records, writing each one on a yellow sticky note: Hamish. Lachlan. Isla. I filled the rest of the bedspread with other names, some crossed out, some circled in red. I drew arrows, built a family tree, then tore it down and rebuilt it to fit the dates. It became clear almost immediately that nothing about the Sutherland legacy was straightforward. Every generation seemed to end in tragedy: fire, fever, sudden violence. Always, the record would skip a decade, and the next branch of the family would pick up as if nothing had happened.

I scanned the digital letter again, "she has not run. She is taken," letting the words ring in my ears. The language was too modern, but the fear felt ageless.

The radiator clanged, echoing through the hollow wall. I barely registered it as I thumbed through the photocopies, piecing together the fragments: a report of "unusual disturbance" at the castle in 1784; a local girl "vanished, presumed dead" in 1857; a post-war suicide, the body never found, just a pair of shoes left at the edge of the ruined chapel. A girl's name in every case. Always in their early twenties, they always disappeared or died.

I took a breath, only realizing now how shallowly I had been breathing. My hands trembled, but not from fear. The trembling came from the thought that I was somehow connected to this — the dreams, the flashbacks, the lingering echo of his touch. I wanted to call it adrenaline, but it felt more like hunger. I felt stupid; I was an educated woman, I knew that curses and ghosts were not real.

I laid down notes along the blanket, creating a timeline, each entry more desperate than the last. Each woman drawn to the castle is then erased from the world in some way.

I scrolled through my own digital search history, the log of names and phrases I'd chased across the internet in the past forty-eight hours. I was halfway through transcribing a news item from 1912, a mention of an "American heiress spirited away during an engagement party on the castle grounds", when the lamp on my desk flickered.

At first, I ignored it and attributed it to old wiring in the building, but the flickering persisted. I looked at the lamp; it brightened, then dimmed until the room was shrouded in shadows. The laptop's fan whined as if protesting an unseen force, then with a soft pop, the lamp went out, and the laptop screen flashed to black.

I was in total darkness. I could feel my heart pulsing, and I could not see my hand in front of my own face.

The laptop rebooted with a high-pitched beep, bathing the room in a cold blue light. The screen was blank except for the faint, mirrorish reflection of my own face, drawn, wide-eyed, mouth slightly open. But behind me, over my left shoulder, was another face.

It hovered just above the curve of my braid, a shape more than a portrait, tall and angular. I stared at it for a heartbeat, then two. It did not move. I turned slowly, every muscle braced for the reality of hands on my body, or a breath at my ear.

Nothing. Only the sound of the radiator, hissing like a threat.

I turned back to the screen. The face was gone, replaced by the familiar desktop. I exhaled, shaky, and reached for the lamp's switch. It did not respond.

The next hour vanished into a kind of trance. I assembled the women's names on the blanket, lined up the years, and drew the lines that bound them all back to the Sutherland Castle and the men who ruled it. The weight of it pressed down on me: the pattern, the repetition, the sense that I was not discovering but remembering, unearthing something my body already knew.

At some point, I realized I was speaking out loud, repeating names over and over to no one but the empty space. With each repetition, the air in the room grew colder, as if the house had been set on a sea of night. I grabbed my sweater and wrapped myself in it, trying to gather some warmth, but the cold was internal now, sitting behind my ribs.

I reread the fragment about Hamish Sutherland, the eldest. His cruelty was not a matter of myth; it was written plainly in the records, in the fines for 'disobedience,' in the stories of his feuds with tenants, his anger at women who spurned him. The scholar in me catalogued the evidence, the part of me that felt the connection to this Isla of the past felt nothing but dread.

I found myself staring out the window toward the castle, part of me expected to see the Highlander's reflection in the glass. But he didn't. Instead, the lights in the hallway flickered, a flicker of yellow against the seam of my door.

I went back to the letter, the warning: let her rest, and gone not taken. I read it again, then again, lips moving, voice dropping to a whisper.

I didn't know who this message was for or who it was from.

My hands restlessly leafed through the last of the printouts, searching for something I couldn't name. I knew I needed it, I just didn't know what 'it' was. At the bottom of the stack, I found a photograph, it was a copy from a local paper, dated 1973. The image was grainy, but the face was clear enough: a woman, flame-haired and narrow-eyed, standing in front of the castle's shattered gates. She wore a tartan scarf. I traced the shape of the jaw, the set of the mouth, and felt an impossible recognition.

The caption read: "Local Lass Fiona MacLeod, winner of the Dornoch Historical Society prize for her essay on Sutherland Castle."

I touched the name. The chill in the room grew teeth and gnawed at my wrist.

The laptop screen flickered again, this time returning to life with a snap. The desktop had changed. The wallpaper, the photo of me at a Red Sox game, had been replaced by a different image: Sutherland Castle, viewed from below, a silhouette against a sky the color of blood.

I did not change that, I don't think I even took that photo.

The radiator hissed. The parlor TV downstairs had gone silent, or perhaps I was too deep in the hush to hear it. I tried the lamp again. No luck.

I stood, legs unsteady, and went to the mirror. The bruises on my neck had darkened. I traced them, fingers trembling, half-expecting to find the marks wet or tender. They were not. I pressed my palm over the pulse at my throat and stared into my eyes in the mirror. I dared my face to change.

It did not.

I exhaled, a shuddering release, and went back to the bed. The research materials looked different in the semi-darkness: not like data, but like an altar. A shrine to something old and hungry.

I sat down and rested my head in my hands in fear and frustration, "Who are you? What do you want from me?" I asked the empty room.

For a moment, nothing answered.

Then the hallway light outside the door went out, followed by the room lights and the laptop shutting down. I was plunged into darkness again, so thick it felt as if it were reaching out to me.

I closed my eyes, and in the hush and darkness, I heard my own name spoken in a voice that wasn't mine.

"Fiona, come back to me," the disembodied voice whispered. I could feel the voice more than hear it; it was both familiar and a stranger's all at once.

And suddenly I knew where I needed to be.

CHAPTER 5
The Highlander in the Dusk

The sky is a bruised purple, swollen with rain that refuses to fall. I stand in the shadow of the Sutherland Keep, the wind biting through my layers like a physical tooth. It gnaws at the exposed skin of my wrists and stings my cheeks, but the cold feels necessary. It is a sharp, grounding thing in a world that has gone soft and fluid around the edges.

In my hand, the notebook is damp. The ink of my notes has begun to bleed, turning names and dates into Rorschach tests. Isla. Lachlan 1608. The numbers smear into the margins. I flip the page, the paper snapping in the wind. My handwriting looks frantic, the loops of the letters too wide, the pressure of the pen indenting the page so deeply I can feel the braille of my own obsession on the reverse side.

I am not supposed to be here. The sign at the bottom of the gravel path said Grounds Closed at 5 PM. It is past seven. The gate was locked, but the drystone wall to the east has crumbled enough to offer a foothold for someone desperate. And I am desperate.

I snap the notebook shut and shove it into my pocket. It offers no answers, only questions that make my head throb. History is a safe distance; this—whatever is happening to me—is too close. It is under my fingernails.

I move deeper into the skeleton of the castle. The tourists are long gone, taking their bright jackets and loud voices back to the warmth of the village pubs. Here, the silence is aggressive. It presses against my eardrums, a heavy, wet wool. The only sound is the crunch of my boots on gravel and the sigh of the wind through the arrow loops. It sounds like the castle is breathing. In. Out. A slow, tubercular rhythm.

I step over a fallen lintel, venturing beyond the roped-off areas. The ground here is uneven, treacherous with slick moss and loose shale. I should be careful. I should be worried about twisting an ankle or falling into one of the uncovered cellar pits. I am not. My body feels light, magnetic, drawn toward the northern tower by a force that hums in my blood.

The shadows stretch out from the walls, long black fingers grasping at the grass. The light is failing fast. The gray stone turns charcoal, then black.

"Come out," I whisper. The wind snatches the words away before they can fully form.

I stop at the entrance to what might have been a chapel or a solar. The roof is gone, the floor carpeted in weeds that look black in the twilight. A single archway remains intact, framing the darkening valley below. The drop is sheer.

I feel it then. The prickle at the base of my neck. The sudden drop in air pressure makes my ears pop. It is the same feeling as in the library, as in my room. A static charge that lifts the fine hairs on my arms.

I am being watched.

I do not turn immediately. I let the sensation wash over me, terrified and thrilling. It feels like a hand hovering just above my skin, the heat of a palm radiating through the cold air. My heart hammers a frantic rhythm against my ribs, a trapped bird battering itself against the cage.

Slowly, deliberately, I pivot.

He is there.

He stands in the deep shadow of a collapsed wall, motionless. He is not a ghost. Ghosts are translucent, vaporous things that belong in Victorian stories. This man is solid. He absorbs the little light remaining in the courtyard. The dark tartan wrapped around his shoulder is heavy, the wool matted and rough. His hair is loose tonight, moving slightly in the wind, black strands cutting across a face that looks carved from the same granite as the keep.

Lachlan.

The name forms in my mind, silent and screaming.

His eyes lock onto mine. Even from this distance, even in this gloom, they burn. They are not the empty sockets of a skull; they are blue fire, intelligent and agonizingly sad. He looks at me with a familiarity that strips me bare. He looks at me as if he has been waiting for four hundred years for me to turn around.

"You," I breathe. The word is a puff of white vapor.

He does not speak. He does not smile. He simply watches, his hands hanging loose at his sides. One hand rests near the hilt of the dirk at his waist. The weapon looks real, heavy iron, and worn leather.

I take a step forward. My boot scuffs loudly on the stone.

The sound seems to break the spell. He flinches, a micro-movement, his jaw tightening. The sorrow in his eyes hardens into something steely. Warning.

He steps back.

"Wait!" I shout, the sound tearing at my throat.

He turns, his plaid swirling around him like smoke, and steps into the absolute blackness of a recessed doorway.

"No!"

I run. I scramble over the wet stones, slipping, catching myself with a hand that scrapes raw against the masonry. I ignore the sting. I reach the spot where he stood seconds ago.

Empty.

There is no doorway.

I stand staring at a solid wall of stone. The masonry is unbroken, the mortar crumbling but intact. There is nowhere he could have gone. No passage. No hidden exit. Just the cold, unforgiving face of the tower.

I slam my hands against the rock. "Where are you?" I scream it this time. The cry echoes around the courtyard, mocking me. Where are you... are you... you...

I press my cheek against the stone. It is freezing. There is no lingering warmth, no scent of leather. Just the damp, earthy smell of ruin.

I spin in a circle, scanning the courtyard. Nothing but shadows and weeds and the rising night.

My chest heaves. I feel foolish. I feel insane. I saw him. I know I saw him. The image of his face is burned onto my retinas, more vivid than the stone I am touching.

I slide down the wall until I am crouching in the dirt, my knees pulled to my chest. I wrap my arms around myself, shivering violently. The wind howls through the archway, a lonely, desolate sound.

I am chasing a hallucination. I am a doctoral candidate in history chasing a projection of my own loneliness. That is the rational explanation. That is what Murray would say. Hysterical, Fi. You're being hysterical.

But as I sit there in the growing dark, tracing the shape of the stone behind me, I feel the lie of it. I am not lonely. I am haunted. And God help me, the emptiness where he stood hurts more than his presence ever could.

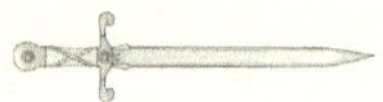

Dornoch in the morning light is a deception. It pretends to be a postcard—slate roofs gleaming with rain, the smell of baking bread warring with the salt tang of the sea, locals nodding politely as they sweep their stoops. But I see the rot beneath the charm. The gray stone of the buildings looks too much like the castle walls. The shadows in the alleyways are too deep.

I walk fast, head down, collar turned up against a drizzle that is more mist than rain. I am trying to walk him off. If I move fast enough, maybe the image of his face will detach from my mind. Maybe the phantom weight of his body on mine from the dream will fade.

I stop in front of a jeweler's shop. The display is filled with silver thistles and amber set in heavy Celtic knots. I stare at a necklace, trying to focus on the craftsmanship, the price tag, the reality of commerce.

In the glass, a reflection moves.

He is standing directly across the street.

I see him clearly in the pane—the dark hair, the white shirt beneath the plaid, the stillness that sets him apart from the bustle of the delivery van passing by. He is looking right at the back of my head.

I whirl around, my boots splashing in a puddle.

A woman with a stroller swerves to avoid me, muttering a curse. A man in a blue courier uniform jumps down from his truck. Two tourists in ponchos consult a map.

The space where he stood—in front of the bakery—is empty.

"Excuse me," I say to the courier, breathless. "Did you see a man? Tall, long hair? Wearing a kilt?"

He looks at me, scanning my frantic eyes, my windblown hair. He shakes his head. "Lots of folks in kilts for the weddings, love. But nobody was standing there."

I turn back to the window. The reflection shows only me, pale and haunted.

I keep moving. My heart is a drum beating a retreat.

I buy a coffee I don't want, just to have something warm in my hands. I sit on a bench in the square, watching the world go by. I lift the cup, the steam rising.

Over the rim, I see him again.

He is leaning against the stone wall of the old kirk yard, fifty yards away. He is not looking at me this time. He is looking at the sky, his profile sharp against the gray clouds. He looks weary. He looks like a man carrying the weight of the earth.

I set the coffee down, spilling it over my hand. I don't feel the burn.

I fumble for my phone. My fingers are clumsy, numb. I unlock the screen, swipe up for the camera. The lens finds him. He is there on the screen, a dark figure against the gray stone.

Click.

I take another. And another. Zooming in. Click. Click.

He turns his head slowly. He looks at the lens.

And then he dissolves. He doesn't fade; he simply steps behind the stone pillar of the gate and does not emerge on the other side.

I lower the phone. I run across the square, ignoring the traffic, ignoring the horn that blasts at me. I reach the Kirk yard gate.

Empty. Just rows of leaning headstones and the wet grass.

I lean against the cold iron of the gate, gasping for air. I pull up the gallery on my phone. My thumb hovers over the last photo.

Proof. I need proof.

I tap the image.

The screen shows the stone wall. The gray sky. The pillar.

There is no man.

There is a blur—a smudge of darkness like a thumbprint on the lens, a shadow that looks like a trick of the light. But no face. No plaid. No eyes burning with centuries of loss.

I swipe to the next photo. The same. An empty wall. A shadow that suggests a shape but confirms nothing.

I laugh. It is a jagged, ugly sound that makes a passing woman clutch her purse tighter and hurry away.

I am losing my mind. That is the only explanation. The stress, the breakup, the isolation—it has finally cracked the porcelain of my sanity. I am projecting my desire for a savior, for a connection, onto the blank canvas of this town.

But even as I think it, I feel the prickle again. The static charge.

I look up.

High on the ridge overlooking the town, the castle ruins loom. And I know, with a certainty that bypasses logic and settles in the gut, that he is up there. He is not in the photos because he does not belong to the light. He belongs to the stone.

He is waiting.

The camera lies. My eyes lie. But the blood—the blood remembers.

I shove the phone into my pocket. I don't need proof. I need him.

The sun has bled out into the western hills, leaving the sky a sickly, bruised violet. I am back at the gate. The sign still says CLOSED, a white rectangle of authority that means nothing to me. I step over the chain.

The path is steeper in the dark. The gravel shifts under my boots, trying to slide me back down to the safety of the normal world. I dig my heels in. I climb.

The castle is a jagged silhouette against the rising moon. It looks like a broken crown. The wind is louder up here, screaming through the gaps in the masonry. It pulls at my clothes, tangles my hair across my face.

Isla...

I stop. The sound is not the wind. It is distinct, low, a vibration that hums against my eardrums.

"I'm here," I say. My voice is snatched away, lost in the gale. "I'm here!"

I push forward, leaving the main path. I scramble over piles of fallen masonry, moving toward the part of the keep that hangs over the precipice. This is dangerous ground. The signs warned of unstable floors, of drop-offs. I don't care. The pull is a physical hook in my navel, reeling me in.

I find a narrow staircase, half-choked with rubble. I climb it on hands and knees, the stone scraping my palms.

At the top, the ruins open up into a chamber I haven't seen before. The roof is partially intact here, a stone vault that shelters the space from the wind. It is quieter. The roar of the gale becomes a muffled backdrop.

The room is small. A single, narrow window—an arrow loop—looks out over the black void of the valley. Moonlight spills through it, cutting a sharp white rectangle across the flagstones.

The air here is different. It is heavy, static. The hair on my arms stands up. The smell is stronger—peat smoke, ozone, the metallic tang of old blood.

I stand in the center of the room, turning slowly.

"I know you're here," I whisper. "I can feel you."

The shadows in the corner deepen. They pool together, knitting themselves into a shape.

He steps out of the dark.

He is not transparent. He is not a trick of the light. He is a wall of presence. He stands in the doorway, blocking the exit, filling the space with his size. He is closer than before. I can see the rise and fall of his chest. I can see the dampness of the rain on the wool of his plaid. I can see the scar that cuts through his eyebrow, a white line on weathered skin.

My breath catches in my throat.

He looks at me. His expression is not angry, not predatory. It is tortured. It is the look of a man who is watching his own heart being ripped out.

"Who are you?" I ask. The question is a formality. I know who he is. My blood knows.

He does not answer. He takes a step toward me. The floorboards do not creak.

I do not retreat. I hold my ground. The fear that should be paralyzing me is absent. In its place is a terrible, aching need. A recognition.

"Tell me," I demand, my voice trembling. "Am I crazy? Are you real?"

He tilts his head. The movement is avian, sharp. His lips part.

Isla.

He doesn't speak the name; he projects it. It blooms in my mind, a dark flower opening.

I take a step toward him. I lift my hand. I need to touch him. I need to know if his skin is cold like the stone or warm like the man in my dream. I need to bridge the gap between the living and the dead.

"Lachlan," I whisper.

His eyes widen. A flash of shock, or hope.

My fingertips brush the rough wool of his plaid.

And then he is mist.

My hand passes through him. There is a sensation of bitter cold, a shock of ice water, and then nothing. I stumble forward, off-balance, falling into the empty space where he stood.

I catch myself on the doorframe.

I spin around.

The room is empty. The moonlight hits only dust and weeds.

"No," I moan. "No, don't go. Come back!"

I claw at the air, grasping at shadows. But the presence is gone. The static charge has dissipated. The smell of peat smoke is replaced by the smell of wet rot.

I slide down the doorframe to the floor. I press my forehead against the cold stone. I am alone.

And that is the horror of it. Not the ghost. Not the haunting. The horror is the silence. The horror is the disappointment that hollows me out, leaving me shivering in the dark, waiting for a monster who refuses to stay.

CHAPTER 6
Shadows Under My Skin

The dark is not empty. It is heavy, pressing against my eyelids, demanding entry. I do not drift into sleep; I fall into it, a stone dropped down a well. The splash is silent.

The air changes instantly. The smell of the B&B—stale lavender and industrial cleaner—vanishes, replaced by the scent of burning pitch and resin. The temperature drops, then spikes with a sudden, suffocating heat.

I am running.

I am not in my room. The floor beneath my feet is uneven flagstone, strewn with dried rushes that catch at the hem of a gown I do not own. The walls are not peeling wallpaper but solid, sweating granite, illuminated by the sputtering rage of torches set in iron sconces. The smoke stings my eyes. It tastes of oak and history.

I know this place. I know the turn of the corridor ahead, the way the shadows pool in the alcoves like spilled ink. This is Sutherland Castle. Not the skeleton I climbed this evening, but the body. Whole. Alive. Breathing.

I round the corner, my heart beating a frantic rhythm against ribs constricted by stays. I am looking for him. I am fleeing from him. The distinction does not exist.

A shadow detaches itself from the wall.

He moves faster than thought. One moment the corridor is clear, the next, a wall of tartan and muscle bars my path. I gasp, skidding to a halt on the rushes, but he does not let me stop. He surges forward, a predator closing the gap.

His arm bands around my waist—hard, unyielding like an iron hoop. The impact slams me backward. My spine meets the unforgiving cold of the stone wall. The air leaves my lungs in a sharp whoosh.

"Running again, lass?"

His voice is gravel grinding on glass. Low. dangerous.

I look up. Lachlan fills my vision. He is terrifying in the torchlight. The scars on his face are stark maps of violence, his blue eyes burning with a fever that mirrors my own. He smells of horses and peat smoke, a raw, masculine scent that overrides my panic and replaces it with a desperate, cloying heat.

"I wasn't running," I lie. My voice is breathless, pitched higher than my own.

He crowds me. His body presses into mine, pinning me to the masonry. I feel the heavy, scratchy wool of his plaid against my bare arms, the cold metal of his dirk digging into my hip through the layers of my skirts. He is heavy, solid. Realer than the life I left in Boston.

"Liar," he growls.

His hand moves. It is large, calloused from the sword and the reins. He grips my jaw, his thumb tracing the line of my throat, pressing into the pulse that flutters there like a trapped moth. His skin is rough, creating friction against mine. It burns.

I should fight him. This is violence. This is a trap. But my hands do not push him away. They fly to his shoulders, gripping the fabric of his shirt, pulling him closer. I want the weight of him. I want to be crushed by it.

He lowers his head. His breath is hot against the sensitive skin below my ear. It scalds me.

"Mo chridhe. Isla."

The name hits me with the force of a physical blow. It vibrates through my sternum, resonating with a frequency my bones remember. Isla. It is not a name I learned in a book. It is the name etched into the marrow of my soul. It fits me better than Fiona ever did.

"Lachlan," I whimper.

He does not wait. He drags me sideways, into the deep gloom of a recessed alcove hidden from the main passage. The shadows swallow us whole.

There is no gentleness here. We do not have time for gentleness. His hands are everywhere—fumbling with the laces of my bodice, bunching the heavy fabric of my skirts in his fists until the cool air hits my thighs. He claims me with a desperation that speaks of centuries of hunger.

I arch into him, my back scraping against the rough stone. The sensation is sharp, grounding. I bite my lip to stifle a cry as his hand finds skin, hot and demanding. He touches me not as a discovery, but as a reclamation. He knows the map of my body. He knows exactly where to press, where to grip, to make my knees buckle.

"Mine," he hisses against my mouth. "Ye belong to the stone. Ye belong to me."

I do not argue. I cannot. The rational world—the dissertation, the plane ticket, the lonely apartment—dissolves into mist. There is only the hard wall behind me and the hard man before me. There is only the friction of wool and skin, the taste of salt and smoke, and the terrible, beautiful weight of being his.

The stone wall dissolves. The heat vanishes.

I jerk upright, gasping, my lungs fighting for air that is too thin and too cold. My hands claw at the darkness, grasping for purchase, but find only the tangled mess of cheap cotton sheets twisted around my legs.

The room is silent. It is a dead silence, broken only by the ragged, tearing sound of my own breathing.

I am back. God help me, I am back.

The digital clock on the bedside table bleeds red numbers into the gloom: 4:23 AM. The light is sallow, sickly, casting long, distorted shadows across the peeling wallpaper.

I collapse back against the headboard, trembling. My body is drenched in sweat, but I am freezing. The perspiration cools rapidly on my skin, turning to ice, but beneath the surface, I am still burning.

I wrap my arms around myself, rocking slightly. The sensation is maddening. I can still feel him. My waist throbs where his arm clamped me to the wall. The skin of my throat tingles, raw and sensitized, as if his beard has just grazed it. The phantom weight of him presses down on my chest, a heaviness I miss with a sickness that churns in my gut.

I drag a hand down my side, my fingers digging into my flank. My flesh feels tender. Bruised.

"It's not real," I whisper. The words crack in the dry air. "Just a dream. Neurochemical firing. Stress."

But my skin remembers. The nerves are still firing, reporting a touch that is no longer there.

I stumble out of bed. My legs are weak, water instead of bone. I navigate the dark room by memory, bashing my shin against the corner of the dresser but barely registering the pain. I need water. I need to wash the smoke and the guilt out of my pores.

The bathroom is freezing. The tile floor bites the soles of my feet. I fumble for the tap, turning the cold handle until it screeches. I cup my hands, splashing the icy water over my face, gasping as the shock hits. I do it again. And again. Until my skin is numb.

I grab a towel and bury my face in it. I do not look in the mirror. I cannot look in the mirror. I am terrified that if I look, I will see eyes that are not mine. I will see Isla staring back, accusing me of waking up. Or worse, I will see nothing at all.

I lower the towel, keeping my gaze fixed on the drain. The water swirls away, clear. No blood. No ash.

I turn off the light and step back into the bedroom.

I freeze.

The shadows in the far corner, near the wardrobe, are wrong. They are not falling naturally. They are gathering. Knitting together.

My breath catches in my throat.

The darkness shifts. It lengthens, stretching upward, taking on the broad, imposing silhouette of a man. The air in the room grows heavy, charged with that familiar static electricity. I can feel him. The pull in my navel snaps tight.

He is watching me. I can't see his face, only the density of his presence, darker than the night around him.

"Lachlan?"

The name leaves my lips before I can stop it. A plea.

The figure does not move. The silence stretches, tight as a bowstring.

Panic flares—sharp and bright. I lunge for the bedside lamp, my fingers fumbling blindly for the switch. I knock a book to the floor but I don't stop. My thumb finds the plastic toggle.

Click.

Yellow light floods the room. It is harsh, unforgiving. It washes out the corners, exposing the dust motes dancing in the air.

The corner is empty.

Just the wardrobe. Just the peeling wallpaper. Just the empty chair where I threw my clothes.

I spin in a circle, my heart hammering against my ribs like a fist. I check behind the door. I check the window, but the latch is fastened tight.

He is gone. Or he was never there.

I stand in the center of the room, shivering in my oversized t-shirt, staring at the empty space. I am alone. But the hair on the back of my neck stands up, and the skin of my waist burns where a ghost held me only moments ago. The room feels crowded, full of eyes I cannot see.

The night does not end; it merely bleeds out.

I sit on the edge of the mattress, wrapped in the duvet, watching the window turn from black to charcoal to a miserable, weeping gray. The dawn here is not a promise; it is an accusation.

I haven't slept since 4:22. I haven't blinked. My eyes feel gritty, lined with sand, but I dare not close them. If I close them, he will be there, waiting behind my eyelids, ready to drag me back into the stone.

And if I close them, he might not be there. That thought is infinitely worse.

The radiator clanks, signaling the start of the day. A delivery truck rumbles past on the street below. The world is waking up, turning its gears, indifferent to the haunting in room 4.

I loosen my grip on the duvet and let it fall. I pull up the hem of my t-shirt.

My skin is pale, untouched. There are no bruises on my ribs. No red marks on my waist where the iron band of his arm crushed me. I trace the line of my ribs with trembling fingers. I press down.

I flinch.

It hurts. The flesh is tender, a deep, bruised ache that lies beneath the surface, in the muscle and the memory of the tissue. I move my hand to my throat. I tilt my head back, looking at the ceiling, and graze the spot where his beard scratched me. It burns. A friction burn that defies the visual evidence.

"What is happening to me?"

The voice is raspy, foreign. It sounds like an old woman's voice. It sounds like her.

I stand up and begin to pace. Three steps to the window, three steps to the door. I am a caged animal. My movements are jerky, agitated.

The scholar in me—the woman who spent six years analyzing primary sources and debunking myths—is screaming. She is listing the symptoms: sleep deprivation, isolation, psychosomatic response to trauma. She is telling me to pack my bag, drive to Inverness, and get on the first plane back to Boston. She is telling me that ghosts are not real, that stone does not hold memory, and that I am having a nervous breakdown.

But the scholar is a liar.

I stop pacing. I turn to the corner by the wardrobe.

It is just a corner. Dust bunnies gather on the floorboards. But I can't look away. I stare at the empty space, willing the shadows to lengthen again. I wait for the drop in pressure, the scent of peat smoke.

Nothing happens.

A growl builds in my throat—frustration, sharp and hot.

I am not afraid of the ghost anymore. The fear has burned off, leaving something harder, darker underneath. A hunger.

My body hums with it. It is a craving that sits in the pit of my stomach, a void that the scone and the tea yesterday couldn't fill. I feel incomplete. I feel like an amputee who has woken up to find her limb restored, only to have it hacked off again the moment she opened her eyes.

I walk to the window and press my forehead against the cold glass. The mist is swallowing the town, hiding the ridge where the castle sits.

"Lachlan," I whisper.

I shouldn't know his name. I shouldn't know the taste of his mouth. I shouldn't miss the violence of his touch.

But I do.

I turn back to the room. I grab my jeans from the chair. My hands are steady now. The trembling has stopped, replaced by a terrifying purpose. I am not going to Inverness. I am not going to the airport.

I am going back to the stone. The hunger is awake, and it demands to be fed.

CHAPTER 7
Returning to the Castle

I stand in the center of the herd, pressed on all sides by damp Gore-Tex and the smell of travel-weary bodies. We are thirty strong, a clumsy organism shuffling through the vaulted entry of Sutherland Castle. The air here tastes of wet stone and the mints the woman beside me is chewing aggressively. I hate them. I hate their casual curiosity, their cameras, their need to be entertained by the wreckage of a family that bled into this soil.

But I need them. They are my camouflage.

"Now, if everyone could just... squeeze in a bit tighter," the guide says. She is not Moira. This one introduced herself as Maggie. She is a flurry of chaotic energy, a woman made of loose ends. Her scarf is unraveling, her glasses slide down her nose every three seconds, and she clutches a sheaf of laminated notes like a shield. "Right. So. The Great Hall. Or what's left of it."

She gestures vaguely toward the soot-stained fireplace. Her flashlight beam wobbles, illuminating a patch of moss instead of the masonry she intends to highlight.

"The Sutherlands were... well, they were a complicated bunch," Maggie says, breathless. "Warriors. Poets. Murderers, some say." She laughs, a nervous titter that bounces off the granite walls and dies instantly. "But aren't we all? In our own way?"

The tourists exchange confused glances. A child in a yellow raincoat kicks the base of a pillar, the dull thud echoing in the cavernous space.

I am not looking at the fireplace. I am scanning the periphery. My eyes dissect the shadows pooling in the corners, the dark mouths of archways leading to nowhere. My skin feels too tight for my body. The memory of the dream—of his hands, his weight, the salt-iron taste of his mouth—is a second skin I cannot shed. I am vibrating with it. A low-grade fever that has nothing to do with a virus and everything to do with the man who isn't here.

Lachlan.

The name is a hook in my gut. I say it silently, testing the air. The castle does not answer, but the temperature seems to drop a fraction.

"Excuse me," a man in a trekking vest calls out. "Is it true about the dungeons? The guidebooks say they sealed people in the walls."

Maggie blinks, startled. She drops a page of her notes. It flutters to the flagstones. "Oh! Well. The history is a bit... murky on that. The records are incomplete. Sutherland justice was swift, usually. Not... architectural." She bends to retrieve the paper, her flashlight beam swinging wildly across the faces of the crowd, blinding a teenager who groans in protest.

I edge toward the back of the group. The herd is distracted, watching Maggie fumble with her papers. She tries to reorder them, muttering about dates and clan feuds.

"And this painting?" an elderly woman asks, pointing her cane at a reproduction hanging crookedly near the archway. "Is this the Earl? He looks remarkably like my dentist."

Maggie abandons her notes, rushing over to the couple with frantic enthusiasm. "Ah! No, that's a Victorian imagining of the third Earl. Pure fantasy, really. The nose is all wrong. The Sutherlands had distinct noses. Roman. Sharp."

The crowd shifts, pivoting toward the painting like iron filings to a magnet. They create a wall of backs, a barrier of synthetic fabric, and hushed whispers.

It is time.

I do not hesitate. I do not think about the rules or the warning signs or the logical part of my brain screaming that I am about to commit criminal trespass. I simply step sideways.

The movement is fluid, soundless. I slide into the shadow of a heavy tapestry that smells of dust and neglect. Behind it, a narrow corridor gapes—dark, unlit, uninvited.

I take one backward step into the gloom. Then another.

The voice of the guide becomes tinny, distant. "Now, over here we have a lovely example of..."

I turn my back on them. The darkness receives me like a lover.

Here, the air is different. It is stagnant, heavy with the scent of earth that has never seen the sun. My pulse kicks against my throat, a frantic bird desperate to escape. I press my fingertips to the wall. The stone is rough, weeping moisture. It scrapes against my skin, abrasive and cold, a welcome shock after the humid warmth of the crowd.

My footsteps change. On the main tour route, the floors are reinforced with wood or packed gravel. Here, it is original stone. My boots strike the floor with a rhythmic *click-clack* that echoes too loudly. I stop, holding my breath, waiting for a shout, a beam of light, a hand on my shoulder.

"Wait, wait, I think I missed a page," Maggie's voice floats down the hall, muffled and pathetic.

No one is coming.

I exhale. The sound is ragged. I am alone in the veins of the beast.

My heart hammers, not with fear, but with a terrible, soaring anticipation. I am not a historian anymore. I am not a tourist. I am a woman hunting a ghost, and for the first time in days, I know exactly which way to go.

I drift deeper into the throat of the castle. The silence here is not empty; it is watchful.

I fish my phone from my pocket and thumb the flashlight on. The beam is a pathetic white cone that slices through the gloom but fails to conquer it. Shadows leap away from the light, stretching long and distorted across the walls, twisting into shapes that suggest limbs, jaws, and grasping fingers. The moss clinging to the masonry absorbs the light, a velvet disease spreading across the grey granite.

To my left, a door bound in iron bands sits heavy in its frame. Locked. I try the handle—a rusted ring the size of a dinner plate—but it refuses to give. To my right, a roped-off chamber filled with crumbling masonry and the skeletal remains of a wheelbarrow.

I don't need to enter them. They are not the way.

I know this because the sensation in my chest has sharpened. It is no longer a vague itch; it is a physical tether attached to the underside of my sternum. A fishing line, pulled taut. It tugs me forward, past a warning sign that has fallen face-down in the dirt, past the rot of a collapsed timber ceiling.

Come.

The command isn't heard. It is felt. A pressure in the sinuses. A vibration in the teeth.

I pause at a junction where the corridor splits. Logic dictates I should turn back. Logic says I am a twenty-eight-year-old doctoral candidate standing in a condemnation-worthy ruin in the dark, chasing a hallucination born of stress and sexual frustration. Logic says I am liable to break an ankle or get arrested.

The pull jerks hard, a sharp pain behind my ribs that makes me gasp.

I turn left.

The voices of the tour group are gone and devoured by the distance and the density of the walls. There is only the sound of water—a slow, rhythmic dripping from somewhere overhead, counting down the seconds. Plip. Plip. Plip. And the wind. It sighs through cracks in the masonry, a low whistle that sounds like a flute played by a dying man.

The floor slopes downward. The air grows colder, losing the damp freshness of the rain and taking on a metallic tang. Old copper. Blood that has dried and turned to dust.

The beam of my flashlight catches the edge of a void.

I stop.

A spiral staircase falls away into the dark. It is narrow, the steps wedge-shaped and uneven, worn smooth in the center by centuries of feet.

There is no railing on the inner curve, just a sheer drop into a black well that seems to have no bottom. On the outer wall, a rusted iron handrail clings to the stone like a severed vine.

I grip the cold iron. It leaves rust flakes on my palm, gritty and sharp.

"This is madness," I whisper. The words are small, swallowed instantly by the shaft.

I lean over the edge, shining my light down. The beam dies before it hits the floor. It illuminates only the first twist of the spiral, the stones slick with moisture, looking like the gullet of a great stone worm.

My stomach rolls. Vertigo tilts the world on its axis. My knees threaten to buckle, urging me to sink to the floor, to crawl back to the safety of the gift shop and the lavender sachets.

But the pull is agonizing now. It is a hunger that dwarfs my fear. It drags at my center, insistent and cruel. He is down there. I do not know how I know, but the certainty is absolute. He is in the dark, waiting.

I put a boot on the first step.

The stone seems to sigh beneath my weight. A draft rushing up from the depths lifts the hair from my neck. It smells of him—peat smoke and winter air—and something else. Something older. It smells like the dream.

I take another step. Then another.

The staircase winds tight. I keep my back pressed to the outer wall, my hand white-knuckled on the rail. I count the steps to keep my mind from fracturing. One. Two. Three.

With every revolution, the air grows heavier. It presses against my skin, a physical weight, dense and gelatinous. It pushes against my eardrums. It is like descending into deep water. The pressure builds. My lungs have to work harder to draw breath.

I am walking into the mouth of the past, and it is swallowing me whole.

I hit the bottom step, and the world levels out.

My flashlight beam stutters, flickers, then stabilizes. I glance at the screen. The battery icon is a sliver of red, bleeding out. Twenty percent. Ten. It drains as I watch, the numbers ticking down like a bomb timer. The castle eats everything: light, heat, power.

I am in a corridor that shouldn't exist. The ceiling is low, heavy beams of blackened oak pressing down, threatening to crush the skull. Along the walls, alcoves have been carved into the living rock. They are empty, mostly, though one holds a pile of rags that might have once been a tunic, and another holds a scattering of small bones. Rat? Bird? They look too delicate to be anything else, but I don't look closer.

The hook behind my ribs yanks me forward. I stumble, catching myself on the wall.

A jolt of heat shoots through my arm.

I recoil, gasping, but then I reach out again. My fingers find grooves etched into the stone at shoulder height. Not random cracks. Symbols. Gaelic knots, rough and jagged, carved with frantic haste. I trace the lines. The stone here is not cold. It is warm. It pulses against my fingertips with the fever-heat of a living body.

Thump-thump. Thump-thump.

The corridor has a heartbeat. Or perhaps it is just my own blood roaring in my ears, deafening and wild.

I push off the wall. My breath comes in shallow, jagged, tearing sounds. Sweat slicks my hairline, stinging my eyes, yet my breath fogs in the air. I am burning and freezing all at once. The light from my phone flickers again, strobing. In the brief flashes of darkness, the shadows in the alcoves seem to detach themselves. They shift. They lean forward.

Get out, a small, sane voice whispers in the back of my skull. Run.

I cannot run. I am a marionette, and the strings are pulled tight.

The corridor ends.

Blocking the way is a door of timber planks thick as railway ties, bound in iron straps that have rusted to the color of dried gore. It is not locked.

It stands ajar, a crack of absolute blackness visible between the wood and the frame.

I stop. My boots scrape on the grit, a sound like a scream cut short.

My hand trembles so violently that the light dances across the wood, making the iron bands writhe. I reach out. My palm hovers inches from the wood.

If I open this, there is no going back. I know this with the same certainty that I know the sun will rise, or that I will never be happy in Boston again. This is the threshold.

"Lachlan?" I whisper. The name shreds my throat.

The silence from the room beyond is heavy. It waits.

I grip the iron handle. It is freezing, cold enough to burn. I shove.

The door groans, the hinges protesting with a shriek of metal on metal that vibrates in my teeth. It swings inward.

A blast of air rushes out to meet me. It is not just a draft. It is a breath—exhaled from the lungs of the earth. It hits me with the force of a physical blow, smelling of musk, and ancient, fermented longing.

My phone light flares once, blindingly bright, and then dies.

Blackness slams down. Instant. Total. The kind of dark that has weight, that fills the mouth and the eyes.

I stand frozen, blind, my hand still gripping the freezing iron of the door. I can hear my own heart; a frantic drum solo in the dark.

Then, from the center of the room, a sound.

The shift of weight. The scuff of a boot on stone. The rustle of heavy fabric moving against the air.

Someone is here.

CHAPTER 8

Are You Looking For Me?

The darkness presses against my skin like a living thing, warm and expectant. I stand motionless in the stone passage, my lungs barely drawing air, my ears straining for any sound beyond the thunder of my own pulse. Time stretches, elastic and unreliable. I feel more than hear a shift in the air behind me, a subtle displacement, the weight of another presence, and every nerve in my body ignites at once.

"Are ye lookin' fer me?" The voice is low and rough-edged. It comes from directly behind me, close enough that I should have felt breath on my neck. But there's no warmth, no stirring of air against my skin.

I turn, my body responding before my mind can process fear. The passage remains dark, but something has changed, a density to the shadows, a coalescence of darkness into the unmistakable outline of a man. Tall, broader than any modern frame has right to be, his silhouette cuts against the faint ambient light from distant torches. My eyes adjust, greedily seeking details I've only glimpsed in dreams and visions, the strong jaw, the proud nose, the eyes that catch what little light exists and reflect it back with unnatural clarity.

"Yes." The word escapes my throat, raw and honest. "I've been looking for you."

He steps closer, and the shadows retreat from his face like water parting. He's exactly as I dreamed and somehow more substantial, more real. His hair falls loose past his shoulders, black as a raven's wing. The tartan wrapped around his torso is woven in muted blues and greens, fastened at his shoulder with an iron brooch. Weathered by Highland winters, he looks live-in, yet his eyes—God, his eyes—are impossibly young, filled with a recognition that borders on reverence.

"I ken." His mouth curves, not quite a smile but something older, more private. "I've felt ye searching. Following the memories. Walking the paths I walked."

My heart slams against my ribs, painful in its insistence. My skin prickles with gooseflesh despite the unexpected warmth of the passage. This close, I can see the fine details of his clothing, the way the fabric hangs with a weight modern reproductions never achieve, the worn leather of the belt at his waist, the dirk sheathed against his thigh. Too perfect to be a costume, too vivid to be a ghost.

"Who are you?" I ask, though part of me already knows, has always somehow known.

He inclines his head slightly, a courtly gesture at odds with the wilderness that clings to him like a scent. "Lachlan Sutherland," he says, and hearing the name spoken in his voice sends a shock through my system, a jolt of recognition that travels from crown to sole. "Though you've known that for some time, I think."

His name settles in my chest like a stone dropped into still water, ripples of certainty spreading outward. "Lachlan," I repeat, testing the shape on my tongue. The syllables feel both foreign and familiar, like a word learned in childhood and long forgotten.

"And yer Fiona MacPherson," he says, not a question but a statement of fact. "But that's no all ye are."

He moves closer still, until barely a handspan separates us. The passage seems to constrict around us, the ancient stones leaning in to listen. I should be terrified—alone in the bowels of a ruined castle with a man who can't possibly exist—but fear feels distant, academic, a concept rather than an emotion.

"What else would I be?" My voice emerges steadier than I feel, though my fingers tremble at my sides.

His gaze travels over my face with painful intensity, as if memorizing features he once knew by heart. "It's no sae much the whit as the who, but that's for ye tae discover, lass. An' I'd say ye're already beginnin' tae remember."

Something in his accent shifts as he speaks, thicker, more authentically Highland than any tour guide or actor I've encountered. This isn't a performance. This is a voice shaped by a Scotland that existed centuries ago, vowels and consonants untouched by modern influences.

"The dreams," I whisper, unable to look away from his face. "They're not just dreams, are they?"

"Och, naw." His words carry the weight of a confession.

My rational mind scrambles for explanations: exhaustion, suggestion, an elaborate hoax, but my body knows better. The same recognition that flooded me in dreams now pours through my veins, hot and undeniable. This man held me, touched me with hands that knew every contour of my body, whispered my name, not Fi, but another name, older and truer.

"This isn't possible," I say, but the protest sounds hollow even to my own ears.

Lachlan's mouth quirks, a flash of unexpected humor in his solemn face. "There are many things possible within these walls...Things the modern world has long since forgotten." He gestures to the passage around us, his movement leaving a faint trail in the air, like smoke disturbed by a hand. "The stone remembers what folk cannae."

I reach out, hesitant, my fingers hovering inches from his sleeve. I want to touch him, to confirm his solidity, but something holds me back, not fear, but a peculiar reverence, as if touching him would commit me to something irreversible.

"Why me?" I ask the question that's haunted me since the first dream. "Why now?"

His expression darkens, sorrow and something fiercer crossing his features like storm clouds. "Because ye came back," he says simply. "As ye always do."

A chill that has nothing to do with the castle's temperature slithers down my spine. The implications of his words open before me like an abyss: past lives, reincarnation, a connection that transcends death itself. My academic training recoils from such concepts, but the part of me that recognized his touch in dreams understands with perfect clarity.

"And what happens now?" I ask, the words barely audible above the rushing in my ears.

Lachlan's gaze holds mine, centuries of waiting distilled into a single look. "That," he says softly, "depends entirely on whether ye're brave enough tae remember wha ye were...wha we were."

The air between us vibrates with possibility, with history, with a tension that makes my skin hum like a plucked string. Whatever comes next, I know with bone-deep certainty that my life will never be the same.

I hesitate only a moment before following Lachlan deeper into the passage. The rational voice in my head has fallen strangely silent. In its place surges something older, a certainty that precedes thought. I watch his broad back as he moves ahead, his outline somehow visible despite the darkness, as if he carries his own subtle luminescence. The stones around us seem to exhale, releasing a breath held for centuries.

"Bide close, lass," he says, his voice low enough that it seems to resonate directly in my bones rather than through the air. "These passages confuse even thae born tae them."

He leads me through an opening I would have missed entirely, a section of wall that appears solid until approached at just the right angle. Beyond lies a corridor narrower than the first, walls pressing close on either side. Unlike the tourist-trodden paths, these stones retain sharp edges, undulled by centuries of hands and shoulders.

"The servants used these ways," Lachlan explains, ducking slightly beneath a low arch. "Invisible passages for invisible folk. The laird could host a feast for fifty, an' the castle's workings would remain unseen."

We emerge into a slightly wider section where ambient light filters through cracks in the masonry. I realize we must be moving parallel to areas still accessible to the public, catching fragments of illumination from the main rooms. I can just make out Lachlan's profile now, the strong line of his jaw, the proud set of his mouth.

"There," he says, pointing to a narrow slit in the stone. "Look."

I press my eye to the opening. Beyond is a vast space I recognize as the Great Hall, though from an angle no tourist would notice. Afternoon light slants through the ruined ceiling, painting golden rectangles on the floor.

"It wisn aye a ruin," Lachlan murmurs, his breath close to my ear. "When I kent it, the hall stood forty feet high, beams blackened wi' smoke frae a hunner fires. The clan gathered here for every purpose, feasts that lasted three days, councils o' war, marriages, funeral rites."

His voice takes on a cadence that mesmerizes, words flowing like water over stone. "The tables stretched tha length o' tha room, oak planks polished tae a shine till they glinted like water in torchlight. Tha laird sat at tha head, his lady beside him, then blood kin in order o' favor, no just by birth."

"Where did you sit?" I ask, the question emerging without thought.

Something flickers across his face—pain, maybe, or regret. "Near the top, though not by ma ain choice. I preferred the lower tables, where men spoke truth instead o' pleasantries."

He guides me onward, one hand occasionally brushing my elbow when the passage turns sharply, or the floor becomes uneven. Each touch, however brief, sends currents of warmth through my skin, as if some dormant part of me responds to a familiar call.

We pass another viewing slit, this one overlooking what was once the armory. Now it stands empty save for a few glass cases containing relics too fragile to be handled, a rotted scabbard, remnants of a shield, and a broadsword eaten by rust.

"We planned our battles here," Lachlan says, his voice droppin' to a rougher tone. "Maps spraed across tables, men arguin' strategy until dawn while wimmen prepared bandages for wounds nae yet inflicted." His hand clenches at his side. "I stood in this room an' watched me brother send men tae die for pride disguised as honor."

I study his face in the diffused light. The sorrow etched there isn't academic or performative; it carries the weight of witnessed horror. "You fought in those battles," I say, not a question.

"Aye, an' led ma share o' it." His gaze fixates on some middle distance, seein' across time rather than space. "The first time I killed a man, I wis sixteen. He was someone's son, just like me. I remember that more than I remember his face."

We move deeper into the hidden heart of the castle, time slipping away as we walk. My academic mind tries to map our route, to place these secret passages within the known layout, but I soon abandon the attempt. The castle Lachlan shows me exists in a different dimension than the one documented in guidebooks and trust records.

"Here," he says, leading me into a small chamber barely large enough for us both. "This was a sanctuary o' sorts."

The room contains a single stone bench built into the wall and, above it, a tiny window admitting a shaft of fading daylight. The walls are carved with symbols I recognize from my research, protection runes older than Christianity but tolerated by priests in remote places like this.

"Women cam' here when birthing was weel-kennèd," Lachlan explains, his voice gentling. "Or when a husband's haun grew tae heavy. The old ways lived longer in these walls than priests wad care tae admit."

He describes rituals carried out by firelight, healing practices passed from mother to daughter, the preparation of hers and poultices in stone mortars that have long since crumbled to dust. His knowledge isn't the rehearsed recitation of a tour guide but the casual intimacy of someone recounting his own household.

"How do you know all this?" I ask, though part of me already understands.

Lachlan's eyes catch the light, reflecting it with unnatural brightness. "The same way ye ken which questions tae ask, though ye haven't the wake why yet."

Our path continues, winding even deeper. I lose track of time, of direction, of everything except the cadence of his voice and the occasional brush of his shoulder against mine. Each contact triggers a cascade of sensation, recognition, longing, a bone-deep certainty that this proximity is right, necessary, somehow coming home.

“The women wore linen shifts beneath their dresses,” Lachlan says, answering another question I asked about daily Highland life. “Wool against the skin chafes, especially when wet. And in the Highlands, everything is eventually wet.”

“What about jewelry?” I ask, my historian’s curiosity mingling with something more personal. “Archaeology shows silver brooches, but what was worn day to day?”

“Simpler things,” he replies, a smile warmin' his voice. “Carved wood, bone beads, polished stones on leather cords. Silver was for lairds’ wives and special occasions.” He glances at me, somethin' knowin' in his expression. "Ye favored a small pendant, amber set in bronze. Ye said it matched yer eyes.”

The casual way he talks of me from the past sends a shock through my system. Before I can question it, a sound echoes from behind us, footsteps, distant but approaching, accompanied by a voice calling indistinct words that bounce off stone.

Lachlan stiffens, his head turning toward the noise. “We’re no’ alone,” he says, the warmth draining from his tone. “The livin’ hae come seekin’.”

I realize with a start that I've completely forgotten about the tour group, about the world beyond these hidden passages. How long have I been walking with him? Minutes? Hours? The light that filters through the cracks has dimmed considerably, afternoon has slipped toward evening while I've been lost in his stories.

His shoulder brushes mine as he turns, the contact sending another wave of warmth through my body. "Come," he whispers. "There's one more place ye need to see."

We reach a junction after descending a narrow spiral staircase, steps worn concave by centuries of use. Three corridors branch from the central point, each identical to the naked eye, dark mouths in ancient stone. The air hangs heavier here, as if we've crossed some threshold into a deeper layer of time. My skin prickles with awareness; each breath draws in cold that seems to settle in my lungs rather than warm to my body.

Lachlan stops so abruptly that I nearly collide with his back. The junction forms a perfect trefoil, corridors radiating like spokes from a hub. Overhead, the ceiling rises into a small dome where faint remnants of paint cling to stone—spirals of blue and green, faded to ghosts of their former brilliance. The floor beneath my feet is different too, inlaid with a Celtic knot, endless and unbroken, worn nearly smooth by countless footsteps.

"The ancient heart," Lachlan says, voice so low I have to strain to hear it. "Three paths for three fates. Choice made manifest in stone."

He turns to face me, and my breath catches. Something has changed in his countenance—a deepening of the sorrow that's shadowed him throughout our journey, but also an intensity I haven't seen before. His eyes seem to hold the weight of centuries, of waiting beyond human endurance.

“Do ye feel it?” he asks, studying my face with painful focus. “The recognition? The memory buried in yer blood?”

I do feel something—a resonance that vibrates through my bones, a sense of déjà vu so profound it makes me dizzy. The junction seems familiar in a way that transcends academic knowledge, as if I’ve stood in this exact spot before, making this exact choice.

“I’ve been here,” I whisper, the words escaping before I can examine them. “But that’s impossible.”

Lachlan’s mouth curves in a smile more sorrowful than any weeping. “No impossible. Just forgotten, ken ye noo.” He steps closer, his presence filling the space between us with a charge that makes the air shimmer. “Ye’ve come hame at last, Isla.”

The name strikes me like a physical blow. Isla. The woman from my dreams, the one who wore my face but lived centuries ago. The one whose memories bled into mine since I first set foot in the castle.

“No,” I say, though I’m not sure what I’m denying—the name, the implication, or the certainty growing in my chest that he’s right. “I’m Fi MacPherson. I’m a doctoral student. I’m from Boston.”

"Ye are aw 'those things,” he agrees, his voice gentle. “And ye are more.” He reaches as if to touch my face, then stops just short, his hand hovering near my cheek. "Ye carry her soul. Ye always have.”

He turns away suddenly, facing the leftmost corridor. "This way leads to the chapel," he says, his back to me. "Where we first met up, where we first—" He breaks off, shoulders rigid with some unspoken memory.

I move without thinking, reaching for him, needing that connection. My fingers extend toward his arm, expecting the solidity of wool and flesh. Instead, they pass through his form like smoke, meeting nothing but colder air and a sensation like static electricity that shoots up my arm and branches through my chest.

I jerk back with a gasp, the shock so complete it freezes me in place. My mind struggles to process what's happened, denial warring with the evidence of my own senses. Lachlan turns slowly, his expression a mixture of resignation and ancient grief.

"You're not—" My words catch. "You can't be—"

"Real?" he finishes for me, the corner of his mouth lifting in that not-quite smile. "I am as real as these stones. More real than most living men. But aye, not flesh and blood, not anymore." He looks down at his own hand, turning it as if examining the lack of substance. "Not for almost five hundred years."

Terror spikes through my system, my body finally catching up to what my mind has refused to accept. The man I've been following, speaking with, nearly touching, isn't a man at all. The intimate stories, the brush of shoulders, the warmth I thought I felt—all impossible, all beyond rational explanation.

"You're a ghost," I whisper, the words sounding absurd even as I speak them. Yet I know they are true. Had known, perhaps, from the first moment I saw him in the archway, from the first dream that pulled me into his arms.

Lachlan's eyes meet mine, blue as winter ice and infinitely sad. "I am whit remains when everything else is tak'd. Memory made manifest. Longin' given form." He pauses, something fiercer cutting through the sorrow. "I am the one wha' ha' waited for ye through lifetimes."

I can't move, can't speak, my entire reality shifting beneath my feet like sand in a tide. The academic who collected evidence and built arguments on verifiable facts—that woman stands in a three-way junction deep beneath a Scottish castle, facing the ghost of a Highland warrior who claims to know her soul.

And the most terrifying part isn't his revelation. It's how deeply, how completely, I believe him.

"The dreams," I manage, voice barely audible. "They were real."

"Aye," he says simply. "Memory breaking through the veil. Yer soul recognizing what yer mind cannae."

From somewhere above and behind us comes a voice, distant but growing clearer—the tour guide, calling for missing visitors. "Hello? Is anyone down here? The castle's closing in fifteen minutes!"

The sound pierces the bubble of unreality that envelops me. I glance toward it reflexively, the modern world intruding into this liminal space between past and present.

When I turn back, Lachlan's form has grown less distinct, the edges of him blurring like watercolor in rain. His eyes remain sharp, though, fixed on mine with an emotion too complex for simple naming.

"They'll find ye soon," he says, his voice fading with his form. "But we are not finished, you and I. The curse binds us still."

"Wait," I call, reaching again, though I know my hand will find no purchase. "What curse? Who am I to you?"

But he is already dissolving, his outline melting into the shadows of the junction. The last thing to remain is his gaze, sorrowful and ancient, filled with a longing that transcends death itself.

"Find me again," his voice whispers, seeming to come from all three corridors at once. "Remember."

And then he is gone, leaving me alone in the junction with the distant voice of the tour guide drawing nearer, and the certainty that everything I believed about myself is about to unravel.

CHAPTER 9
The Ghost Her Loves Her

The walls pressed closer as the ancient stones exhaled centuries of trapped breath. The chill settled deeper, not just on my skin but in my marrow, as if my body suddenly remembered what it meant to be mortal in the presence of eternity. My pulse hammered in my temples, each beat a denial, another failed attempt to process the impossible.

He was a ghost. I had walked with a ghost, listened to a ghost, and nearly touched a ghost. Worse, I had recognized him, felt his pull in my dreams, responded to a name that wasn't mine. What did that make me?

"Hello? Is anyone down there?" The voice echoed down the spiral staircase, sharp and modern, shattering the silence. "The castle's closing in five minutes!"

I turned back to Lachlan, a desperate plea forming on my lips. Stay, explain, don't leave me with just questions. But the space where he had stood was empty. Not fading, not dissolving into mist. Simply gone, as if he'd never been there at all. Only the lingering cold marked where he'd stood, a pocket of winter in the already chill air.

"Oh, thank God. Here you are!"

A young woman with a red lanyard and a pinched expression emerged into the junction, clipboard clutched to her chest. Her flashlight beam swept over me, then darted to each of the three corridors, checking for other strays.

"You can't be down here," she said, her voice tight with professional irritation. "This area is strictly off-limits. There's structural damage; it's not safe." She glanced nervously at the ceiling, as if expecting it to collapse at any moment.

I couldn't speak. My tongue felt alien in my mouth, too thick to form words. I stood rooted there, my hand still outstretched where it had passed through his arm.

Her expression softened slightly, professional concern replacing annoyance. "Are you all right? You look like you've seen a..." She stopped herself, flushing. "Sorry. Bad joke in a place like this."

A ghost. The unspoken word hung between us.

"I'm fine," I manage finally, my voice distant in my own ears. "I got... lost." Even I could hear how hollow it sounded.

"Well, we need to get back to the group. They're waiting at the exit." She gestured toward the staircase. "How did you even find your way down here? The gate was locked."

I lowered my hand at last, the movement requiring conscious effort, as if my arm had forgotten how to obey my brain. "I don't...I'm not sure."

She frowned but didn't press. "Come on, then. Watch your step on the stairs. They're uneven."

I followed mechanically, my body on autopilot while my mind remained in that dark junction with the ghost of Lachlan Sutherland. Each step away felt like tearing something vital, as if I were leaving pieces of myself behind in the darkness.

We ascended the spiral staircase in silence, her flashlight carving a path through shadow. I studied the back of her jacket, focusing on mundane details—the slight fraying at the shoulder seam, the way the fabric bunched at her waist—anything to anchor me to the present.

But my mind kept replaying the moment my fingers passed through his form, the shock of it, the impossible cold. The sudden, devastating knowledge that the man who had haunted my dreams, who had shown me the castle's secrets, who had spoken of intimate things across centuries—he was dead. Had been dead for hundreds of years.

And yet I had known him. Not just recognized his face but the cadence of his voice, the way he moved, the set of his shoulders when he spoke of his brother.

The corridor widened, leading back to the public areas of the castle. Ahead, I could see the tour group gathered near the exit, faces turned toward us, expressions ranging from boredom to mild concern.

"Found her," the guide called, relief in her voice. "She was just... exploring."

I stepped into their midst, a ghost among the living. Their chatter washed over me—questions, comments, a joke about getting lost in time—but none of it penetrated the fog in my mind. I nodded when appropriate, murmured apologies, accepted reproving looks with the automatic grace of someone operating on instinct alone.

But inside, where no one could see, I was falling through darkness, Lachlan's final words echoing in my bones.

Find me again. Remember.

I can't even recall the drive back to the B&B. The road unspooled beneath my rental car's tires, miles vanishing into a blur of headlights and mist. My body handled the wheel while my mind stayed trapped in that underground junction, replaying the moment my fingers passed through his arm with the obsessive precision of a scholar examining an artifact that shouldn't exist.

I parked crookedly, tires crunching gravel as I lurched to a stop. The B&B sign blinked above me—VACANCY, then nothing, then VACANCY again—its fluorescent stutter matching the fragmented rhythm of my thoughts. I sat motionless behind the wheel, key in the ignition, until the engine's ticking as it cooled finally registered.

The night air bit into my skin as I stepped out, my jacket suddenly insufficient against the Highland chill. I walked toward my room with the careful, deliberate steps of someone navigating unfamiliar terrain in darkness. The hallway lights flickered as I approached my door, casting jumping shadows that made my heart stutter with memories still too fresh.

The key trembled in my hand, scraping against the lock without finding purchase. I tried again, focusing on the simple mechanics of metal sliding into metal—trying to anchor myself in this mundane task. It took three attempts before the tumblers finally clicked.

I pushed the door open and slipped inside, immediately leaning back against it as if to bar entry to something pursuing me. The latch clicked shut with a finality that broke something inside me. My legs, which had carried me through castle corridors and back here, suddenly gave way. I slid down until I sat on the worn carpet, knees drawn to my chest, back pressed against the only barrier between me and a world that no longer made sense.

My breath came in shallow gasps that didn't seem to reach my lungs. The room tilted around me, its cheap furniture and generic art swimming in and out of focus. I pressed my palms against the carpet, feeling its rough texture, trying to ground myself in the physical sensation.

"Breathe," I whispered. "Just breathe."

But each inhale brought the memory of cold stone and ancient passages, of stories told in a voice that carried the cadence of centuries. Of eyes that had looked at me with recognition across an impossible divide of time. Of a hand that wasn't solid enough to touch, yet had somehow touched me more deeply than any living man ever had.

The truth settled into my bones like winter frost: Lachlan Sutherland was a ghost. Not a tour actor in period costume. Not a hallucination conjured by my exhausted mind. A ghost—the lingering spirit of a man who had died centuries before I was born.

The radiator in the corner clanked to life, its fan pushing tepid air that did nothing to dispel the chill rooted inside me. I wrapped my arms tightly around my knees, making myself smaller, as if that might somehow contain the enormity of what I'd experienced.

I rocked slightly, a primal self-soothing rhythm, as fragments of our encounter played through my mind in disjointed flashes. How he'd appeared in the corridor, tall and solid in the darkness. How he'd described the castle not as a ruin but as a living place, full of sounds and scents and people long vanished. The casual way he mentioned details no historian could know—the feel of wool against skin, the taste of meat preserved in cold cellars, the exact cadence of prayers over winter graves.

How he said "you" when describing a woman who had lived and died hundreds of years ago.

The academic in me—the part that built my identity around evidence and verification, that learned to question, to doubt, to demand proof—struggled to categorize what had happened. Sleep deprivation. Suggestion. The power of folklore on a susceptible mind. Maybe I'd been drugged or was in the early stages of a neurological condition. There had to be rational explanations.

Yet none of them accounted for the specific gravity of his gaze, or the way my body recognized him before my mind could name him. None explained how he knew secret passageways missing from every blueprint or tour map. None explained the sensation of my fingers passing through his form—denser than air, colder than flesh.

"His clothes," I whispered to the empty room. "The details were wrong for a costume."

Modern reproductions always missed small things—the weight of the wool, the way tartan draped, the weathering of leather exposed to Highland winters. His plaid was worn at the edges, darkened by smoke, marked by real time rather than artificial aging. His shirt was hand-stitched, seams uneven in places. His boots bore the specific wear pattern of Highland terrain, not modern pavement.

And his knowledge of the castle was intimate, personal—the knowledge of someone who had lived there, not someone who had studied it.

I pressed my palms against my eyes, trying to block the evidence my mind kept cataloguing. But the darkness behind my lids only summoned the memory of his face—the sorrow etched there when he spoke of battles long ago, the tenderness in his voice describing the women's chamber, the raw longing when he looked at me.

"Find me again," he had said. "Remember."

Remember what? Who was Isla, and why did the name resonate in my blood? What curse bound us across centuries? What did he want from me?

The walls of this small room seemed to pulse with these questions, the space too confined to hold the vastness of what I was confronting. I lowered my hands from my eyes, gazing at my palms as if they might still bear the imprint of that impossible touch.

"He's real," I whispered, the words both surrender and revelation. "He's actually real."

The academic in me protested, but weakly, drowned out by the certainty taking root in a deeper, more primal part of my consciousness—the part that recognized Lachlan before I even saw him. The part that drew me to Sutherland Castle, to that specific corridor, to the exact junction where three paths met.

The part that, even now, was already planning how to find him again.

CHAPTER 10
The Nightfall Possession

I lie rigid beneath the thin blanket, watching shadows crawl across the textured ceiling. The digital clock's red numerals ticked past midnight an hour ago, but sleep remains a distant shore. My mind churns with the truth I discovered in the castle's depths: Lachlan Sutherland is real. Not flesh and blood, but something that persists beyond death, something that knows me by another name.

The single bedside lamp casts elongated silhouettes across the walls, distorting the mundane furniture into looming sentinels. I left it on deliberately, unwilling to face the Highland darkness that presses against my window like a living thing. The radiator hums its mechanical drone, yet fails to dispel the persistent chill I brought from the castle.

I shift, sheets rustling beneath me. My academic training offers explanations: stress, suggestion, the power of place on the imagination. But none can account for the sensation of my fingers passing through his arm, or the recognition that blazed in his eyes when he called me Isla.

The temperature in the room plunges without warning. One moment the air is merely cool; the next, my breath fogs before my face. The lamp's light dims, then surges, casting jittery shadows across the walls. My pulse quickens, my body responding before my mind can process what's happening.

"Who's there?" I whisper, the words materializing as vapor in the suddenly arctic air.

Nothing answers but the faint drip of the bathroom faucet and the muffled sound of a car passing on the distant road. Yet the sense of presence intensifies—not a threat, but an awareness, a weight to the air that wasn't there before. The hairs on my arms lift, skin prickling with gooseflesh that has nothing to do with the cold.

I am being watched.

I push myself up against the headboard, scanning the corners of the room. The shadows have deepened, gathering most densely near the foot of my bed. As I stare, the darkness there seems to thicken, coalescing into a shape more substantial than mere absence of light.

A silhouette forms, tall and broad-shouldered, the outline unmistakable even before details emerge. The plaid draped across his shoulder, the loose hair falling past his collarbone, the proud set of his jaw—all exactly as I remember from the castle passageway.

"Lachlan." His name escapes my lips without conscious intent.

He materializes further—not solid, never solid, but present in a way that defies rational explanation. The air around him wavers like heat rising from summer pavement, distorting the reality behind him. His edges remain indistinct, as if parts of him exist in another dimension, or another time.

Only his eyes are sharp and clear—blue as Highland winters, fixed on me with an intensity that steals my breath. They hold centuries of waiting, of watching, of remembering what I've somehow forgotten.

The scholar in me recoils, cataloging the impossibility of a ghost in my hotel room with the precision of an academic defense. This isn't happening, can't be happening. Spirits do not cross the veil. The dead do not return. Yet my body knows differently, responding to his presence with a recognition that bypasses reason and lodges directly in my marrow.

Lachlan moves toward the bed, his steps soundless on the worn carpet. The air ripples around him like water disturbed by a stone. He pauses beside me, looming above where I sit frozen against the headboard. His expression carries such naked longing that I have to look away, overwhelmed by the intimacy of it.

"Ye found me again," he says, his voice like wind through stone passageways— not quite sound, but something my mind translates into words I can understand.

He reaches toward my face, hand hovering just above my cheek. Though his fingers don't touch me—couldn't touch me—warmth radiates from the space between us, a phantom caress that defies the room's chill. My skin prickles beneath the almost-contact, nerve endings firing as if responding to actual touch.

I shiver, unable to reconcile the contradiction: the absence of physical contact and the undeniable sensation it produces. Part of me wants to pull away, to deny this breach of natural law. But a deeper part, a part I'm only beginning to recognize, leans toward the ghostly hand, seeking more of that impossible warmth.

"What do you want from me?" I whisper, voice strained with the effort of maintaining control.

His mouth curves into a half-smile that carries more sorrow than joy. "Whit I've always wanted. Whit was taken from us."

The words resonate beyond their simple meaning, vibrating through my chest like the aftershock of a blow. Time seems to stretch between us, elastic and unreliable. The digital clock still reads 1:17, though minutes must have passed since I last looked at it.

Lachlan's gaze never wavers, holding me captive more effectively than any physical restraint. I feel pinned beneath the weight of his attention, examined down to the cellular level by eyes that somehow know me better than I know myself.

"Isla," he whispers, the name sliding into my consciousness like a key into a lock.

The sound of it—not Fi, not Fiona, but Isla—sends a jolt through my system. It isn't just a name. It's an invocation, a summoning of something that slumbers within me, something that recognizes the call and stirs in response. My rational mind fights against it, denying the implication that I am someone other than who I believe myself to be. But my body betrays me, warmth spreading through my limbs as if my blood itself remembers what my mind cannot.

“I’m not her,” I insist, but the protest sounds hollow even to my own ears.

“Ye are,” Lachlan counters, voice gentle but unyielding. “Ye always have been. In every lifetime, in every form, ye carry her soul.”

The conviction in his words terrifies me, not because I fear it’s a lie, but because I fear it’s the truth. What would it mean if I weren’t just Fi MacPherson, if my identity were merely the current iteration of something much older, something bound to this ghost by ties that transcend death itself?

His hand moves from my cheek to hover above my forehead, and the warmth intensifies. My eyelids grow suddenly heavy, as if weighted by unseen hands. I fight against the sensation, struggle to maintain consciousness, but exhaustion crashes through my system like a wave. Sleep pulls at me with irresistible force.

“Rest now,” Lachlan murmurs, his form beginning to fade at the edges. “Remember in dreams what you cannae yet face in waking.”

I want to protest, to demand answers, to understand what is happening to me. But my body surrenders to the overwhelming fatigue, limbs growing leaden, thoughts blurring at the edges. The last thing I see before sleep claims me is Lachlan’s face, watching over me with the patient devotion of one who waited centuries and can wait a few hours more.

I slip beneath consciousness like a stone through dark water, sinking past the thin barrier between present and past. The room dissolves, replaced by cold stone and flickering torchlight. I am no longer Fi—the name, the identity, the century all fall away. I am Isla now, my back pressed against the rough wall of a hidden alcove, my heart hammering against my ribs as Lachlan's solid, warm body pins me there.

The alcove is barely large enough for two, carved into the thickness of the castle wall where a window was bricked over decades ago. A single torch gutters in a sconce at the corridor's turn, casting just enough light to find our way but not enough to expose us. The space smells of damp stone and old smoke, but I notice only the scent of him—peat and heather, leather and male sweat, the particular tang of Highland winter caught in the wool of his plaid.

"They'll be looking for me," I whisper, though I make no move to leave the circle of his arms. "My absence will be noted."

Lachlan's eyes catch the distant torchlight, reflecting it back like a wolf in darkness. His hand slides to my waist, fingers splaying possessively across the small of my back, pulling me closer until the rough weave of his kilt abrades my skirts. The friction sends a shiver through me that has nothing to do with the castle's perpetual chill.

"Let them look," he murmurs, breath hot against my ear. "I've waited three days to hae ye alone."

His other hand finds mine, fingers intertwining with a desperate strength that walks the line between pleasure and pain. He lifts our joined hands above my head, pressing them against the stone, using the leverage to align our bodies more completely. I feel the hard planes of his chest against my breasts, the solid weight of his thigh wedged between my own, the heat of him burning through layers of linen and wool.

The castle breathes around us—distant footsteps echoing through corridors, the creak of ancient timber settling, the faint strains of a servant's song drifting up from the kitchens. Each sound is a reminder of our danger, of eyes that might discover us, of the consequences that would follow. Yet the threat only sharpens my awareness, makes each touch more acute, each stolen moment more precious.

Lachlan lowers his head, mouth finding the sensitive hollow beneath my ear. His lips trace a path down the curve of my neck, teeth grazing my skin just hard enough to send a jolt of sensation straight to my core. My free hand clutches at his shoulder, fingers digging into the muscle there, anchoring myself against the flood of feeling.

"We cannae keep meeting like this," I whisper against his temple, even as my body arches into his touch, contradicting my words. I mean it—each encounter risks everything. My reputation, my future, perhaps even my life if my father discovers my dalliance with the younger Sutherland brother instead of the elder who owns my hand.

Lachlan raises his head, gaze burning into mine with an intensity that robs me of breath. "I would rather die than stop," he says, voice rough with desire and something deeper, something that transcends mere wanting. His hand tightens on mine, his thumb stroking the inside of my wrist where my pulse races beneath thin skin.

The declaration should frighten me, should remind me of the stakes. Instead, it unleashes something wild and reckless in my blood. I surge forward, closing the last breath of space between us, my mouth finding his with unerring precision.

The kiss isn't gentle. It can't be, not with the wanting behind it, not with the constant threat of discovery hovering at our backs. Our lips meet in desperate hunger, open and demanding. Lachlan groans into my mouth, the sound vibrating through my body like a plucked string. His hand releases my wrist to tangle in my hair, dislodging pins that clatter unnoticed to the stone floor.

My freed hand finds the nape of his neck, fingers threading through hair that feels like silk despite its warrior's length. I pull him closer, deepening the kiss, my tongue meeting his in a dance as old as desire itself. He tastes of cloves and whisky, of forbidden things I was raised to avoid but now can't imagine living without.

His hand at my waist slides lower, gathering the fabric of my skirts, bunching them in his fist until he can touch the bare skin of my calf, my knee, my thigh. The calluses on his palm catch against my skin, the slight abrasion sending ripples of pleasure up my spine. His touch is possessive, certain, mapping territory he considers rightfully his.

"Ah dream o' ye," he murmurs against my mouth between kisses. "When we're apart, I see yer face in the flames, hear yer voice in the wind."

His words unleash a flood of heat through my body. I press myself harder against him, one hand sliding beneath his shirt to find the warm skin of his back, to feel the flex of muscle as he moves against me. My nails scrape lightly down his spine, marking him as surely as he's marked me with his mouth at my throat.

"And I dream of ye," I confess, words torn from my throat on a gasp as his fingers trace patterns on the sensitive skin of my inner thigh. "I wake reaching for ye in the darkness."

The admission breaks something in his control. Lachlan presses me harder against the wall, mouth reclaiming mine with renewed hunger. One hand cradles the back of my head, protecting me from the rough stone, while the other continues its maddening exploration beneath my skirts.

I hook one leg around his, pulling him impossibly closer, feeling the hard evidence of his desire pressing against my hip. The position opens me further to his touch, a vulnerability I would allow no other. His fingers trace higher, finding the damp heat at my center, and I bite my lip to stifle the sound threatening to escape.

"Let me hear ye," he whispers, voice like a command I can't resist. "I need to ken I'm not alone in this madness."

I turn my face into his shoulder, muffling my moan against the wool of his plaid as his fingers continue their exquisite torture. The scent of him fills my lungs—smoke and sweat and something uniquely male that calls to something primal within me. My hands clutch at him, one tangling in his hair, the other gripping his hip with bruising force.

A distant shout echoes through the corridor—a servant calling to another, still far away but a stark reminder of the world beyond our alcove. Lachlan stills, body tense with the instinct to protect. For a heartbeat, we both freeze, listening. The voice recedes, moving away rather than toward us.

The interruption doesn't cool our passion but transforms it, lending renewed urgency to our touches. Time is our enemy, each second precious and fleeting. I pull Lachlan's mouth back to mine, pouring everything I can't say into the kiss—the longing, the fear, the certainty that whatever lies between us is worth any risk.

"If they find us—" I begin against his lips.

They shannae,", he interrupts, fierce and certain. "And if they did, I'd fight the warld tae keep ye.

The declaration hangs between us, heavy with promise and peril. I know the truth of it—Lachlan Sutherland would indeed defy family, clan, and God himself to claim what he considers his. The knowledge should terrify me. Instead, it feels like coming home after a lifetime of wandering.

I press my forehead to his, our breath mingling in the narrow space between us. Our bodies remain locked together, hands still exploring, hearts beating in desperate synchrony. In this moment, stolen from time itself, we are not Sutherland and Grant, not hunter and prey, not forbidden lovers risking destruction. We are simply Lachlan and Isla, two halves of a whole that somehow found each other despite the world's determination to keep us apart.

"I would rather die than stop," I echo his words back to him, sealing the vow with another kiss that tastes of promise and fate and something eternal that neither life nor death could sever.

I wake with a gasp, body jackknifing upright in the bed. My heart slams against my ribs, and sweat slicks my skin, plastering the thin cotton nightgown to my body. For one disorienting moment, I can't place myself in time or space—the cold stone of the castle alcove still pressing against my back, Lachlan's hands still gripping my wrists, his mouth still claiming mine with desperate hunger. The sensations are too vivid, too immediate to be merely a dream.

Reality asserts itself in fragments: the synthetic comforter twisted around my legs, the drone of the ancient heating unit, the faint glow of the digital clock. The hotel room is empty now, the spectral figure gone from the foot of my bed. Yet the air retains a lingering warmth where Lachlan stood, a pocket of heat that defies the room's otherwise persistent chill.

I press trembling fingers to my lips, which still tingle as though the kisses in my dream were real. The physical sensation is undeniable—a slight swelling, a phantom pressure, the ghost of a passion that happened centuries ago and also minutes before. My nightgown clings damply to my flushed skin, my body still humming with an arousal that belonged to another woman in another time.

I push tangled hair from my face, trying to orient myself. The dream—if it can be called that—didn't feel like imagination or fantasy. It carried the unmistakable texture of memory: specific, detailed, laden with emotional weight that invention couldn't replicate. I remember the exact pattern of the stones in the alcove, the precise route through the servants' corridors that led us there, the small scar at the base of Lachlan's throat that I traced with my fingertip during previous encounters.

Previous encounters that I, Fi MacPherson, doctoral student from Boston, never experienced.

I swing my legs over the side of the bed, the carpet rough beneath my bare feet. My body feels simultaneously my own and not my own, as if I'm inhabiting a space between two existences. The muscles in my thighs ache slightly from being pressed against the stone wall, though I spent the entire night in bed. A tender spot at the juncture of my neck and shoulder throbs where Lachlan's teeth grazed my skin—not hard enough to mark, but with enough pressure to send lightning through my blood.

I lift my hands, turning them over in the dim light. I examine my wrists, half-expecting to find bruises where Lachlan pinned me against the castle wall. The skin is unmarked, yet I can still feel the precise shape of his fingers, the strength in his grip, the contrast between his callused palm and the soft pad of his thumb that stroked the inside of my wrist.

"This isn't possible," I whisper to the empty room, but the words lack conviction.

What is happening to me defies rational explanation, yet carries a certainty that transcends logic. I am Fi MacPherson, a woman of the twenty-first century with a life and identity entirely my own. Yet I am also Isla—a woman who loved Lachlan Sutherland with a desperation that defied centuries, whose memories now surface in my dreams with the clarity of lived experience.

The boundaries are dissolving between us, between then and now, between dream and waking. I can't determine where my own consciousness ends and Isla's begins. Have I always carried these memories, dormant until proximity to the castle and to Lachlan's spirit awakened them? Or is something more inexplicable occurring—a possession, a merging, a remembrance of something my rational mind can't comprehend?

The digital clock on the nightstand flashes 4:17 AM in harsh red numerals—the hour when the veil between worlds grows thin in countless legends. I stare at the numbers, wondering if they hold significance. The time itself seems suspended, the minutes refusing to advance as I watch, as if this moment exists outside the normal flow of time.

I draw my knees to my chest, wrapping my arms around them. The scent of peat and heather still clings to my skin, though no fire burns in the hotel room, no Highland flora grows for miles. The smell isn't from my own body but transferred from his—from a dream-touch that somehow bridged the gap between past and present, between life and whatever existence Lachlan now inhabits.

"Lachlan?" I whisper into the darkness, voice barely audible even to myself.

No answer comes, at least not in words. But across the room, the curtains stir slightly, lifting and settling as if disturbed by a gentle breath. The window is closed, sealed against the Highland winter—no draft possible from that source. Yet the fabric moves again, a deliberate ripple that travels its length before subsiding.

My skin prickles, but not with fear. The sensation is closer to recognition, to the awareness of being seen by eyes I can't detect. He is still here, just beyond the threshold of my perception, watching over me as he promised to do.

"I felt you," I say to the apparently empty room. "Not just in the dream. Before that. Your hands, your—" I break off, heat flooding my cheeks at the memory of his touch beneath my skirts, of the pleasure he drew from my body with such practiced skill.

The curtains remain still this time, but the air near the foot of the bed seems to thicken slightly, gathering substance without forming a visible shape. I have the distinct impression that if I reached out, my fingers might encounter something more substantial than empty space.

I don't reach. Not yet. The space between us—between Lachlan and me, between present and past, between reality and whatever lies beyond it—feels sacred somehow, a threshold not to be crossed without understanding what waits on the other side.

Instead, I press my palm to my chest, feeling the drumbeat of my heart beneath my nightgown. The rhythm seems to echo with a second pulse, as if two hearts beat within my ribcage—my own, and one that ceased its natural rhythm centuries ago but somehow continues in another form.

Outside, the first tentative calls of early birds pierce the darkness, though dawn remains hours away. The sound anchors me in the present, reminding me of the world beyond this room, beyond this strange communion with a past I'm only beginning to understand. Yet even as I acknowledge the reality of the modern night, of my own identity, I can't dismiss what I experienced.

The dream was a message, a reminder, perhaps even a warning. Lachlan showed me who we had been to each other—the passion, the secrecy, the willingness to risk everything for moments together. What he didn't reveal was how our story ended, what curse he mentioned in the castle passage, what tragic fate bound us across centuries.

I settle back against the pillows, eyes fixed on the still-rippling curtains. I know with bone-deep certainty that sleep will not return tonight, nor will I be alone in my vigil until dawn. Whatever journey began in Sutherland Castle's hidden passageway is only beginning to unfold.

The boundary between my world and Lachlan's has worn thin, allowing him to cross over, allowing me to remember. What remains unclear is whether that boundary can ever be restored—or if I will even want it to be.

CHAPTER 11

Tell Me Who I Am

I return to Sutherland Castle as dusk bleeds across the Highland sky, my skin still warm with the ghost-touch of last night's dreams. The tourists cluster at the entrance, cameras flashing against the fading light, oblivious to the current that pulls me deeper, not toward the approved paths with their helpful plaques and safety ropes, but to the forgotten places where the stones remember their secrets. My fingers tremble as I check my watch, waiting for the perfect moment to slip away unnoticed.

The tour guide's voice drifts toward me, reciting facts about restoration efforts and architectural styles. I let it wash over me, meaningless as rainfall. When she turns to lead the group toward the Great Hall, I step sideways into shadow, my body remembering a path I've never consciously walked.

The corridor opens before me, darker than mere absence of light should allow. I trail my fingers along the damp stone wall, feeling each imperfection like braille. The chill seeps into my skin, but beneath it runs a contradictory warmth, as if my blood recognizes these passages even as my mind struggles to map them. With each step, the pull behind my sternum grows stronger, that invisible hook lodged between my ribs, drawing me forward with a certainty that bypasses thought.

"I know you're here," I call, my voice bouncing off ancient stone. "No more games. No more dreams. I want answers."

The silence that follows feels watchful, heavy with intention rather than emptiness. I continue deeper, guided by that inexorable tug, until I reach the junction where the three corridors meet. The trefoil pattern on the floor seems to pulse beneath my boots, though I know it's merely a trick of the fading light filtering through cracks in the masonry above.

"Lachlan," I speak his name with more command than I feel, my academic training falling away in favor of something older, more instinctive. "Show yourself."

The air thickens at the edges of my vision, shadow gathering substance like water condensing from vapor. He forms gradually, first the broad outline of shoulders, then the details filling in: the plaid draped across his chest, the leather belt at his waist, the proud set of his jaw emerging from darkness. His eyes appear last, blue as winter ice, fixed on me with an intensity that makes my skin prickle.

"You came back." His voice carries the weight of centuries, each word shaped by Highland winds long silent.

"I never left," I reply, surprised by my own certainty. "Not really."

We stand facing each other across the junction, separated by more than mere physical space. My fingers press white against the cold stone wall, seeking support as my knees threaten to buckle.

My pulse drums in my ears, each beat a counterpoint to the silence stretching between us.

"Tell me about Isla," I demand, forcing strength into my voice. "Tell me why I dream her memories. Why I wake with the taste of you on my lips."

Lachlan steps forward, the motion fluid despite his insubstantial form. His warrior's stance softens imperceptibly. Sorrow etches lines around his eyes that weren't visible before, revealing the weight of time on a spirit that cannot age.

"Ye ken already, " he says, each word deliberate. "Yer body remembers whit yer mind refuses tae accept."

"Say it," I insist, though my voice breaks on the words. "I need to hear it."

He moves closer still, his outline wavering like a reflection in troubled water. "Ye are Isla," he says simply. "No a descendant. No a resemblance. Ye carry her soul, just as ye hae in every life since she died after bein' taken frae my arms."

The words should sound absurd, the ravings of a mind fractured by time or a deliberate manipulation. Yet they settle into me like stones dropping through still water, creating ripples of recognition that spread outward from my center.

"That's not possible," I whisper, but the protest lacks conviction. My breath catches as he steps closer, near enough that I should feel the heat of him, the displacement of air by his body. I feel nothing but a slight cooling, as if he draws warmth rather than generates it.

"Yer soul returns," he continues, his voice gaining strength. "Different body, different name, different life—but aye, it's aye ye. Always findin' yer way back to these stones. Back to me."

My chest aches with a pain that belongs to no medical textbook, a hollowness that feels ancient and familiar at once. "Why? Why would a soul do that?"

"Love," Lachlan says, his voice barely a whisper, yet it fills the space between us. "A love that even death couldnae end. A bond that his curse couldnae break."

"Whose curse?" I ask, though part of me already knows the answer.

"My brother's." His form dims slightly, as if the memory itself has power to weaken him. "Hamish cursed us as he died, binding our souls to this place, to this endless cycle of finding and losing each other."

Fragments of dreams flash behind my eyes—not just last night's vivid encounter, but older dreams, half-remembered upon waking. A man's face twisted with jealous rage. Blood on stone floors. A knife that glinted in torchlight. My hand flies to my throat, fingers tracing the phantom sensation of steel against skin.

“I’ve died before,” I whisper, the knowledge surfacing from some deep well within me. “Many times.”

Lachlan nods, his expression a mixture of tenderness and ancient grief. “Each time ye return, pulled back tae these stones whaur it all began. Each time, we find each other. Each time, he finds us.”

“But I don’t remember,” I protest, even as contradictory memories flicker at the edges of my consciousness—faces I’ve worn, lives I’ve lived, deaths I’ve died.

"Ye begin to,” he counters. “The dreams. The recognition. The way ye followed hidden passages no livin' soul remembers.” His form solidifies slightly as he speaks, as if my growing belief lends him substance. "Yer soul knows the way, even when yer mind rebels against it.”

I close my eyes, letting the sensations wash over me—the castle’s peculiar gravity that’s pulled me since I first saw it, the dreams too vivid to be mere fantasy, the recognition that blazed through me when I first saw Lachlan in the archway. When I open them again, he’s watching me with eyes that have waited centuries for this moment of understanding.

“We’re bound,” I say softly, testing the truth of it against my tongue. “My soul to yours. To this place.”

“By love,” he says. “And by blood. By vows we made and by the curse that twisted them.”

The invisible tether between us pulls tighter, a connection I can neither see nor deny. My body hums with it, a resonance that makes the stone beneath my palm vibrate in sympathy. I stand at the edge of a precipice, knowing that to accept what he's telling me means abandoning everything I thought I knew about myself, about reality.

Yet I can no more resist this pull than the tide can resist the moon.

"I feel it," I admit, the words dragged from some place deeper than thought. "I've always felt it, even before I knew what it was."

Lachlan's expression shifts, centuries of waiting giving way to something close to hope. "Then ye're beginnin' tae mind," he says. "And this time, perhaps, we micht break the cycle."

The words hang between us, a promise and a warning both. I don't know if I believe everything he's told me, but I can't deny the recognition that flows through my veins, stronger than blood, older than reason. Whatever brought me to this castle, to this moment, to this man who exists between worlds, it transcends the rational mind I've spent my life cultivating.

It belongs to the soul I'm only beginning to remember.

We move deeper into the castle's heart, passing through narrow archways where centuries of hands have worn the stone smooth. The shadows gather more densely here, pooling in corners where modern visitors never venture. Lachlan leads me to a small chamber I recognize from my dreams—a room with a single arrow-slit window that frames a sliver of darkening sky. His form seems more substantial in this enclosed space, as if proximity to these particular stones strengthens him.

“This was once a guard post,” he explains, his voice steadier than before. “Then, a storage room for winter provisions. Then forgotten entirely.” He gestures to markings carved into the wall—tallies, names, crude drawings that span centuries of human presence. “Now it’s where I wait, when I’m no' searchin’ for ye."

I trace the markings with my fingertips, feeling the indentations where desperate hands once pressed against stone. “How is this possible? How are you still here after all this time?”

Lachlan’s expression darkens, the shadows beneath his cheekbones deepening. “The curse,” he says simply. “Hamish bound my spirit tae these stones as he died. My body is dust, but my soul remains—tethered tae this place like a dog tae a post.”

The crude comparison sends a chill through me. “You can’t leave?”

“Aye, I can, but no far. No for long.”

He moves toward the arrow-slit, his outline blurring slightly as he nears the opening to the outside world.

“The further I travel frae the castle, the weaker I get. Beyond the valley, I fade entirely.”

To demonstrate, he steps closer to the window. His form dims immediately, becoming transparent enough that I can see the wall behind him. The rich blue of his eyes dulls to gray, the details of his face growing indistinct, like a painting left in rain.

“Stop,” I say, alarmed by his fading. Instinctively, I reach for him, my hand passing through his arm with a cold shock that races up to my shoulder.

The sensation isn't simply absence—it's a negative pressure, a vacuum that pulls at my warmth, my substance. I jerk back, gasping.

Lachlan steps away from the window, his form solidifying again as he moves deeper into the chamber. "Forgive me," he says softly. "I forget sometimes that touch between us is...complicated."

I stare at my hand, which trembles visibly in the dim light. My breathing has grown shallow, my chest constricted as if bands of iron have tightened around my ribs. I press my palm against my sternum, where an inexplicable ache blooms—not pain exactly, but a hollowness that feels both fresh and centuries old.

"What happens when I leave?" I ask, though I already suspect the answer. "Do you just...wait?"

"I exist," he says, the word weighted with all that it doesn't encompass. "I patrol these wa's. I watch the seasons change, the stanes crumble, the visitors come and go." His mouth twists into something too bitter to be a smile. "And I search for signs o' yer return, in every red-haired wuman that passes through th' gates, in every lass that lingers tae lang in the chapel ruins."

"But how do you know?" My voice drops to a whisper. "How can you be certain I'm her? That I'm Isla?"

Lachlan's warrior eyes soften with a longing so intense it makes me look away. "The same way the needle kens the north. The same way the tide kens the moon." He moves closer, careful to maintain the space between us. "Our souls ken each ither across time, across death itsel'. We aye find each ither."

The certainty in his voice resonates through me like a struck bell. Fragments of memory flicker at the edges of my consciousness, not just the intimate scene from last night's dream, but older impressions, moments viewed through different eyes. A castle bright with torchlight, not the ruin that it later became. A feast hall where music played, men's voices raised in songs now lost to time. The weight of wool and linen against skin unaccustomed to modern fabrics. The taste of heather honey, sharper and more complex than anything sold in today's markets.

"I remember..." I begin, uncertain how to articulate impressions that feel more like sense memories than coherent thoughts. "Not everything. Just...fragments. Feelings."

"It comes in pieces," Lachlan agrees. "Different in each lifetime. Sometimes ye remember almost naething until the end. Sometimes..." He hesitates, something like fear crossing his features. "Sometimes ye remember a' too much, a' too soon."

"What happens then?"

His gaze slides away from mine. "The burden o' too mony lives, too many deaths, it can overwhelm a single mind."

The implication sits heavily between us. I think of multiple lives, multiple deaths, all carried within one consciousness. No wonder he fears my remembering. “Is that why you haven’t told me everything? Why you waited until I came to you?”

“Partly,” he admits. “But also 'cause words alone couldnae convince ye. Ye needed tae feel it yerself, the pull o' this place, the dreams, the recognition in yer blood that transcends logic.” His voice drops lower. "Ye've aye been thrawn, Isla. In every life.”

I smile, “Thrawn? That means stubborn, doesn’t it?” I ask with a knowing smirk; it’s not the first time I have been accused of that.

Aye, Isla, that it does,” he nods.

The name no longer sounds foreign when he speaks it. Something in me responds to it, a part of myself I’m only beginning to uncover. I close my eyes, letting the sensations wash through me, the cold of the stone, the scent of ancient dust, the weight of centuries pressing down. When I open them, Lachlan is watching me with an expression that’s weathered five hundred years of waiting.

“I was a historian before,” I say, the realization surfacing from nowhere. “In another life. I came to study the castle then, too.”

Lachlan nods. “In 1973, yer name was Fiona MacLeod then. Ye stayed six months, researchin' the Sutherland clan's history.” His voice catches. “Ya found auld letters in the parish records. Ye were gettin' too close to the truth when—”

He breaks off, but the unspoken end hangs between us when you died. Again.

I sink onto a stone ledge that runs along one wall, my legs suddenly unsteady. The full weight of what he's telling me—what I'm beginning to believe—settles onto my shoulders. Not just one past life, but many. Not just one death, but a repeating cycle. A curse that spans centuries, claiming me each time I return.

"How many times?" I ask, my voice barely audible. "How many times have I come back?'

"Thirteen," he says after a hesitation. "This is the fourteenth since..." He doesn't finish the sentence, but his hand rises, opening his shirt slightly, where I now notice a thin line, paler than the surrounding skin, the ghost of a wound that ended his mortal life.

I absorb this information, turning it over in my mind like a stone worn smooth by water. My academic training suggests a dozen rational explanations, delusion, suggestion, an elaborate hoax, but none account for the bone-deep recognition I feel, or the memories that aren't mine yet sit alongside my own like books on a shelf.

"I don't know if I can believe all of this," I admit finally. "It contradicts everything I've built my life around—evidence, verification, the limits of what's possible."

"Aye, I ken," he says, and the simple acknowledgment contains multitudes. "I dinnae ask ye to forsake yer mind. Only to listen when yer soul speaks."

In the silence that follows, I hear the distant voices of the last tourists leaving the castle, the guide's keys jingling as she locks the main gates.

Soon, the ruins will be empty save for us. A woman from Boston and the ghost who claims to have loved her across lifetimes.

A ghost I'm beginning to believe.

"I should go," I say, though I make no move to stand. "They're closing the castle."

Lachlan's expression tightens with familiar fear, the fear of watching me walk away, of being left alone in these stones for another night, another year, another lifetime. "Will ye return?"

The question contains centuries of longing, of loss, of hope renewed and dashed and renewed again. I look at him, this warrior out of time, this spirit who has waited for me through a dozen lifetimes, and feel something shift inside me, a quiet acceptance of what I've been fighting since I first dreamed of him.

"I'm not leaving Dornoch," I tell him, the decision forming even as I speak it. "Not yet. Not until I understand...this." I gesture between us, indicating a connection I can neither explain nor deny.

The relief that washes over his face is so raw, so human, that for a moment I forget he isn't flesh and blood. In that expression, I see not just the warrior who has waited centuries, but the man who loved Isla with enough ferocity to transcend death itself.

"I'll be here," he says simply. "I'm always here."

I stand, gathering my bag, aware that I need time to process all I've learned. But as I turn to leave, I pause at the chamber's threshold, looking back at him one last time. In the fading light, his outline has already begun to blur, edges softening as darkness reclaims the room.

"Tomorrow," I promise. "I'll come back tomorrow."

The word hangs between us, not a causal promise but a covenant, a recognition that whatever binds us has already taken hold, stronger than doubt, deeper than fear. As I navigate the darkening corridors toward the exit, I feel the tether between us stretch but not break, guiding me through passages my conscious mind doesn't remember.

Something pulled me to Sutherland Castle, to Scotland, to this moment in time. Whether fate or curse or the desperate love of a ghost, I can no longer pretend it's a mere coincidence. Whatever brought me here has roots deeper than my academic curiosity, older than this lifetime.

And I'm done running from it.

CHAPTER 12
The Original Sin

Sleep takes me like a stone dropped through dark water, my consciousness spiraling down through layers of time. The room dissolves around me, replaced by the not-so-gentle sway of a carriage, the clop of hooves on muddy ground, and the scent of damp wool and horse sweat. I'm no longer Fi MacPherson from Boston; I am Isla, daughter of the Grant clan, arriving at Sutherland Castle on a gray autumn day in 1608. My father's hand covers mine, his finger cold through the thin fabric of my gloves. "Remember, daughter," he says, "This match will secure oor clan's future." But as the carriage door opens to reveal the castle looming above us, something inside me already knows my future holds something else entirely.

The castle stands proud and whole, not the crumbling ruin I know from my waking hours. Its stones gleam wet from recent rain, banners snapping in the wind above towers that reach completely into the steel-gray sky. Servants rush to meet us, faces pinched with cold but eyes bright with curiosity. I step down, my slippers immediately dampened by the courtyard's stones. Father follows behind me, his hand at my elbow, guiding me as I might flee. Perhaps he senses my reluctance.

“Chin up, Isla,” he murmurs, his breath forming clouds in the chill air. “The Sutherland alliance brings us protection. Their clan is powerful, their lands vast. And Hamish—” he pauses, squeezing my arm, “Hamish will make a fine husband.”

I nod, unable to form words around the stone in my throat. This journey has been inevitable since my sixteenth year, when Hamish had journeyed through our village. Now, at eighteen, I’ve been delivered like cattle to market, my dowry packed in trunks that servants unload behind us as we approach the door.

“Isla, straichten yer shooders, lass,” my father said as we waited for the door to open.

The great hall swallows us whole. Firelight dances across dark wooden beams, casting long shadows that stretch like fingers across stone floors. Tapestries line the walls, faded huntsmen forever pursuing stags through forests woven in thread. The room hushes as we enter, faces turning toward me—some curious, some calculating, some openly pitying.

At the far end of the hall, a man stands before the massive hearth. Even from this distance, I can see the rigid posture, the shoulders squared with what might be pride or merely the expectation of obedience. Hamish Sutherland. My betrothed. My future.

He steps forward as we approach, his movements precise and measured. Every inch the laird, from his immaculate plaid to the silver brooch fastening it at his shoulder. His face might be considered handsome by some—strong jaw, straight nose, eyes clear and cold as winter pools. But his smile stops at his lips, never warming those eyes as he takes my hand.

"Isla, lass, it's a pleasure tae meet ye. Let me hae a look at ye," he says as he drops my hand and circles me.

"Aye, m'laird," I give a small curtsy.

He takes my hand again, his hand is dry and cool around mine, his grip firm but careful, as though I am a possession he fears might break before he's properly claimed it. I cast my eyes down as befitting a proper bride, though something in me rebels against this display of submission.

"Ye've grown much fairer sin' I first saw ye." Hamish says, his gaze traveling the length of me in a way that makes my skin go cold.

Before I can form a response suitable for the assembled crowd, the heavy side door bursts open. Laughter spills into the hall, rich and unrestrained, followed by two men—one clearly a stable boy by his dress, the other—

My breath catches in my throat.

He is Hamish's opposite in every way that matters. Where Hamish stands straight and proper, this man moves with the fluid grace of a predator. His dark hair falls loose about his shoulders rather than neatly tied. His tunic, clearly once fine, is torn across the chest, revealing skin slick with sweat and the ripple of muscles beneath. A training accident, perhaps, though he seems entirely unconcerned by the damage or the exposure.

The hall, so silent moments before, erupts in muted whispers. The newcomer notices, his grin widening as he claps the stable boy on the shoulder and sends him on his way. Then he turns toward us, his stride confident as he approaches.

"Brother, we've guests. Keep yer horseplay outside," Hamish growls, clearly displeased at his brother's arrival.

"Ooch, Brother, ye need tae learn tae hae a bit o' fun," the man says as he pokes Hamish in the ribs playfully.

"Lachlan," Hamish acknowledges, his tone noticeably cooler. "Your timing is impeccable as always."

Lachlan Sutherland—this must be the younger brother I've heard mentioned in hushed tones—slings an arm around Hamish's shoulders. The contrast between them is stark, light and shadow, winter and summer, restraint and abandon.

"Who is this lassie? Lachlan asks, his voice dropping to a playful rumble that seems to vibrate through the stone beneath my feet.

"My betrothed," Hamish replies, his arm sliding possessively around my waist. "Isla Grant, daughter of Alasdair Grant of Glenmor." His grip tightens slightly. "My future bride."

Lachlan's eyes find mine for the first time, and the hall around us seems to dim. His gaze is blue, not the pale, frozen blue of his brother's but deep and warm as summer skies. Something flickers there, a recognition that makes no sense, for we have never met before this moment.

"Isla," he says, my name transformed in his mouth to something precious, something secret. He steps forward, taking my hand from his brother's grasp. "Welcome to Sutherland Castle."

His fingers close around mine, and the world stops.

Heat flares between our palms, racing up my arm and spreading through my chest like whisky. The sensation is so unexpected, so overwhelming, that I gasp aloud. Lachlan's eyes widen, his pupils dilating until only a thin ring of blue remains. He feels it too—this impossible connection, this recognition of something that should not exist.

We stand frozen, our hands joined, our eyes locked, as something ancient and inevitable passes between us. In that moment, I know him, not as the younger Sutherland brother, not as my betrothed's kin, but as something essential to my own existence. A missing piece suddenly found.

"Brother." Hamish's voice cuts through the spell, sharp as a blade. "You forget yourself."

I withdraw my hand with effort, feeling the loss of contact like a physical wound. Lachlan steps back, but his eyes never leave mine. The corner of his mouth lifts in a half-smile that speaks of secrets yet to be shared.

From the corner of my eye, I see Hamish's hand tighten on the pommel of his sword, his knuckles white with strain. The air between the brothers crackles with tension I don't yet understand but instinctively fear.

"Forgive me," Lachlan says, though nothing in his tone suggests regret. "I was merely welcoming our new addition to the family."

"A welcome best left to me," Hamish counters, his other hand returning to my waist, fingers digging into the fabric of my dress. "As her future husband."

The words fall like stones into still water, ripples of consequence spreading outward. I stand between them, already caught in currents I cannot control, already lost though I've only just arrived. My heart hammers against my ribs with a truth my mind rejects but my soul already knows: I have been promised to one brother while my entire being has recognized the other.

And in Hamish Sutherland's cold eyes, I see that he knows it too.

The memory shifts like mist over water, time slipping forward without warning. Weeks have dissolved into a blue of stolen glances and forbidden moments, conversations in shadowed corners that ended too quickly when footsteps approached. Now I stand in the great hall once more, but transformed beyond recognition. Hundreds of candles flicker in iron sconces, their light catching on threads of gold woven through elaborate tapestries brought down from storage. The hall smells of beeswax and pine boughs, of spiced wine and roasting meat. And beneath it all, the scent of my own fear, sharp as vinegar. Today I become Isla Sutherland, wife to Hamish, lady of these lands. My white dress feels like a shroud, the silver circlet on my head heavy as a crown of thorns. I stand beside my new husband, my face a mask of demure pleasure that hides the screaming within.

The ceremony itself passes in a fog. I speak when prompted, my voice a hollow thing that echoes strangely in my ears. The priest's Latin washes over me, ancient words binding me to a man whose touch leaves my skin cold. Hamish's fingers grip mine with crushing force as we exchange rings—silver bands that gleam in the candlelight, beautiful manacles that will hold me for life.

"You look pale, wife," Hamish whispers as guests come forward to offer congratulations. His mouth curves in what might pass for concern, though his eyes remain watchful, calculating. "I trust you are not taken ill on our special day."

"Just overwhelmed, husband," I reply, the new title bitter on my tongue. "So many people, so much attention."

He seems satisfied with this answer, his hand settling at the small of my back, a gesture that appears loving to observers but serves as a constant reminder of his claim. I scan the crowd, unable to help myself, though I know I should not seek what I most wish to see.

And then I find him.

Across the hall, half-hidden in the shadow of a stone pillar, Lachlan stands perfectly still. He has not approached to offer congratulations. Has not joined in the drinking or dancing that grows louder as the evening progresses. He simply watches, his face a study in careful emptiness that does nothing to disguise the agony in his eyes.

Our gazes lock across the crowded space, and for a heartbeat, the hall falls away. The music dulls, the voices fade, and we exist in a pocket of silence created by shared pain. He looks different today, his usual dishevelment replaced by formal attire that sits unnaturally on his frame. His hair is tied back neatly, his plaid arranged with uncharacteristic precision. The effort only emphasizes how wrong it is to see him constrained, like watching a wolf in a collar and chain.

I force myself to look away, turning my attention to a clan elder offering slurred blessings for fertility and prosperity. But my awareness of Lachlan never fades. I feel his presence like a flame at my back, a constant warmth in a room that grows increasingly cold despite the roaring fires.

The feast begins in earnest, trestle tables groaning beneath platters of venison and salmon, bowls of root vegetables swimming in butter, loaves of dark bread still steaming from the ovens. Wine flows freely, voices grow louder, laughter more raucous. On any other occasion, the abundance would be impressive, the merriment infectious. Tonight, each bite of food turns to ash in my mouth. Each burst of laughter feels like mockery.

Hamish keeps me close as we make our way through the hall, greeting guests, accepting gifts. His arm never leaves my waist, his fingers occasionally digging into my side when my attention wanders. "Smile, wife," he murmurs during one such moment. "People will think you unhappy with your match."

I force my lips to curve upward, though the effort makes my face ache. "Forgive me, husband. The day has been long."

"It will be longer still," he replies, his meaning unmistakable in the way his gaze drops to my bodice. "But I am a patient man. For now."

The implied threat sends ice through my veins. Night will come, and with it, duties I cannot avoid. Duties that fill me with dread rather than the anticipation a bride should feel. I reach for my wine goblet, draining it in a single swallow that earns a raised eyebrow from my husband.

"Careful," he says, refilling the cup with his own hand. "I want ye tae be aware o' aal that's transpirin' tonight."

My gaze betrays me again, drawn across the room as if pulled by invisible threads. Lachlan has moved, now standing near one of the smaller hearths. The firelight catches his profile, highlighting the tension in his jaw, the rigid set of his shoulders. As if sensing my attention, he turns, eyes finding mine unerringly through the crowd.

The look we exchange is too long, too laden with things that cannot be spoken. His face softens for an instant, the mask slipping to reveal such naked longing that I have to grip the table to steady myself. In that moment, I know with certainty that what passes between us is not one-sided. Not a girlish infatuation or a young man's passing fancy. It is recognition, soul-deep and ancient, of something that should have been but now can never be.

"You find my brother fascinating."

Hamish's voice slices through my thoughts. I turn to find his eyes—so like his brother's in color yet so different in expression—fixed on my face. There is no question in his tone, only cold observation.

"I was merely noting who has attended," I lie, the words weak even to my own ears. "So many guests to remember."

"Indeed." His hand covers mine on the table, thumb pressing into the center of my palm hard enough to hurt. "Yet your gaze returns to him with remarkable regularity."

I force myself to meet his eyes, to keep my expression neutral though my heart races beneath my ribs. "I know not what you mean, husband."

"Do not play me for a fool, Isla." His voice drops lower, meant for my ears alone. "I have watched you these past moons. Both of you."

The implication hangs between us, a blade suspended by the thinnest thread. My mouth goes dry, the taste of fear metallic on my tongue. I wonder what he has seen—the accidental meetings in the castle corridors, the lingering conversations about books and music, the way Lachlan taught me to handle his favorite hunting falcon when Hamish was away attending to clan business. Nothing improper has occurred, yet everything about our interactions feels like betrayal when viewed through Hamish's suspicious eyes.

My gaze flicks involuntarily across the room again, seeking Lachlan like a compass finding north. He stands straighter now, watching our exchange with naked concern. Our eyes meet for the third time that evening, a silent conversation flowing between us. His stance shifts subtly, ready to move, to intervene, though what he thinks he could do, I cannot imagine.

The sound of Hamish's goblet slamming onto the table startles everyone nearby into silence. Wine sloshes over the rim, spreading across the white linen like blood from a wound. Conversations falter, heads turn toward the high table.

“Enough,” Hamish says, his voice controlled but threaded with steel. He rises to his feet, pulling me with him. “The hour grows late, and my bride and I have duties to attend to.”

A chorus of suggestive cheers and whistles follows his announcement. Men raise their cups in bawdy toasts; women titter behind their hands. But I see only Lachlan’s face across the room, the devastation there so complete it steals my breath.

Hamish’s fingers dig into my arm as he leads me toward the staircase that will take us to the laird’s chambers, to our marriage bed. As we ascend the first steps, I glance back one last time. Lachlan has moved into the center of the hall, watching our departure with fists clenched at his sides, body tensed as if physically restraining himself from following.

Hamish shoves me into the bedchamber with such force I stumble against the bedpost. The heavy oak door crashes shut behind us. When he turns to face me, his eyes glitter in the candlelight—not with desire but with something darker, more primal. The iron key scrapes in the lock with terrible finality. "Tonight," he says, voice dropping to a whisper that somehow frightens me more than shouting, I claim wha’s mine by richt an’ blood.” His fingers work methodically at his belt, each movement deliberate. My throat constricts as he approaches. His lips curve upward at whatever he sees in my expression, and he reaches out to trace my jawline with calloused fingertips. “Ach, well, wife. These walls hae stood for centuries, but they’re not thick enough to keep my brother hearin’ exactly what happens in this room tonight.”

Hamish's snores fill the chamber as I ease from beneath his arm. Each movement sends fresh pain spiraling through my body. I pause at the door, listening for any change in his breathing before slipping into the corridor. The stone floor chills my bare feet as I limp toward the kitchen. In the dim light of a single candle, I fill a wooden cup with water, wincing as it touches my split lip. My torn shift clings to places where blood has dried—evidence of violations beyond the claiming of my maidenhood. I lower myself onto a bench in the corner, curling inward like a wounded animal. Tears fall silently into my cup, rippling the water's surface. Tomorrow night he will wake again, and the night after, and all the nights that follow.

A shadow falls across the floor. I look up through swollen eyes to find Lachlan standing in the doorway, his tall frame rigid. The candlelight catches the muscle twitching in his jaw as his gaze travels over my torn shift, the darkening bruises, and the blood-crusted split in my lip.

"Christ Almighty," he whispers, crossing the stone floor in two strides and kneeling before me. "What has he done tae ye?"

I turn away. "Nothing unusual for a wedding night. I am merely... unaccustomed."

His fingers hover near my cheek but don't touch, as if afraid I might shatter. "Nay, Isla. This isnae what happens 'twixt man and wife. This is..cruelty."

He rises without another word and retrieves water from the kitchen trough, returning with a dampened cloth. When he lifts it toward my face, I flinch involuntarily. His hand freezes mid-air, eyes never leaving mine.

"May I?" he asks, voice gentle as a prayer.

I manage a small nod. The cool cloth touches my skin with such tenderness that tears spring fresh. "He made certain ye'd hear," I whisper. "He wanted it that way."

"I ken." His voice breaks on the words.

When he finishes, he sets the cloth aside and carefully draws me against his chest. I feel his heart hammering beneath my cheek. "It was punishment," I confess into the rough wool of his shirt. "For looking at another."

He pulls back just enough to study my face. "And who did ye look at, lass?"

The question hangs between us. I cannot speak the truth we both know. Instead, I lift my gaze to his, letting him read the answer there.

"Mo chridhe," he breathes, tilting my chin upward with a gentleness I had forgotten could exist. His lips hover a breath from mine, waiting.

I close the distance between us. In that kiss, the night's horrors recede like shadows before dawn.

CHAPTER 13
Secrets in the Stone

I wake gasping, the dream of Isla's wedding still burning behind my eyelids. The digital clock reads 4:37 AM, but sleep has now abandoned me completely. Outside, the Highland darkness has just begun to soften toward dawn, the blackness turning to deep indigo at the edges. My body moves before my mind can catch up, fingers already reaching for clothes, for my notebook, for car keys. The tug beneath my breastbone has grown stronger overnight, a physical ache that points me toward the castle like a compass finding north. I don't fight it anymore. What's the point? The castle calls, and like every version of me that came before, I answer.

The rental car crunches over gravel, headlights carving a narrow path through the mist that clings to the valley floor. My research notes sit on the passenger seat, pages dog-eared and covered in my increasingly desperate scrawl. Last night's dream has left me raw, my skin too tight for my body, as if Isla is pressing outward from inside me, desperate to escape.

I park at the empty visitor's lot, the castle's jagged silhouette just visible against the lightening sky. The ruins aren't technically open for another five hours, but the gate's padlock has a weakness, a slight give if you pull it just right while turning it, something I discovered two days ago during my increasingly frantic visits. The metal yields with a soft click, and I slip inside, careful to close the gate behind me.

Dew soaks my boots as I cross the outer courtyard, notebook clutched to my chest like a shield. Birds are just beginning to stir, their tentative calls breaking the silence. The castle feels different at this hour, more itself somehow, without tourists trampling its stones or guides reciting sanitized versions of its history. The weight of centuries presses down, the past so close I can almost taste it in the air, smoke from long-dead fires, the metallic tang of old blood, the ghost of heather honey carried on a phantom breeze.

"I know you're here," I whisper, my breath visible in the chill. "I can feel you watching."

Nothing answers but the soft drip of condensation from stones above, yet the air around me thickens, as if gathering substance in response to my words. The hook behind my sternum pulls harder, drawing me toward the east tower, the most precarious section, cordoned off with warning signs and barriers. I duck beneath the caution tape without hesitation, my steps sure despite the uneven ground.

The first hints of daylight filter through the roofless chambers, catching on something that glimmers at the edge of my vision. I turn, heart leaping to my throat, but see only the empty archway. When I face forward again, the shimmer has moved to my periphery, always just beyond direct sight. Not light reflecting off stone, but something with intention, something watching.

"Lachlan," I call, my voice steadier than I feel. "Enough games."

A cold draft brushes the back of my neck, raising gooseflesh along my arms. The sensation isn't unpleasant, more like fingers trailing across my skin with careful reverence. I close my eyes, breathing through the sudden tightness in my chest. When I open them, he stands before me, ten feet away, near the crumbling wall.

The dawn light passes through him, revealing the stone behind his form, yet he appears more solid than in my dreams. His eyes fix on me with an intensity that makes my knees weaken, hunger, recognition, and something deeper that I can't name but recognize in my blood. His hands clench at his sides, as if physically restraining himself from moving toward me.

"Ye should na be here alone," he says, voice barely audible above the stirring breeze.

I blink, and he vanishes like mist burned away by sunlight. Before I can call out, a cold pressure settles behind me, the air condensing into his presence so close I can almost feel breath on my neck. I gasp, spinning around to find him inches away, his form wavering like a reflection in troubled water.

"You should na be here alone," he repeats, closer now, voice rumbling through me like distant thunder. "These stones grow treacherous with age. The fall would kill ye."

The concern in his voice sounds genuine, yet beneath it runs a current of something possessive, something that whispers: Not yet. Not this way. Not before I've had my fill of you.

"Would that be so terrible?" I ask, surprising myself with the question. "If I died here? Would we be together then?"

Anguish flashes across his features, quickly masked. "Death is nae the answer, Isla. It ne'er has been."

"Stop calling me that," I snap, though the name resonates in my chest like a struck bell. "I'm Fi. Fiona MacPherson. A doctoral student from Boston, not some woman who died centuries ago."

"Are ye sure of that?" His mouth curves slightly, not quite a smile. "Yer dreams suggest different."

I reach for him without thinking, my hand passing through his chest as if through cold water. The sensation sends shockwaves up my arm, not simply absence, but a negative pressure that pulls at my warmth, my substance. I gasp, jerking back, fingers tingling with pinpricks of electricity.

"Why can't I touch you?" I demand, frustration breaking my voice. "If I'm really her—if we're really bound across time or whatever you claim—why can't I feel you?"

Lachlan's eyes darken, the blue deepening to the color of the ocean at dusk. "Tha curse was designed tae be cruel. Tae let us find each ither in every lifetime, tae recognize whit we've lost, but nevair tae reclaim it." He lifts his hand, hovering it near my cheek without making contact. "Tae see, tae want, but nivver tae hold."

The chill of his almost-touch sends shivers down my spine, not entirely unpleasant. My skin seems to remember his, responding to his proximity with a longing that transcends the physical barrier between us.

“Tell me about the curse,” I say, fighting to keep my voice steady. “Tell me how to break it.”

"Ye've asked that in every lifetime,” he responds, sorrow etching deeper lines around his eyes. “Always searchin' for answers, for escape. The historian, the archaeologist, the folklorist—ye've come tae me wearin' different faces, different names, but aye wi' the same questions.”

“And you’ve never answered them,” I counter, anger flaring hot in my chest. “Not in any way that matters.”

His gaze shifts past me, toward the horizon where the sun now crests the distant hills. “Time grows short,” he says, his outline already thinning as dawn light strengthens. “The veil thickens with daylight.”

“Don’t you dare disappear on me again,” I say, stepping closer despite knowing I can’t hold him here. “Lachlan, please, I need to understand what’s happening to me. Who I was. Who I am to you.”

“Ye are everything,” he says simply, his voice fading with his form. “Ye hae aye been everything.”

His edges blur, features growing indistinct as sunlight pours through the broken walls. I reach for him again, a futile gesture that meets nothing but colder air. “Will I see you tonight?” I ask, desperation making my voice small.

The ghost of a smile passes across his fading lips. "Ye'll always find me, Fi. In every lifetime, through every barrier. Yer soul knows th' way hame, even when yer mind rebels against it."

And then he's gone, the space where he stood empty of everything but strengthening sunlight and ancient stones. I stand frozen, arms wrapped around myself, trembling with an emptiness that feels too vast for my body to contain. The loss cuts deeper than logic should allow—how can I miss someone I barely know, someone who isn't even properly alive?

Yet as I make my slow way back across the courtyard, my research notes forgotten in my hand, the ache in my chest feels older than this body, deeper than this lifetime. Something ancient and familiar stirs beneath my modern skepticism, a certainty I can neither explain nor deny.

My soul remembers what my mind cannot. And it's tearing me apart.

My room door clicks shut behind me, sealing me in with thoughts that feel too large for these four walls. It's barely noon, but exhaustion drags at my limbs after hours of wandering the castle grounds, searching for traces of Lachlan long after he vanished with the dawn. My laptop sits accusingly on the desk, dissertation notes untouched for days. I should work. I should call my advisor with some excuse for my imminent deadline extension. I should do anything but what I'm actually doing, pacing the worn carpet, checking the mirror every few minutes as if expecting to see his face materializing behind my reflection.

I pause at the bathroom doorway, caught by my own image in the harsh fluorescent light. Dark circles shadow my eyes, my skin pale as parchment. I look haunted, which seems fitting. Leaning closer, I search my features for traces of someone else, for Isla's spirit peering out through my eyes. The woman I see is still me, yet somehow not entirely me anymore, as if something ancient has awakened beneath my skin, stretching toward the surface.

"This is insane," I tell my reflection, voice cracking with fatigue. "He's a ghost." I pause my scholarly brain trying to take over. "No, he's a hallucination. A manifestation of stress and sleep deprivation."

But even as I form the words, my fingers rise unconsciously to my neck, tracing the spot where dream-Lachlan's mouth pressed against Isla's skin. The phantom sensation makes my pulse jump, heat blooming beneath my touch. My body remembers something my mind insists is impossible.

I turn away from the mirror abruptly, crossing to the desk where my research materials lie scattered. My dissertation on Highland clan disputes seems childishly inadequate now, built on fragmentary historical records that capture nothing of the reality I've glimpsed through Lachlan's eyes and Isla's memories. What's the point of academic analysis when the past breathes down my neck, when history haunts me in the most literal sense?

Still, I force myself to sit, to open my laptop, to stare at the cursor blinking accusingly on the page I abandoned days ago. The words blur before my eyes, meaningless strings of letters that fail to capture the weight of centuries, the complexity of human hearts. I type a sentence, delete it, type another. My scholarly voice sounds foreign to my own ears, detached and bloodless compared to the visceral truth of Lachlan's presence, of Isla's memories flooding my dreams.

Sleep ambushes me between one blink and the next. My head drops forward, then jerks up. The room tilts around me, walls breathing in and out like lungs. I should move to the bed, set an alarm, and fight this pull toward unconsciousness. Instead, I surrender, letting darkness swallow me whole.

I am Isla again, but not at the wedding. Not yet trapped in a marriage to a man whose touch leaves frost on my skin. This is earlier, the first time Lachlan sought me out alone, a week after my arrival at Sutherland Castle. He finds me in the corridor near the chapel, his body crowding mine against the stone before I can cry out. Not that I would have. Something in me recognizes him from our first meeting and has been waiting for exactly this moment.

His hands frame my face, thumbs tracing my cheekbones with a reverence that makes my knees weaken. I should protest, should push him away, should remember my betrothal to his brother. But I dont, or can't, my fingers clutch at his shoulders, pulling him closer, erasing the space between us.

"Do ye feel it too lass?" he whispers as he tilts my head up to face him.

"I feel it," I whisper back, the admission torn from some place deeper than thought. "I've felt it since I first laid eyes on ye."

The confession breaks something in his restraint. His mouth claims mine with desperate hunger, teeth grazing my lower lip, tongue seeking entrance. I open to him without hesitation, my body arching into his touch like we have done this a hundred times before, as if our bodies have a magnetic pull to each other.

His hands are everywhere, tangling in my hair, skimming down my sides, gripping my hips with possessive strength. He lifts me slightly, pressing me harder against the wall, his knee sliding between my thighs to support my weight. The position is shockingly intimate, opening me to the hard press of his body in a way that sends lightning through my veins.

"Isla," he groans against my throat, the name vibrating through my skin. "My Isla."

His teeth scrape gently down the column of my neck, finding the sensitive hollow where my pulse hammers against thin skin. He nips there, then soothes the sting with his tongue, the dual sensation pulling a sound from my throat I've never made before, half gasp, half-moan, wholly abandoned.

My hands find their way beneath his shirt, nails scoring lightly down the muscled plane of his back. His skin burns beneath my touch, as if fever runs in his blood. He responds with a growl, his own hands gathering my skirts, bunching the fabric until his fingers find bare skin above my knee. His touch brands me, calluses catching against my flesh as he traces upward with agonizing slowness.

"Tell me tae stop," he whispers, voice ragged with restraint. "Tell me tae leave ye be."

But I can't form the words, can't even pretend I want them spoken. I pull his mouth back to mine, my kiss the only answer I can give. My body knows what my mind is still struggling to accept, that whatever lies between us is inevitable as tide following moon, as death following life. Some bonds cannot be broken, not by propriety, not by family, not even by time itself.

I wake gasping, sheets twisted around my legs, my skin flushed and hypersensititve. The dream clings to me like smoke, Isla's desire flowing through my veins as if her blood and mine are one and the same. My nightgown sticks to sweat-dampened skin, my heart hammering against my ribs with a rhythm that belongs to another century.

"Dreams cannae sustain ye forever."

The voice comes from the foot of the bed. I jerk upright, pulling the sheet to my chest, though the gesture feels futile. Lachlan stands watching me, his form more solid in the darkened room than it was in morning light at the castle. His eyes burn with an intensity that steals my breath, possessive, hungry, ancient with waiting.

"You're in my room," I manage, voice hoarse.

He moves closer, the air rippling around his form like heat above summer pavement. "Yer soul remembers what yer mind cannae." he says, echoing his words from the castle. "Yer body kens mine, even across death."

He reaches toward my face, hand hovering just above my cheek. The air between us crackles with invisible energy, static electricity raising the fine hairs on my arms. When his fingers pass through my skin, the contact isn't physical in any normal sense, yet I feel it, a cold fire that races from the point of almost-touch down my spine, pooling low in my belly.

I gasp, jerking back, the sensation too intense to process. "Don't," I whisper, though I'm not sure if I'm asking him to stop or begging him to try again.

"I would give anything to feel yer skin beneath my hands," he says, voice rough with frustrated desire. "Tae hold ye, as I aince did, tae taste yer mouth, tae feel yer heart beatin' against mine."

The naked longing in his voice matches the ache in my own chest—a hollowness that's grown more acute with each encounter, each dream, each moment of connection that falls just short of true touch. I fear him, yes. Fear what his presence in my life means, what it might cost me. But I fear his absence more, fear returning to a world where I never knew the peculiar gravity of his gaze, the recognition that flows between us deeper than words can capture.

"What's happening to me?" I ask, my voice small in the darkness.

His smile is terrible in its tenderness. "Yer remembering," he says simply. "And memory, once awakened, cannae be buried again."

I cancel my trip to Inverness with a terse email, citing research needs. My phone buzzes with a call from my advisor – the third this morning – but I silence it without looking. The tour to the stone circles, the whisky distillery visit, the dinner reservation at that restaurant my guidebook insisted was unmissable – all abandoned without a second thought. The notebook where I once meticulously planned each day of my research trip now contains only variations of his name, scrawled across pages in handwriting that grows increasingly frantic, increasingly unfamiliar. Lachlan. The only appointment I keep is with the castle, arriving the moment the gates open, heart racing with anticipation that disgusts and thrills me in equal measure.

The ticket seller recognizes me now, offering a small nod as I approach. "Back again, Miss? Fourth day in a row, isn't it?"

"The dissertation," I mutter, the excuse automatic though my research hasn't progressed in days. "Clan histories. The Sutherlands, specifically."

She nods, uninterested in my academic fabrications, and waves me through. I'm grateful for her indifference, for the fact that she can't see the hunger that drives me here has nothing to do with scholarship and everything to do with the ghost who waits within these walls.

The morning tour group clusters near the entrance, tourists with sensible shoes and expensive cameras, guidebooks open to pages that contain nothing but sanitized history. I drift away from them at the first opportunity, veering left where they go right, seeking the older sections where restoration hasn't yet begun. My boots know the path now, carrying me unerringly toward the places where the veil between worlds grows thin, where Lachlan's presence feels strongest.

A barricade blocks the corridor leading to the north tower – a new addition since yesterday, complete with a fresh sign: DANGER – STRUCTURAL INSTABILITY – ABSOLUTELY NO ENTRY. I glance over my shoulder, confirming I'm alone before ducking beneath it. Two weeks ago, I would have obeyed without question, the rule-following academic respecting barriers and authority. Now I brush past them as if they're cobwebs, meaningless obstacles between me and what I seek.

The staircase beyond spirals upward, steps crumbling at the edges, mortar reduced to powder by centuries of Highland winters. Caution whispers that each step might be my last, that a fall from this height would shatter my body beyond repair. I climb anyway, one hand trailing along the wall for balance, the other reaching into empty air as if expecting someone to catch me should I slip.

"I know you're here," I murmur to the seemingly empty stairwell. "I can feel you watching."

Nothing answers, but the air thickens slightly, the temperature dropping several degrees in the space of a heartbeat. Not cold enough to see my breath, but enough to raise gooseflesh along my arms despite the heavy sweater I wear. His way of acknowledging me without materializing fully.

I continue upward, emerging onto what was once a parapet walkway, now open to the elements where the outer wall has partially collapsed. The view stretches for miles – rolling hills fading to distant mountains, the loch glittering like hammered silver in the morning light. Beauty that would have captivated me a week ago now registers as merely the backdrop to my vigil, scenery to occupy my eyes while my senses strain for evidence of Lachlan's presence.

Movement catches my eye – not on the parapet with me, but in the courtyard below. A small puddle from last night's rain reflects the overcast sky, but as I watch, the water's surface ripples without wind or disturbance. The ripples coalesce into a face I know too well – sharp cheekbones, proud mouth, eyes that have watched me across centuries. I lean over the crumbling edge, heart pounding, but the image disperses as quickly as it formed.

"Stop playing games," I call, voice echoing off ancient stones. "Show yourself properly."

A tour group emerges into the courtyard below, their guide gesturing animatedly toward features I can't distinguish from this height. Their voices drift upward in fragments – "...sixteenth century..." "...clan warfare..." "...tragic history..."

They know nothing. Their history is a fairytale, sanitized and simplified, missing the blood and bone and heartbreak that I've glimpsed through dreams, through Lachlan's eyes. I watch them with newfound contempt, these tourists who walk through the past but never feel its weight, never hear its whispers.

One breaks away from the group, a woman with a camera who looks upward, directly at me. She raises her hand in greeting, then gestures toward the stairs I've climbed, her meaning clear – Is it worth the view? Should I come up too?

Before I can respond, a shadow moves across the parapet, coalescing between me and the edge. Though invisible to my eyes, I feel Lachlan's presence like a solid thing, a barrier between me and the woman below. The temperature plummets, my next breath emerging as white vapor despite the mild day. The tourist below visibly shivers, her smile faltering as she hugs her arms around herself. She backs away, rejoining her group with one last uneasy glance toward my perch.

"That wasn't necessary," I say to the empty air. "She wasn't a threat."

"O' them are," comes his voice, sourceless yet surrounding me completely. "They would take ye from these walls, back to yer world, away from me."

A doorway at the far end of the parapet darkens, shadow gathering substance until Lachlan stands framed within the arch. His form seems stronger today, more defined, though still translucent enough that I can see the stones behind him. He looks different in daylight – less the romantic specter of my dreams, more the Highland warrior who fought and died for love.

"I'm not going anywhere," I tell him, the declaration both reassurance and recognition of my own deepening obsession. "I've canceled everything else. The castle is all that matters now."

His expression softens, centuries of longing visible in the way his gaze travels my face, as if memorizing features he's seen a dozen times before in different iterations. "Not the castle," he corrects gently. "What lies between us. The bond that death itself cannae break."

I turn away, unable to bear the naked emotion in his eyes. Below, the tour group moves on, disappearing into the great hall. Their absence leaves the courtyard eerily silent, the only sound the distant cry of ravens circling the broken towers.

“I should be working,” I say, more to myself than to him. “My dissertation deadline is in three weeks. My advisor has left four voicemails I haven’t returned. There’s a conference in Edinburgh next month where I’m supposed to present preliminary findings.”

“Does your work still matter to ye?” Lachlan asks, voice gentle but probing. “Does anything beyond these walls?”

The question strikes too close to a truth I’ve been avoiding. I walk to the parapet’s edge, fingers tracing crumbling stone. “I don’t know anymore,” I admit. “It should. It was my whole life before I came here. Now it feels...” I struggle for the right word. “...hollow. Like I’m studying shadows when I’ve glimpsed the substance that casts them, or maybe this connection was what drew me to study this subject in the first place.”

I turn back to find him standing closer, close enough that if he were flesh, I would feel his breath on my face. "I know I'm behaving irrationally. I know what this looks like, abandoning my work, my friends, spending every waking hour in ruins talking to a man no one else can see." I laugh, the sound brittle in the Highland air. "If one of my colleagues described these symptoms, I'd suggest immediate psychiatric evaluation."

"Yet here ye stand," he says, the words neither question nor accusation, simply acknowledgment.

"Yet here I stand," I echo, watching a raven land on the broken wall nearby, its black eyes regarding us with ancient wisdom. "Talking to empty rooms, following a ghost through dangerous ruins, dreaming of a woman I both am and am not."

The raven cocks its head, then takes flight with a harsh cry that echoes across the valley. I track its path until it becomes a black speck against the gray sky, envying its freedom, its certainty of purpose.

"I'm becoming as obsessed with you as you are with me," I whisper, the admission torn from some place deeper than conscious thought. "And I don't know if that terrifies me or thrills me anymore. The line is blurring." I meet his gaze, finding both understanding and hunger there. "I'm losing myself, Lachlan. Losing Fi to find Isla."

He moves closer still, the air between us crackling with potential energy. "Not losing," he corrects softly. "Remembering. Becoming whole again."

My hands rise of their own accord, hovering just shy of where his chest would be if he were solid. The space between us hums with electricity, with longing, with something deeper than either. "Is this how it happened before? In my other lives? Did I always fall this fast, this completely?"

"Each time different," he says. "Each time the same at its core." His hand rises to mirror mine, not quite touching. "The curse ensures we find each other, recognize each other. What comes after has always been yer choice."

"And what did I choose, those other times?" I ask, though part of me already knows the answer, can feel it humming in my blood, a warning and a promise both.

His eyes hold mine, centuries of longing distilled into a single look. "Ye chose me," he says with a blunt tone. "Every time, despite the cost. Despite knowin' how it must end."

The words settle into my bones, heavy with implication. I should be running, should be packing my bags and fleeing this castle, this country, this man who offers only a love cursed to end in tragedy. Instead, I find myself leaning toward him, drawn by a gravity older than reason, stronger than self-preservation.

"And what if I choose you again?" I whisper, the words emerging from some deep, ancestral part of me that remembers what my conscious mind cannot. "What happens then?"

The smile that crosses his face contains equal measures of triumph and sorrow. "Then we begin again," he says. "The dance that has claimed us thirteen times before. The love that death could not end."

His form flickers slightly, like a candle flame in draft. "The fourteenth time," he adds, voice dropping lower. "Perhaps this time, we break the cycle."

I stand on the precipice, literally and metaphorically – one step from a deadly fall, one choice from surrendering to a destiny I'm only beginning to understand. The rational part of me screams warning, reminds me of my life beyond these walls, my identity beyond these memories. But that voice grows fainter with each passing hour, drowned out by the certainty that flows through my veins, by the recognition that pulses between us stronger than blood, older than time.

"I'm afraid," I admit, the words barely audible above the Highland wind.

"As am I," he answers, surprising me. "Fear has walked with us through every lifetime." His gaze holds mine, unwavering. "But so has love."

And in that moment, standing on ancient stones with a ghost who has waited centuries for my return, I realize the true danger isn't what might happen if I surrender to this connection.

It's that I no longer care.

CHAPTER 14
The Dungeon

The world tilts and slides away from me, the parapet and modern day dissolving like mist in morning sun. I am no longer Fi standing on crumbling stone—I am Isla, my skirts tangled around my legs as I race through the twisting bowels of Sutherland Castle, desperate terror clawing at my throat. Hamish's voice echoes off the walls, a roar of betrayal and rage that bounces through the corridors, guiding my frantic steps. The stone beneath my slippers is slick with damp, and somewhere ahead, I know with bone-deep certainty, Lachlan is suffering for our sins.

I pause at a junction of three corridors, heart hammering against my ribs like a trapped bird. The torches flicker, throwing monstrous shadows that leap and sway across ancient stone. Which way? I strain to hear, closing my eyes to better trace the source of Hamish's fury. There—to the left—a hoarse cry that can only be Lachlan's.

My skirts whisper against the walls as I run, the sound obscenely delicate against the background of distant shouting and the drip of water onto stone. The smell hits me next—the metallic tang of blood mingling with mold and unwashed bodies. The dungeons. Of course Hamish would take him there, away from prying eyes, away from servants who might whisper of the laird's brother stripped and beaten.

My fingers trail along the wall for balance, coming away slick with moisture that glistens black in the meager light. Rats scuttle through the shadows, their small claws clicking against stone. I should be afraid of them, perhaps, but how can I spare terror for vermin when Lachlan lies in chains?

"You dare question me?" Hamish's voice, suddenly clearer, echoes up the spiral stairs that lead to the lowest level. "My own brother, rutting with my wife like a common animal."

A dull thud follows, then a grunt of pain that slices through me sharper than any blade. I clutch at the front of my dress, pressing against the physical ache blooming beneath my breastbone. What have we done? What have I led us to with my weakness?

I force myself forward, down the winding stairs, each step bringing me closer to a confrontation I fear more than death itself. My breath comes in ragged gasps that seem too loud, surely betraying my approach to anyone listening. But there's no time for caution. Every second I delay is another Lachlan spends under Hamish's hand.

A guard stands at the foot of the stairs, his face impassive in the torchlight. He watches my descent without expression, making no move to stop me. Does he pity me? Or perhaps he sees justice in this—the adulterous wife forced to witness her lover's punishment. I lift my chin, summoning dignity I no longer deserve.

"Move aside," I command, voice steadier than I feel.

He hesitates only a moment before stepping back, his eyes deliberately looking past me rather than meeting my gaze. "The laird expected you would come," he says, voice flat. "He waits below."

Expected me. Of course. Hamish knows me too well, knows I couldn't stay hidden in my chamber while Lachlan suffered. Is this part of his punishment, then? To make me watch?

More guards line the narrow corridor that leads to the central chamber, their faces carved from the same emotionless stone as the walls themselves. They stand rigid, torches held high, eyes fixed on points beyond my shoulder. None speak as I pass. None need to. Their silence carries all the judgment of the clan, all the contempt for a woman who would betray her husband with his own brother.

The corridor narrows, the ceiling dropping so low I must duck my head. Water drips from above, cold droplets striking my neck and sliding down my spine like fingertips of ice. The smell grows stronger—blood and fear and human waste. My stomach turns, but I swallow the bile that rises in my throat. I will not show weakness, not now.

"Did you think I wouldn't discover you?" Hamish's voice, dangerously soft now, carries through the darkness ahead. "Did you think me blind as well as betrayed?"

I quicken my pace, pulse thrumming in my ears so loudly it nearly drowns out Lachlan's response—too low to distinguish words, but the defiant tone is unmistakable even through obvious pain. My Lachlan, proud even in chains.

My Lachlan. The thought stabs through me, sharp with guilt. How easily I think of him as mine, when I belong to another by sacred vow. Yet those vows feel hollow now, empty words spoken before I knew what true feeling was. Before I understood that some bonds transcend ceremony and obligation.

Memory flashes through me as I round the final bend—Lachlan's mouth on mine in the shadow of the east tower, his hands tangling in my hair, the weight of his body pressing me against cool stone. "I would rather die than stop," he whispered against my throat, and I believed him. We both believed our love worth any price.

How foolish we were. How arrogant to think passion could overcome centuries of clan law, of sacred bonds, of a brother's rightful claim.

My foot catches on an uneven step, nearly sending me sprawling into the darkness below. I catch myself against the wall, palm scraping rough stone, the slight pain centering me in this nightmare. I press myself flat, trying to steady my racing pulse. Three more steps to the chamber door. Three more steps before I must face what we've wrought.

Through the gloom, I see a rectangle of torchlight marking the entrance to the central chamber. The guards stationed on either side of the opening glance at me, their expressions a mixture of pity and disgust. One shakes his head slightly, a warning I dare not heed.

I gather my skirts in trembling hands, lifting the hem above the filthy floor. My legs feel leaden, each step requiring more will than I thought I possessed. But I move forward anyway, drawn by a force stronger than fear, stronger than shame.

At the threshold, I pause, lungs aching for air that isn't fouled by damp and blood. Beyond this point, there is no return to who I was, to the life I had. Beyond this door waits the consequence of love that defied all bonds of family and honor.

I take one last shuddering breath and step from shadow into cruel light.

I step into the chamber and my world contracts to a single point of agony. Lachlan kneels in the center of the room, wrists raw and bleeding where iron shackles bite into his flesh. His once-fine shirt hangs in tatters around him, revealing broad shoulders streaked with red lash marks, skin torn open in cruel, methodical lines. His head hangs forward, dark hair matted with sweat and blood, but I know the moment he senses my presence—his shoulders straighten infinitesimally, a warrior's pride asserting itself even now.

Hamish paces before him, boots clacking against stone with sharp, angry precision. My husband's hands are flecked with blood not his own, his knuckles split and swollen. He has done some of this work himself, then. Not content to let his men deliver the punishment, he needed to feel my lover's flesh yield beneath his fists, needed to make this pain personal.

"Finally," Hamish says, turning toward me with eyes colder than winter loch water. "The faithless wife arrives to view her handiwork." His voice drops to something terrible in its softness. "Come closer, my dear. See what your lust has purchased."

I cannot move, my feet seemingly rooted to the filthy stone. Lachlan lifts his head at last, and the sight of his face steals what little breath remains in my lungs. One eye is swollen shut, his cheekbone purpled and distended beneath it. Blood crusts at the corner of his mouth, yet somehow he finds the strength to offer me the ghost of a smile.

"Don't look at her," Hamish snarls, backhanding Lachlan across his already-ruined face. The sound—flesh striking flesh—echoes obscenely in the chamber. "You've forfeited any right to gaze upon her."

Lachlan spits blood onto the stones, then raises his head again, defiant. "I forfeit nothing," he says, voice rough but steady. "Least of all her."

From the shadows along the walls, guards chuckle—low, cruel sounds that speak of entertainment found in others' misery. How long have they watched this spectacle? How much of my shame and Lachlan's pain have they consumed like morsels at a feast?

"My own brother," Hamish continues, resuming his pacing, each word precise as a blade being sharpened. "With my wife." He stops directly before Lachlan, reaching down to grip his hair, wrenching his head back to expose his throat. "Did you laugh together afterward? Share jests about the cuckold you made me?"

"It was never about ye," Lachlan answers, each word clearly causing him pain.

Hamish's laugh holds no humor, only the brittle edge of a man whose control has fractured beyond repair. "Everything has always been about me," he hisses. "The elder son. The heir. The rightful master of these lands and all who dwell upon them." His grip tightens, tearing strands from Lachlan's scalp. "Including her. Especially her."

I find my voice at last, though it emerges thin and trembling. "Hamish, please. This solves nothing. Let him go and we can—"

"We can what?" Hamish releases Lachlan's hair and turns his fury on me, closing the distance between us in three long strides. His fingers close around my arm, bruising even through the fabric of my sleeve. "Return to our marriage bed as if you haven't spread your legs for my brother? Pretend I don't know the taste of his kiss still lingers on your mouth?"

His grip tightens as he drags me forward, forcing me closer to Lachlan's kneeling form. "Look at him," Hamish commands, giving my arm a vicious shake. "Look at what your betrayal has wrought."

I try to turn my face away, but Hamish's other hand comes up to grip my jaw, fingers digging into soft flesh, forcing my gaze toward Lachlan. "Is this what you wanted?" he demands, voice cracking with genuine pain beneath the rage. "Is he worth betraying your vows?"

Lachlan's eyes meet mine—the one not swollen shut still that impossible blue, clear and fierce despite everything they've done to him. I see no regret there, no plea for forgiveness, only the same consuming fire that drew us together against all reason, all loyalty, all sacred bonds.

"Answer me!" Hamish shouts, his spittle striking my cheek.

What can I say that isn't a lie? That I regret the pain but not the love? That I would take back the betrayal but not the moments in Lachlan's arms? That some part of me recognized him from the first moment, as if my soul had been waiting for him across lifetimes?

"She doesn't need to answer." Lachlan's voice cuts through the heavy air between us. "The blame is mine, brother. I pursued her. I seduced her. Yer quarrel is with me alone."

"Liar." Hamish's fingers tighten on my jaw until I taste blood where my teeth cut into the inside of my cheek. "I saw how she looked at you that first night. How she trembled when you took her hand." He turns back to me, eyes searching my face with desperate intensity. "Did you ever feel for me even a fraction of what you clearly feel for him?"

The raw honesty of the question penetrates the haze of fear and guilt that surrounds me. In this moment, Hamish isn't the laird, the husband, the vengeful master. He's simply a man discovering he was never truly loved.

"I tried," I whisper, the closest to truth I can offer.

Something breaks in Hamish's expression. His hand falls away from my face, leaving behind the ghost-impression of his fingers on my skin. "Not hard enough," he says, voice hollow.

Lachlan lurches forward suddenly, chains clinking as he strains toward me. "Isla," he gasps, my name a prayer on his bloodied lips.

Hamish's control shatters. He shoves me backward, sending me stumbling against the rough wall, then turns and delivers a vicious kick to Lachlan's ribs. The sound of cracking bone turns my stomach. Lachlan curls inward with a grunt of pain but makes no further sound—denying Hamish even the satisfaction of his screams.

"Is this love?" Hamish demands, gesturing between us as Lachlan struggles to breathe through what must be broken ribs. "This destruction? This betrayal of everything sacred?" He turns to me, eyes wild with something beyond rage. "You've made a mockery of our marriage, of clan bonds, of my very name. And for what?"

In the shadows, the guards shift uncomfortably, some looking away from this raw display of their laird's wounded pride. One whispers to another, too low for me to hear the words but not the derisive tone. Hamish hears it too, his shoulders stiffening as he realizes how this scene must appear to his men—not just a husband's righteous anger but the pathetic flailing of a man discovering his inadequacy.

Pride wounded beyond bearing, Hamish straightens, cold calculation replacing naked emotion. "Enough of this spectacle," he announces, voice steady once more. "Take her back to her chambers. Lock her in until I decide her fate."

"Hamish, please," I begin, but he cuts me off with a slashing gesture.

"One more word and he dies now," he says, voice so soft only I can hear. "Is that what you want, wife? His blood on these stones before the night is through?"

I press my lips together, trapping the pleas that rise in my throat. Across the chamber, Lachlan watches me with that one clear eye, something like a warning in his gaze. Don't provoke him further. Don't sacrifice yourself. The silent communication flows between us with an ease that only confirms everything Hamish suspects.

"Guard," Hamish calls, his voice once more the composed command of a laird. "Escort Lady Sutherland to her chambers. Post men at her door. No one enters or leaves without my express permission."

Two guards step forward from the shadows, their faces carefully blank as they move to flank me. Before they can take my arms, I cast one last desperate look at Lachlan, trying to pour a lifetime of feeling into a single glance.

I love you, I mouth silently.

Always, his split lips form in return.

I wrench myself from the guard's grasp with strength born of desperation, lunging toward the barred cell where they'll leave him to suffer through the night. My feet barely touch the ground as I half-run, half-stumble across the chamber, ignoring Hamish's shout of rage behind me. Nothing matters now—not my safety, not my future, not the consequences that will surely follow this final defiance. All that exists is Lachlan and these precious seconds before they tear us apart forever.

The cell door stands half-open, ready to receive him once Hamish tires of his public display of punishment. I reach it before the guards can recover from my sudden movement, fingers wrapping around cold iron bars as if they might somehow protect me, might somehow keep me anchored to him.

"Lachlan," I whisper, his name a prayer on my lips, a confession, an absolution.

He raises his head, chains rattling as he shifts toward me. Blood trails from his temple, tracking a crimson path down his cheek, yet his gaze burns with an intensity that transcends his broken body. He inches forward on his knees, every movement clearly agony, until he kneels directly before me on the other side of the bars.

"Isla," he breathes, the sound barely audible above the sudden commotion of guards rushing toward us.

I thrust my arm through the bars, reaching for him with trembling fingers. He stretches his own hand as far as the shackles allow, the iron cutting deeper into his already raw wrist. Our fingertips hover a breath apart, straining toward a connection we both know might be our last.

"I would do it all again," he tells me, voice low and fierce, meant for my ears alone. "Every moment. Every touch. Every consequence."

Tears blur my vision, carving hot paths down my cheeks. "As would I," I confess, the truth of it burning in my chest like swallowed fire.

Our fingertips brush—the barest whisper of contact, yet it sends a jolt through my entire body, as if lightning has found earth through the point where our skin meets. Something passes between us in that touch, something that transcends flesh and bone, something eternal.

"Enough!" Hamish's roar shatters the moment. He appears beside me, face contorted with rage too vast for his body to contain. "Have you no shame? No remorse?"

His hand closes around my upper arm, fingers digging into flesh with bruising force. I don't flinch, don't look away from Lachlan's face. If these are our final moments together, I will commit every line, every shadow, every drop of blood to memory.

"Take her upstairs," Hamish orders, giving me a violent shove toward the waiting guards. "And if she resists, drag her."

Rough hands grasp my shoulders, pulling me backward. I fight them, feet scrabbling for purchase on the slick stone floor. "Lachlan!" I cry, no longer caring who hears the naked desperation in my voice.

"This isn't over," Lachlan calls, surging forward against his chains, muscles straining as if he might tear the iron from stone through sheer force of will. "What lies between us cannae be broken, not by him, not by death itself!"

The guards haul me toward the stairs, my heels dragging against stone. I twist in their grip, desperate for one last glimpse of him. Hamish steps between us, deliberately blocking my view, his back rigid with fury.

"You think this pain is the end," Lachlan continues, voice growing stronger with each word, rising above the sounds of my struggle. "But I will find you again, Isla! In this life or the next!"

I'm halfway up the stairs now, my body fought over by guards who push from behind and pull from above. My throat burns raw from screaming his name, my dress torn at the shoulder where someone has gripped it too roughly. Through a gap in the men surrounding me, I catch one final glimpse of the chamber below.

Lachlan kneels in a shaft of torchlight, face raised toward where I struggle on the stairs. Our eyes lock across the growing distance, and in that moment, something impossible happens—the dungeon walls seem to fade, stone becoming translucent as mist. I am both Isla being dragged from her lover and Fi standing in ruins centuries later, watching this memory unfold. The distinction between us blurs, time itself seeming to stutter and fold.

His voice reaches me across this impossible divide, across stone and time and death itself: "I will wait for you. Always."

The guards drag me through the doorway at the top of the stairs, but not before I see Hamish draw his dirk, the blade catching torchlight as he approaches his brother with murder in his eyes.

The vision fractures. I am falling, spinning, my consciousness torn between Isla's body being hauled through castle corridors and my own—Fi's—body standing in the ruins of what will become a tourist attraction centuries later. My mouth opens in a scream that belongs to both of us, to all of us, to every incarnation that has loved and lost and found him again.

I blink, and the dungeon is gone. I stand alone on the parapet of present-day Sutherland Castle, my hands gripping ancient stone that's warm beneath the afternoon sun. My cheeks are wet with tears I don't remember shedding, my throat raw as if I've been screaming. Before me, Lachlan's ghost shimmers in the daylight, more substantial than I've ever seen him, his face a mirror of the anguish I just witnessed in his past self.

"Now ye ken," he says simply.

I press my palm against my chest, feeling my heart hammer beneath my ribs—my heart, yet also Isla's, the distinction meaningless now that I've felt what she felt, seen through her eyes, loved with her soul.

"He killed you both," I whisper, the knowledge settling into my bones with terrible certainty. "After they took her away, he murdered you, then her, then himself."

Lachlan nods once, the motion carrying the weight of centuries. "More or less, ye left this earth before me; what he did bound us. Always to find each other. Always to recognize what we've lost. Always to end in blood."

I step toward him, hand outstretched before I remember the futility of the gesture. "But why? What purpose does our suffering serve?"

"Punishment," Lachlan answers, eyes ancient with sorrow. "His final vengeance. That we should find each other in every life, love each other with the same consuming fire, and always be torn apart before that love can flower into the life we should have had."

My fingers curl into a fist, dropping back to my side. "Thirteen times," I whisper, recalling his earlier words. "I've found you and lost you thirteen times before."

"And now the fourteenth," he confirms, something like hope flickering beneath the sorrow in his gaze. "Perhaps this time..."

He doesn't finish the thought, but he doesn't need to. I can feel the question hanging between us, vibrating in the air like the aftermath of a struck bell: Will this time be different? Can we break a curse that has claimed us through thirteen other lifetimes?

The rational part of me—the doctoral student, the skeptic, the woman who built her life on verifiable facts—has fallen completely silent. In its place surges something older, a certainty that precedes thought, a recognition born of Isla's memories now fully integrated with my own.

"I know what he did to us," I say, my voice steadier than I expect. "I know what we've suffered. But Hamish was wrong about one thing."

Lachlan's form flickers slightly in the strengthening sunlight, but his eyes remain fixed on mine, waiting.

"He thought his curse would be our punishment," I continue. "But what he never understood—what I'm only now beginning to grasp—is that finding each other, even briefly, even tragically, was never the curse." I take another step toward his shimmering form, close enough that if he were flesh, I would feel his breath on my face. "It was the blessing that made the curse bearable."

CHAPTER 15
The Curse Revealed

The fluorescent hum of my room lights feels abrasive against my raw nerves, a modern annoyance that fails to chase away the ancient shadows gathering in the corners. I sit on the edge of the mattress, my hands gripping the cheap polyester bedspread until my knuckles turn white. Across from me, sitting in the worn armchair that shouldn't be able to support his weight, is Lachlan.

He looks more solid tonight than he ever has, the blue of his tartan vivid against the beige wallpaper, the dark fall of his hair casting real shadows across his face. But his eyes are windows into a hell I am only just beginning to understand.

"Tell me," I whisper. The command hangs in the air, heavy and suffocating. "I need to know the end of it."

Lachlan leans forward, elbows resting on his knees, hands clasped together. Those hands—large, scarred, capable of wielding a claymore or touching a woman with reverence—tremble slightly. "It is not a story for the faint of heart, mo chridhe."

"I am not faint of heart," I counter, though my pulse flutters like a trapped bird against my ribs. "I died." The words tumble out before I can check them, a memory surfacing that isn't quite mine yet feels like a scar on my soul.

He winces, a flicker of pain crossing his features. "Aye. You did." He takes a breath, and the air in the room drops ten degrees, frost forming delicate patterns on the windowpane. "It began the night he found us. Not the suspicions, not the rumors. The truth."

As he speaks, the walls of the hotel room seem to stretch and warp. The smell of stale carpet and cleaning solution fades, replaced by the scent of damp stone, burning tallow, and fear.

"We were careless," Lachlan's voice becomes a low rumble, vibrating in my chest. "Love makes fools of warriors."

The flashback hits me not as a picture on a screen, but as a physical displacement. I am yanked backward through the centuries. The beige wallpaper dissolves into rough-hewn granite. The humming light becomes the crackle of a torch guttering in a sconce.

I am Isla, and I am screaming.

Guards—men I have known since childhood, men who have eaten at my father's table—have their hands on me. Their grip is bruising, disrespectful in a way that signals my fall from grace is absolute. But my struggle is not for myself.

"Lachlan!" My voice tears at my throat, raw and bloody.

Down the corridor, in the flickering interplay of light and shadow, they have him. Four men struggle to contain the fury of the younger Sutherland brother. He fights with the desperation of a wolf cornered, landing a blow that sends a guard stumbling back with a shattered nose. But there are too many of them.

Hamish stands apart, a silhouette of rigid control amidst the chaos. He watches his brother be subdued, his face a mask of cold, imperious judgment.

"Take him below," Hamish commands. His voice is not loud, but it cuts through the clamor of the struggle like a blade. "Chain him to the wall. Deep."

"No!" I lunge forward, but the guards holding me jerk me back, my arm twisting painfully in the socket. "Hamish, please! He is your blood!"

Hamish turns his gaze to me. There is no love in it now, only a terrifying, possessive void. "And you were my wife."

The scene fractures and shifts, following Lachlan. I am Fi, watching, feeling the cold bite of iron as if it were my own skin.

They drag him down the spiral stairs, his boots scraping helplessly against the stone. Each impact jars through me. The dungeon air is stagnant, heavy with the stench of mildew and old misery. They throw him against the wall, the force of it knocking the breath from his lungs.

The shackles are rusted, cruel things. I feel the phantom bite of cold metal snapping around my wrists as I watch the guards hammer the pins home. Lachlan strains against them, the iron cuffs digging into his flesh, grinding against bone. He roars—a sound of pure, impotent rage—and pulls until blood weeps from his wrists to slick the chains.

Hamish descends the stairs slowly, a predator savoring the trap. He stops just out of reach, the torchlight catching the silver brooch at his shoulder, gleaming like a malice-filled eye.

"You thought you could take her from me," Hamish says softly. The dungeon amplifies his voice, turning it into a serpentine hiss. "My title. My lands. My wife."

"She was never yers," Lachlan spits, blood flying from his split lip. "You owned her name, not her heart."

Hamish steps closer, unbothered by the ferocity in his brother's gaze. He reaches out, trailing a finger along the line of Lachlan's jaw, a mocking caress before he strikes—a sharp, backhanded blow that snaps Lachlan's head to the side.

"Heart?" Hamish laughs, a dry, mirthless sound. "Hearts are fickle, brother. Flesh is what matters. Flesh can be bound. Flesh can be broken." He leans in close, his breath ghosting over Lachlan's battered face. "She will never be yours again. I will make sure of it. While you rot here in the dark, imagining what I do to her, remember this: you bought her suffering with your lust."

"Touch her," Lachlan growls, the sound rising from the depths of his soul, "and I will tear this castle down stone by stone to bury you."

"Empty threats from a chained dog," Hamish sneers. He turns his back, the heavy wool of his plaid swirling around him. "Enjoy the silence, Lachlan. It is the last companion you shall ever have."

The heavy oak door slams shut with a sound like a coffin lid falling. The darkness is total, suffocating, a physical weight that presses against my eyes, against my mind. I am back in the hotel room, gasping for air, tears tracking hot paths down my cheeks, but the cold of the dungeon remains in my marrow.

The vision morphs again. I am no longer watching; I am living it. I can feel the guard's fingers digging into my flesh as they drag me from the dungeon, and the tears feel cold against my heated cheeks. I fear what Hamish will do to Lachlan. The guards push me into the bedchamber and close the door behind me.

My heart hammers a frantic rhythm against ribs that feel too fragile to contain it. I am Isla, and I am trapped.

I pace the length of the room, my silk slippers silent on the rush mats. The door is barred from the outside. Every sound from the corridor makes me flinch. Time passes slowly, I press my hands to my stomach, a protective instinct born of a secret I have kept hidden for two moons.

The lock grinds, a harsh, metal-on-metal screech that sets my teeth on edge. The heavy timber door swings open, crashing against the stone wall.

Hamish fills the doorway.

He has shed his plaid, standing in his shirt and breeches, looking more like an executioner than a husband. His chest heaves, and his eyes...his eyes are voids where the soul should be. He steps inside and kicks the door shut behind him.

"Hamish," I start, backing away until my spine meets the cold stone of the hearth. "Please, let us discuss this sensibly."

"Sensibly?" He crosses the room in two strides, invading my space, his scent of musk and stale wine overpowering. "Was it sensible to spread your legs for him? Was it sensible to humiliate me before my own clan?"

"It was not..."

His hand moves faster than thought. The back of his knuckles connects with my cheekbone, a flash of white-hot pain that explodes behind my eyes. The force of it throws me sideways. I crumble, my skirts tangling around my legs, the rough stone of the floor biting into my palms as I catch myself.

The room spins. I taste copper.

"Get up," he snarls, looming over me like a storm cloud. "Do not cower like a beaten dog. You had courage enough to betray me."

I scramble backward, crab-walking away from him, one hand raised in futile defense, the other cradling my belly. He reaches for me, his fingers tangling in the fabric of my bodice, hauling me up as if I weigh nothing. He shakes me, my head snapping back and forth.

"Who seduced wha, Isla? Did ye gang tae him? Did ye beg for.?"

"Please!" I sob, the words fracturing. "Please, do not hurt me! I am with child!"

Hamish freezes. The violence in him pauses, suspended in a terrifying stillness. He releases me so abruptly I stumble back against the bedpost. He stares at my stomach, his face draining of color, leaving him looking like a corpse animated by hate.

"With child?" he whispers. The hope in his voice is the most twisted thing I have ever heard. "My heir," he breathes.

I cannot lie. Not now. Not with Lachlan's life and our child's hanging by a thread. I lift my chin, trembling but defiant.

"No," I whisper. "Not yers."

The silence stretches, thick and poisonous. A vein throbs in Hamish's temple. "Whose?" he asks, although he knows the answer.

“Lachlan’s,” I confess, the name a prayer and hopefully a shield. “It’s Lachlan’s.”

The transformation is instantaneous. The man vanishes, replaced by a monster. His face contorts, a rictus of pure, unadulterated fury. He lunges, grabbing my upper arms, his fingers digging so deep I feel the bruises forming instantly. He shakes me until my teeth rattle.

“Ye carry his bastard in me house? In the womb that belongs tae me?”

“I belong to nae one but him!” I scream, the truth bursting out of me.

Hamish stops shaking me. He draws me close, his face inches from mine, his eyes wide and wild. A smile stretches his lips, cruel, triumphant, broken.

“I’ll be havin’ his bastard lashed daily; he’ll be a maid, not with name nor title; he’ll pay his father’s debt, as will ye.”

“Lachlan will no allow it.” I say through my teeth. “We belong to him.”

“Him?” Hamish laughs, a wet, breathless sound. “Ye belong to a ghost, then.”

The world stops. The air leaves the room. “What?”

”I killed him,” Hamish lies, the words sliding out smooth as oil. “Befor’

I came up here. I slit his throat in the dark. He died callin' for our mother, not ye."

"No," I gasp, my legs giving way. He holds me up, refusing to let me fall. "Ye lie. I wid feel it. I wid."

"Ye feel nought but what I allow ye tae feel," he hisses. "He is dead, Isla. Gone. And ye..." He drags a hand down my front, over the child that he thinks is an abomination. "Ye are bound tae me noo. Only me. I will raise this bastard, and every day I will make ye watch as I beat the Sutherland spirit oot of it. Ye will live in this room, and ye will serve me, and ye will never, ever be free."

The horror of it, the life he paints, the death of my love, it claws at my mind, tearing through sanity.

"No," I whisper. "No, no, no."

"Yes," Hamish whispers back, leaning in to kiss my forehead, a Judas kiss that burns like a brand. "Forever."

Something snaps inside me, not bone, but the tether that holds me to this world, to this life of duty and fear. If Lachlan is gone, the world is nothing but ash and pain.

I scream, a primal sound of grief that startles Hamish. I shove him with every ounce of strength in my body. He stumbles back, catching his heel on the edge of the hearth rug. It is enough.

I run.

I fly out the chamber door, my skirts billowing like heavy sails. The guards at the end of the hall shout, but they are too slow, too surprised by the spectacle of the Lady Sutherland sprinting like a madwoman. I do not turn toward the main stairs. I turn toward the narrow, winding service stair that leads up.

Up to the wind. Up to the sky.

"Isla!" Hamish's roar chases me, closer than I would like.

My slippers slap against the stone steps. The staircase spirals tight and steep, a dark throat swallowing me whole. My lungs burn as if I have inhaled fire. My hand scrapes against the rough-hewn wall for balance, leaving a smear of skin and blood on the granite, but I feel no pain. I feel only the desperate need to escape the cage he has built for me.

I hear his boots crashing on the steps behind me. He is faster and stronger, but he is driven by hate. I am driven by the need to join my heart.

The wooden door at the top of the stairs is swollen with damp. I throw my shoulder against it, sobbing with exertion. It gives with a groan, bursting open into the grey, swirling violent sky.

The wind hits me like a physical blow, tearing the pins from my hair, whipping the long red strands across my face, blinding me. I stumble out onto the parapet. The stone is slick with rain. Below, the loch churns, dark and unforgiving, and the courtyard stones wait, hard and final.

"Isla, stop!"

Hamish bursts onto the roof, chest heaving, his face slick with sweat. He stops near the doorway, seeing me standing on the precipice. For the first time, the rage in his eyes is replaced by sudden, stark panic.

"Come awa' frae the edge," he orders, though his voice wavers. "Dinna be a fool."

I turn to face him. The wind pulls at my gown, urging me backward, whispering of freedom. I press my hands to my belly one last time, apologizing to the life that will never be. "Forgive me, wee one. We're goin' tae find yer faither." I whisper.

"Ye cannae keep me," I say. My voice is steady, snatched away by the gale but loud enough for him to hear. "Ye can chain ma body, ye can bruise ma skin, but ye cannae keep me."

"Isla, please," he steps forward, hand outstretched. "I...I lied. He lives. I lied to hurt you. Come down."

"It matters no," I tell him, and I realize it is true. If Lachlan lives, Hamish will destroy him slowly. If he is dead, I must follow. There is no version of this life where we are allowed to exist. "I only belong to Lachlan. I will join him in the next life."

"No!" Hamish screams, lunging for me.

I look at him one last time, etching his face into my soul so I might know my enemy when we meet again. Then, I look up at the sky, endless and gray.

"Lachlan," I whisper.

I step backward into the empty air.

Gravity claims me instantly. The stomach-turning drop, the rush of wind roaring in my ears like a thousand screaming voices. The gray sky recedes. The dark stone rushes up to meet me. There is a moment of perfect, weightless clarity, a suspension of time where I am neither alive nor dead, simply falling.

Then, the earth strikes me. A shattering impact. Darkness absolute.

The darkness does not last. It reforms, thick and suffocating. I am no longer falling; I am chained. I am Fi, but I am weeping with grief that belongs to a man. I see through Lachlan's eyes, feel the cold iron biting into his wrists, and the throb of his broken face.

He hangs from the wall, exhausted, listening to the castle above. He felt it, a severing. A sudden, sharp void in the world where a light used to be. He pulls at the chains, groaning, denial warring with instinct.

The door creaks open.

Hamish enters. He does not stride this time. He walks with the mechanical, jerky movements of a marionette whose strings are tangled. His shirt is soaked through with rain, his hair plastered to his skull. His face is the color of old ash.

Lachlan lifts his head. "Isla?" The name scrapes out of his throat.

Hamish stops just out of reach. He stares at Lachlan, but his eyes look through him, seeing something broken on the courtyard stones.

"She was with child," Hamish says. His voice is hollow, devoid of inflection. "Your child."

The words strike Lachlan harder than any fist. A child. A piece of them both. But the phrasing...the grammar of the dead.

"Was?" Lachlan whispers, the blood draining from his face. "What dae ye mean, was?"

Hamish's face twists, a spasm of grief and madness contorting his features until he barely looks human. "She jumped," he says, the words vomiting out of him. "She threw hersel' fae the tower. She chose death. She chose death over me."

Lachlan freezes. The world tilts. And then he screams.

It is a sound that tears the lining of the throat, a sound that shreds the soul. It echoes off the damp stone walls, a cacophony of pure, distilled agony. He thrashes against the chains, not to escape, but to destroy himself, to tear his arms from their sockets, to dash his brains against the granite. He needs to go to her. He needs to follow.

"No!" Hamish draws the broadsword at his hip. The steel hisses against the leather scabbard. "Stop it! Do not think you can escape so easily."

"Unchain me, brother! I'll bother ye no more. I'll end meself to join her!" Lachlan roars, tears streaking through the blood on his face. "Let me go to her, ye bastard!"

"Ye life will be forfeit," Hamish says, his eyes wide and wild with a terrible resolve. He steps forward, leveling the point of the blade at Lachlan's heaving chest. "But not by your hand sae you can join her where she noo haunts, ye widna run tae her ghost in the heather."

Hamish grips the hilt with both hands. The madness settles into a cold, diamond-hard focus.

"I will no' let ye end yer life to meet her in the next life, brother," Hamish declares, his voice trembling with the weight of the curse he is about to cast. "I bind ye here. I bind ye to the stane. Ye will no' find her. Ye will wait. Ye will rot."

He thrusts.

The blade punches through skin, through muscle, grating between ribs to find the heart.

I feel it. I feel the invasion of cold steel, the sudden, shocking arrest of the heartbeat. Lachlan gasps, his eyes locking onto his brother's, wide with shock and hatred. The pain is absolute, blinding white, and then—

Cold.

The dungeon dissolves. The memory shatters like glass.

I gasp, lurching forward off the bed, my hands clawing at my chest, searching for a wound that isn't there. The hotel room rushes back in—the hum of the fridge, the traffic outside, the smell of dust. I am on my knees on the carpet, heaving for breath, my face wet with tears that have been falling for hundreds of years.

"Lachlan," I choke out.

He is there, by the window. He is fading, his form translucent, his expression one of infinite, weary sorrow. He has shown me the end. He has shown me the beginning.

And the weight of it crushes me to the floor.

Sleep takes me.

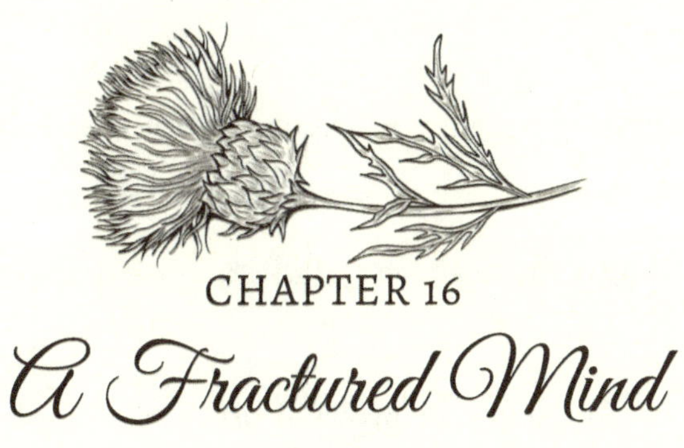

CHAPTER 16
A Fractured Mind

The bristles scrape against my gums, a mundane rhythm, a scrubbing of bone that feels obscenely normal. I spit foam into the porcelain basin, the white turning pink with a trace of blood. I rinse, water swirling down the drain, and lift my head to check my reflection.

My face is pale, eyes bruised by sleeplessness. A stranger's face.

Then the light shifts.

He is there.

Standing just behind my left shoulder, filling the narrow space of the bathroom with a darkness that swallows the fluorescent hum. Lachlan. He does not flicker. He does not fade like a dream at dawn. He is solid, imposing, his Sutherland plaid dark with rain, his hair falling in wet tangles around a face etched with centuries of wanting. His eyes meet mine in the glass—piercing, demanding, a blue so cold it burns.

My toothbrush falls from my hand, clattering into the sink.

"Lachlan," I mouth, the steam on the glass absorbing the sound.

He reaches out. In the mirror, his hand rises toward my neck, large and scarred, the fingers slightly curled as if to graze the pulse hammering beneath my skin. I see the dirt under his nails, the tension in his forearm.

I spin around, gasping, my back slamming against the counter.

Empty.

Nothing but the peeling beige wallpaper and the damp towel hanging on the rack. The air is still cold, vibrating with a static charge that raises the hair on my arms, but he is gone. I grip the edge of the sink, my knuckles white, staring at the space where he should be. My heart kicks against my ribs, a frantic, irregular beat.

"Stop it," I hiss at the empty room. "Stop it."

But he doesn't stop. He never stops.

I leave the bed and breakfast, desperate for the solidity of the outside world, for noise, for other living, breathing people. But Dornoch is a trap of mirrors.

I walk past the bakery. The plate glass front reflects the gray street, the passing cars, and him. He walks beside me in the reflection, matching my stride. A spectral escort. I turn my head sharply to the left. No one. I look back at the window. He is there, looking straight ahead, his jaw set in that stubborn, warrior line.

I hurry past a parked sedan. In the chrome of the bumper, his face warps and stretches, watching me.

I step over a puddle in the cracked pavement. The water is dark, an oil-slick mirror. For a second, it isn't the leaden sky reflected there, but his eyes, looking up from the earth as if he is buried beneath the tarmac, waiting to drag me down.

My breath comes in short, jagged tearing sounds. I need to sit. I need anchor points.

I duck into a small café near the harbor. The bell chimes—a cheerful, innocent sound that grates on my nerves. I order black coffee, my voice sounding thin and foreign to my own ears. I take a table in the corner, away from the windows, away from the glass.

The mug arrives, steam rising in lazy spirals. I stare down into the black liquid.

The surface ripples, though the table is steady. The dark circle of coffee transforms. It becomes a pupil. An eye. His eye.

The ripples smooth out, and his face forms in the crema and shadow. He is smiling—not the cruel smile of Hamish, but the soft, devastating smile of the man who loved Isla in the dark. He mouths a word I cannot hear, but I feel it resonate in my marrow. *Come.*

"Lachlan," I whisper.

It isn't enough. The whisper catches in my throat, choking me. I need to speak it. I need to acknowledge the haunting.

"Lachlan," I say, louder this time. A plea. A confession.

The clinking of silverware stops. The low hum of conversation cuts off.

I look up. The couple at the next table is staring. The woman behind the counter has paused, a rag suspended over a plate. They look at me with that specific, pitying wariness reserved for the mad. The American woman talking to her coffee. The obsession.

Heat floods my face, burning and shameful. I scrape my chair back, the sound screeching like a wounded animal.

"I... I have to go," I mutter to no one.

I grab my bag, leaving the coffee untouched, and flee. The bell chimes again as I exit, mocking me, but I don't look back. I don't look at the windows. I keep my eyes on my boots, but even there, in the shine of the leather toe, I catch the flash of a tartan that hasn't been woven in four hundred years.

Back in my room, I fall asleep to the synthetic, smelling of industrial detergent, but as my eyes close, the texture changes. The polyester weave becomes linen, rougher, heavier. The mattress hardens, transforming into the unforgiving solidity of the past.

The transition is a physical hook behind my navel, yanking me down.

I am not Fi. I am Isla. And I am trembling.

The torchlight is dying, casting long, erratic shadows against the dressed stone of the alcove. We are deep in the castle, in the spaces between spaces, a narrow service passage forgotten by everyone but the rats and the lovers.

Lachlan presses me into the corner, his body a wall of heat shielding me from the draft. There is no gentleness tonight. There is only the frantic, clawing need of two people who know the hourglass is running out of sand.

"Isla," he groans, the sound vibrating against my collarbone.

His hands are on my waist, large and demanding, bunching the fabric of my gown until he finds the skin beneath. His palms are rough, calloused from the sword hilt, from the reins. When they slide over my ribs, the friction strikes sparks in my blood.

"Quiet," I whisper, though I tilt my head back, baring my throat to him. "Hamish is in the hall."

"Let him come," Lachlan growls. He buries his face in the crook of my neck. His beard, days of growth he hasn't bothered to shear, scrapes deliciously against my sensitive skin, a raw counterpoint to the wet heat of his open mouth. "Let him see whit belongs tae me."

He bites me—not enough to break the skin, but enough to mark. A sharp, stinging claim just above my pulse point. I gasp, my fingers digging into the wool of his plaid, dragging him closer until there is not a breath of space between us.

The smell of him floods my senses—peat smoke from the hearth, the iron tang of his armor, the musk of a man who has ridden hard to be here. It is an intoxicant stronger than wine.

He lifts me, his hands grasping my thighs, hitching me up until my back is braced against the cold stone. I wrap my legs around his waist, the position leaving me open, vulnerable, aching. He fumbles with the lacings of his breeches, his movements jerky with haste.

When he enters me, it is a collision.

I cry out, the sound muffled by his mouth crushing down on mine. He tastes of cloves and desperation. He fills me completely, stretching me, grounding me. The cold stone bites into my spine, but I don't care; the fire in front of me consumes everything.

We move with a rhythm that has no music, a primal, frantic cadence.

"Look at me," he commands, pulling back just enough to stare into my eyes. His pupils are blown wide, swallowing the blue, leaving only black wells of want. Sweat beads on his forehead, catching the dying torchlight.

"Lachlan," I sob.

He thrusts harder, driving into me, seeking the deepest part of my soul. It is worship and it is war. Every slide of skin, every friction, is a defiance of the brother who thinks he owns us. We are stealing this pleasure. We are thieves in the night, stealing moments of eternity.

I arc against him, my nails scoring the muscles of his shoulders. The pleasure coils tight in my belly, a golden wire pulling taut. It snaps. I shatter, my body clenching around him, milking him. He groans, a sound of ruin, and follows me over the edge, pouring himself into me, binding us together with seed and sweat and sin.

For a moment, as we hang there in the aftermath, lungs heaving, hearts beating a shared tattoo, we are immortal.

Then the darkness rushes in.

I wake with a scream trapped in my throat.

I sit bolt upright. The air conditioning hums. The red numbers of the clock leer at me: 3:33 AM. My body is slick with sweat that isn't entirely mine. My thighs ache with a phantom stretch. The skin on my neck burns where he bit me.

"Lachlan?"

I reach out into the dark, my hand grasping at the empty pillow beside me. Cold. Just cotton and emptiness.

I collapse back against the headboard, chest heaving. Tears prick my eyes, hot and fast. He isn't here. But as I inhale, shaking and raw, the scent fills the room—unmistakable, heavy, and real.

Heather. Peat smoke. And the musky, iron scent of sex.

He was here. He is here.

The days bleed into a gray smear of rain and stone. I walk the streets of Dornoch, but I am not really here. I am a ghost haunting the living world; the real world is the one I visit when I close my eyes.

I stand before the antique shop on the High Street. The glass is rain-streaked, blurring the displays of rusted farming tools and cracked china. But beyond the display, inside the locked and darkened shop, he stands. Lachlan. He is not a reflection this time. He is on the other side.

He presses his palm against the glass. I lift my hand, matching his spread fingers. The glass is cold, but I feel the warmth radiating through it, a phantom heat that travels up my arm and settles in my chest. He mouths my name. I nod. "I know. I'm coming." I whisper.

Back in the room, I sit before the vanity. The brush pulls through my hair, crackling with static. I look up.

It is not Fi MacPherson staring back. The woman in the glass wears a shift of fine, unbleached linen. Her hair is not loose and frizzy, but heavy, copper waves waiting to be braided.

Lachlan steps out of the shadows of the room behind her—behind me. He wears his tunic, open at the neck. He stands close, his chest brushing her back. He lifts his hands, hovering them just above her shoulders, a caress that doesn't quite land.

"The wind is rising tonight," I say to the mirror.

"It will bring the snow," he answers, his voice sounding in my head, not my ears.

"I must finish the mending before the light fails," I murmur. I blink, and the reflection shimmers back to jeans and a flannel shirt. I don't even find it strange.

Hunger drives me out at dusk, a biological nuisance I resent. I sit in the small bistro, a white tablecloth separating me from the empty chair opposite. I have ordered wine—two glasses. One for me, one for him.

The waiter approaches, a young man with a notepad and a frown. "Excuse me, miss? Are you expecting someone else? We usually need the table if—"

I look up, annoyed by the interruption. "My husband," I say, the word slipping out smooth as a river stone. "Lachlan will be here soon. He is just stabling the horses."

The waiter stares at me. The noise of the restaurant seems to warp, slowing down. Horses?

"I mean..." I blink, the modern world rushing back in a headache-inducing tide. "I mean... parking the car. Sorry. I'm... tired."

He takes the menu away, eyeing me with suspicion. I drink both glasses of wine.

I hurry back to my room. I do not fight the exhaustion. I welcome it. I strip off my clothes, leaving them in a pile on the floor—vestments of a life I no longer want. I slide into bed naked, shivering, and close my eyes with a prayer on my lips. "Take me back." I whisper.

The stone walls rise up to embrace me.

We are not in the alcove. We are in a chamber I know better than my own childhood bedroom. A massive hearth dominates the wall, a fire roaring with logs thicker than a man's thigh. The floor is covered in furs —wolf, stag, sheepskin. A nest.

Lachlan lies back on the furs, the firelight painting his skin in strokes of orange and gold. He holds his hand out.

"Come here, wife of my heart."

I crawl to him. The fur is soft against my knees, the heat of the fire roasting one side of my body while the draft from the window cools the other. I straddle him, sinking down onto him with a sigh that empties my lungs.

This is not the frantic coupling of the alcove. This is slow. Heavy. We move like tectonic plates, grinding together, ancient and inevitable. I lean forward, my hair creating a curtain around us, shutting out the rest of the world.

He touches me with reverence. His hands map every inch of my skin, memorizing me for the darkness he knows is coming.

"Stay," he whispers, thrusting up into me, filling the void that has been inside me since I was born. "Stay here."

"I am trying," I weep, my tears falling onto his chest, mingling with the sweat. "I am trying to hold on."

We rock together, the friction building a heat that threatens to melt bone. I ride him, losing myself, my identity dissolving. I am not Fi. I am not Isla. I am just...this.....this connection, this fire, this man.

When the end comes, it is a collapse. I fall forward onto him, burying my face in the crook of his neck, inhaling the smoke and the salt.

"Don't let me wake up," I beg into his skin. "Lachlan, please. Keep me here."

"I have ye," he promises, his arms tightening like iron bands. "I have ye."

But the light comes anyway. Cruel, gray, morning light.

I wake curled in a fetal ball around a pillow that is damp with my tears. My body is cold. I am alone in my room. The grief hits me like a physical blow, a fresh amputation. I clutch the pillow to my chest and wail, rocking back and forth.

I don't know who is crying. I don't know whose heart is breaking. The line is gone. I am drowning in her memories, and God help me, I don't want to swim to the surface.

CHAPTER 17
The Return of the Old

The carpet smells of dust, a rough texture against my cheek. I am lying on the floor, the grief of a murdered love pressing the air from my lungs, when the sound cuts through the silence.

Knock. Knock. Knock.

Three sharp raps. Precise. Yet Demanding.

I flinch, the noise scraping against raw nerves. I drag myself up, my limbs heavy, my head swimming with the afterimages of the dungeon. Lachlan is gone from the window, fading back into the ether, leaving me exposed.

“Housekeeping?” I croak, my voice wrecked.

No answer. Just the silence waiting on the other side of the wood.

I stumble to the door. My hand shakes as I reach for the chain, then the knob. I don't check the peephole. I am too drained for caution. I pull the door open, expecting a towel, a complaint about the noise, anything mundane.

I stop breathing. What I do not expect is to see Murray standing there.

He is wearing a slate-gray pea coat over a crisp button-down, the collar stiff, the fabric expensive. He smiles, showing teeth that are too white, too straight. It is the smile he used to wear at faculty mixers, the one that says, I am charming, I am harmless, but it doesn't reach his hazel eyes. His eyes are flat, devoid of the warmth I once thought existed there. They are watching me with the intensity of a hawk sighting a mouse in the grass.

"Fi," he says. His voice is smooth, polished, but there is a hitch in the cadence, a slight delay as if the words are being translated from another language before reaching his tongue. "You look terrible, darling."

"Murray?" The name feels alien. "How... how did you find me?"

"You're not hard to track when you leave digital breadcrumbs," he says, stepping forward.

I instinctively step back, and he is inside before I can process the intrusion. He closes the door behind him. The sound of the latch clicking into place is loud, final.

The temperature in the room plummets.

It happens in a heartbeat. The stale warmth of the heater vanishes, replaced by a glacial chill that bites through my thin t-shirt. My breath blooms in a white cloud between us.

Murray pauses, his head tilting to the side in a jerky, bird-like motion. He sniffs the air. "Drafty in here. You should complain to management."

A shadow detaches itself from the corner near the bathroom.

Lachlan materializes. He does not shimmer this time; he is a dense, dark void in the room's atmosphere. His face is twisted in a snarl of recognition and revulsion. The lights in the bedside lamps flicker, buzzing like trapped wasps.

"Get away from him," Lachlan warns. His voice is not a sound but a vibration in my skull, a pressure against my eardrums.

I stare at Murray, then at the ghost. Murray doesn't see Lachlan. He walks right through the space where Lachlan's arm is raised, shivering slightly as he passes, rubbing his upper arms.

"Christ, it's freezing," Murray mutters. He turns his back to me, surveying the mess of papers on the small desk.

Lachlan moves, placing himself between me and my ex. The ghost is agitated, his form flickering like a candle in a gale. He stares at Murray's back—at the set of his shoulders, the arrogant tilt of his head. Lachlan's eyes widen, the blue fire in them turning to horror.

"It is not him," Lachlan whispers, the words rushing at me with urgent terror. "Fi, look at him. Look at how he stands."

I look. Murray stands with his weight on his back foot, one hand resting on his hip—not in his pocket as he usually does, but resting on the invisible hilt of a weapon that isn't there. His posture is rigid, commanding. Imperial.

"Hamish," I breathe.

Murray turns. The movement is too fast. His hazel eyes lock onto mine, but the light behind them has shifted. It is ancient. It is cold. It is the same gaze that watched me fall from the tower.

"Did you say something?" Murray asks softly. The timbre of his voice drops, resonating in a lower register that vibrates through the floorboards.

"He has found a vessel," Lachlan roars, though Murray hears nothing. "He has found you again! Run, Fi! You must run!"

But I can't run. My feet are rooted to the cheap carpet. I am staring at a man wearing a Patagonia jacket and seeing a laird in a plaid who murdered his own brother.

"I said get out," I try again, backing toward the window.

Murray smiles again, but this time the corners of his mouth twitch, fighting against the muscle memory of the face he is wearing. "But we have so much to discuss," he says, taking a step toward me. "History has a way of repeating itself, doesn't it?"

The lights flicker violently, plunging the room into strobing darkness. In the flashes, I see Lachlan screaming silently, clawing at the air, trying to grab a man he cannot touch. And I see Murray—or the thing wearing Murray—walking toward me with hands that ache to wrap around my throat.

The lock engages with a metallic click that sounds like a bone snapping. Murray slides the brass key into his pocket, patting the fabric smooth. He turns to me, blocking the only exit.

"Now," he says, the word heavy and wet. "Let's see what you've been up to in this godforsaken wasteland."

He begins to circle me. It is a slow, deliberate orbit. He moves around the perimeter of the small room, his fingers trailing over the furniture—the TV stand, the dresser, the desk. He claims the space simply by walking through it.

"I'm working on my dissertation," I say, my voice tight. I calculate the distance to the bathroom door. Too far. The window inside is a slit, barely wide enough for a cat. "Clan history. You know that."

"History." He spits the word. He stops at the desk, looking down at the scattered papers, the hand-drawn maps of Sutherland Castle. "You always were obsessed with the past. Obsessed with dead things."

He picks up a sheet of paper. It is a sketch of the tower. My handwriting scrawls in the margins: Lachlan's fall. The betrayal.

Murray's hand tightens, crumpling the paper into a tight ball. "Lachlan," he reads from another page, his voice curdling. "Always that name. Even after four hundred years, you scratch it into the margins like a lovestruck schoolgirl."

I freeze. Murray shouldn't know about four hundred years. Murray thinks I'm studying medieval politics.

"He sees the notes," Lachlan whispers. He is frantic, his form swirling around Murray like smoke. He swipes his hand through Murray's head, trying to disrupt the connection, trying to blind him. Nothing happens. Murray doesn't even blink. "He is too strong here. I have no purchase on this ground."

Murray picks up my laptop. The screen glows, displaying a digital archive of the Sutherland lineage. The light reflects in his eyes, turning them into flat, gray discs.

"He was weak," Murray says. It isn't Murray's critique of an academic subject. It is a brother's verdict. "He was a traitor and a thief."

"Don't," I warn, stepping forward. "That's my work."

Murray looks at me, and for a second, his face blurs. I see the sharp angles of Hamish's jaw, the cruel set of his mouth superimposed over Murray's softer features.

"It is garbage," he snarls.

He lifts the laptop high and brings it down on the corner of the desk. Plastic shatters. The screen spiderwebs, black liquid crystal bleeding across the glass. He strikes it again, and again, a mechanical, rhythmic violence. Crunch. Crunch. Crunch.

Lachlan screams a soundless cry of fury. He throws himself at Murray, swinging a spectral fist that should shatter jawbone. It passes harmlessly through Murray's shoulder. Lachlan stumbles, his momentum carrying him through the wall. He recoils, staring at his own hands in despair.

"I cannae touch him!" Lachlan cries. "Fi, he is flesh and I am mist! You must get out!"

Murray drops the ruined computer. He is breathing hard, nostrils flaring. He looks at me, and the hunger in his face makes my stomach turn over.

"Why do you force me to be this way?" he asks, stepping over the debris. "I only ever wanted to protect you. To keep you proper. To keep you mine."

He lunges.

I scramble back, knocking into the nightstand, the lamp crashing to the floor. His hand shoots out, grabbing my wrist. His grip is iron. It is not the grip of a finance manager from Boston; it is the grip of a man who has wielded a claymore, who has crushed throats.

"Let go!" I scream, twisting my arm.

He yanks me closer, until his face is inches from mine. I smell the stale coffee on his breath, and beneath that, the rot of the grave.

"You think you can hide from me?" His voice drops, the Boston accent dissolving into a rough, rolling burr that hasn't been heard in centuries. "You think death is an escape? I will hunt you through a thousand lives, Isla. I will break you in every single one of them."

Pain flares in my wrist, his fingers bruising the bone. I look at Lachlan. He is hovering by the door, his face a mask of agony.

"He can't touch you here," Lachlan says, his voice breaking. "But I can't either. The castle, Fi. You must get to the castle. The stone remembers me. The stone will give me strength."

Murray—Hamish—shakes me, his eyes wide and manic. "Say it," he hisses. "Say you belong to me."

"You always find him," he whispers, the voice shifting, layering, a chorus of two damned souls speaking through one mouth. "But you always belong to me in the end."

I go limp.

It is the hardest thing I have ever done. Every instinct screams at me to fight, to claw at his eyes, to knee him in the groin. But I know Hamish. I remember him. He feeds on resistance. He delights in the breaking.

I lower my head. I let my shoulders slump. I stop pulling against his grip.

"You're hurting me," I whimper. The fear is real, but the submission is a weapon.

Murray blinks. The tension in his jaw slackens just a fraction. He misinterprets my surrender, just as he did four hundred years ago when he thought locking me in a tower would make me docile.

"Pain is necessary for instruction," he says, his voice softening to a patronizing croon. He loosens his grip on my wrist, sliding his hand up to cup my elbow, a parody of a gentleman's escort. "Look at this mess. You've made such a mess of things, Isla."

He turns his head, glancing toward the desk where my notes lie scattered—the evidence of my "betrayal."

I look at Lachlan.

He is hovering by the light switch near the door. He sees my eyes. He understands.

He closes his eyes. His translucent hands clench into fists. The air in the room begins to vibrate, a low hum that rattles the windowpane. The shadows in the corners stretch and twist, drawn toward him. He is pouring his very essence, the scraps of his soul that remain, into the current.

“Now,” his voice whispers in my mind.

The overhead bulb surges. It glows with a blinding, magnesium-white intensity for a split second, casting stark, jagged shadows against the walls. Then—

POP.

Glass showers down. Sparks rain from the fixture. Darkness slams into the room, absolute and disorienting.

Murray shouts, flinching back, his hand falling from my arm as he covers his face.

I move.

I lunge for the door, my hands scrabbling for the deadbolt. My fingers feel numb, clumsy blocks of wood. I find the latch. I twist.

"No!" Murray roars. It is a beast's sound.

He grabs blindly in the dark. His hand catches the back of my flannel shirt. He yanks, pulling me backward off my feet. I stumble, choking as the collar digs into my windpipe.

I don't stop. I throw my weight forward, twisting violently.

The fabric shrieks. It tears from collar to hem.

I burst free, stumbling forward into the door. I shove it open, spilling out into the hallway's harsh, yellow light. The cool air hits my sweat-dampened skin.

"You bitch!"

I scramble to my feet and run.

My boots pound against the thin carpet of the corridor. Doors line the hallway, indifferent wooden sentinels. I hear him behind me—heavy footsteps, the crash of his body against the doorframe as he pursues.

"You can run!" he screams, his voice echoing, distorted, bouncing off the walls. "But you will never escape me! I will burn the world to find you!"

I hit the push-bar of the exit door at a dead sprint. It clatters open, and the night swallows me.

The parking lot is wet with rain. The streetlights halo in the mist. I fumble for my car keys, but my hands are empty. I left them. I left them in the room.

"The castle!" Lachlan's voice is a whisper in my ear, faint, sounding like it comes from the bottom of a well. "Go to the stones, Fi! I cannae follow... I am fading..."

I don't look back. I turn toward the dark bulk of the hills, toward the jagged silhouette of the ruins that loom over the town. I run.

My breath tears at my throat. My side aches. But the terror driving me is older than my body. Behind me, I hear the hotel door slam open again, hear the shout of a man who has chased me across centuries.

I run into the dark, toward the only place where the dead can fight back. The tether to Lachlan thins, stretching to its breaking point, his presence dissolving into the mist the further I get from his prison.

"Wait for me," I gasp into the wind.

I run until the lights of the town are behind me, and only the ancient dark lies ahead.

CHAPTER 18
Cat and Mouse

The wind off the North Sea tastes of salt and iron, biting at the exposed skin of my neck where my shirt is torn. I run. I do not look back at the lights of the hotel fading into the mists behind me. The asphalt of the highway yields to the uneven, slick cobblestones of Dornoch, the town huddled at the base of the glen like a congregation of stone mourners.

Dusk is not a gentle transition here. It is a bruising, a darkening purple that bleeds across the sky, drowning the world in shadow. My boots strike the stones with a rhythm that sounds too loud, a frantic drumbeat announcing my location to anything that listens in the dark.

Click. Click. Click.

The sound cuts through the wind. Not running. Walking. A measured, deliberate cadence.

I glance over my shoulder. Murray is there, a silhouette carved from the twilight. He is fifty yards back, strolling with his hands in the pockets of his pea coat. He does not look like a man chasing a fleeing ex-girlfriend. He looks like a laird inspecting his estate, ensuring the livestock is properly corralled. His movement is wrong—too fluid, too balanced. Murray had a rolling, loose-limbed gait. This thing moves like oil sliding over glass.

I turn the corner, ducking into a narrow lane lined with tall, narrow houses. The windows are dark, the shutters drawn tight against the coming night. Dornoch has always been a quiet town, but tonight it feels abandoned, as if the residents sensed the ancient malice walking their streets and fled.

My lungs burn. The cold air saws at my throat. I press my back against the rough harling of a building, trying to silence my breathing.

Click. Click.

He is turning the corner. He knows. He doesn't need to see me; he smells the fear. He tastes the blood memory of a woman he killed four centuries ago.

I push off the wall and scramble deeper into the alley. It smells of wet stone and old fish. I am Fi, the academic, the woman who navigates archives and libraries. But I am also Isla, the woman who knows the weight of a man's hand, the woman who knows that mercy is a myth invented by poets. The two identities grind against each other in my skull, fracturing my focus.

I stumble past a shop front, the glass darkened by grime and age. A display of dusty tartans and souvenir shortbread tins sits in the gloom. I stop, gripping the window ledge, my legs trembling so violently I fear they will buckle.

I need a weapon. I need a car. I need Lachlan.

As if summoned by the thought, the surface of the glass ripples. It is not a trick of the light. The reflection of the street behind me—the empty, cobbled dark—dissolves.

Lachlan stares back from the other side of the glass.

He looks wretched. His image is faint, like smoke caught in a bottle. The blue of his eyes is dim, the fire dampened by the distance from his stone prison. He presses his hands against the glass, and I see the phantom blood staining his wrists where the iron bit deep.

"Fi," he mouths. No sound reaches me, but the word resonates in the hollow of my chest. "The castle. I cannae protect ye here."

I place my hand against the pane, desperate for the warmth I felt before, the static charge of his presence. the glass is just ice-cold barrier.

"He's coming," I whisper, my breath fogging the space between our faces. "He's going to kill me, Lachlan. Just like before."

Lachlan's expression twists in anguish. He shakes his head, the motion leaving a trail of gray vapor. “Dinna Fash. Run to the stones. Run to where I am strong."

Behind me, the footsteps stop.

The silence is heavier than the sound. It is a physical weight, pressing down on my shoulders.

In the reflection, Lachlan looks past me, over my shoulder. His eyes widen. He shouts something, a silent scream of warning, and then he shatters. The image disintegrates into mist, leaving me staring at my own face—pale, wild-eyed, blood smeared on my cheek from a scratch I don't remember getting.

And behind my reflection, in the deep black mirror of the shop window, a second face appears.

It hangs in the darkness, floating just above my left shoulder. Murray's face. But the smile is Hamish's—a curling, cruel thing that exposes teeth too white for the gloom.

"Found you," the reflection whispers.

I spin around, swinging my arm out in a blind, terrified arc.

Empty air.

The alley is vacant. The cobblestones glisten with damp. There is no one there.

But the voice didn't come from behind me. It came from everywhere. It dripped from the gutters. It rose from the drains.

"Do you think I need to see you to find you?" The voice is Murray's Boston tenor wrapped around a core of Highland granite. "I have hunted you through the dark before, little bird. I know the rhythm of your heart better than I know my own."

I back away, my heels scraping on the stone. The fear is a cold fluid in my veins, replacing my blood. He is playing with me. He is the cat with the mouse, batting it between his paws before the final crunch.

I turn and run. I run not with a plan, but with the primal, animal need to put distance between the prey and the hunter. The castle. Lachlan said the castle. It looms somewhere above the town, a jagged tooth of rock and ruin, but from down here in the maze of Dornoch, it feels a world away.

I scramble toward the end of the alley, toward the next street, running blindly into the deepening night.

The town of Dornoch is a puzzle box designed by a madman. The streets do not follow the logic of modern grids; they twist and coil like entrails, turning back on themselves, leading into dead ends and courtyards that smell of rot.

I careen off a stone corner, my shoulder taking the impact. Pain flares, sharp and grounding, but I keep moving. The streetlights are sparse here, casting pools of sickly yellow light that only deepen the shadows between them.

"Isla..."

The whisper slides along the walls. It is not Murray's voice. It is the town itself speaking, remembering the woman who walked these stones four hundred years ago.

I take a left, then a right, my boots slipping on wet refuse. The houses lean over the street, their upper stories nearly touching, blocking out the sky. There are no lights in the windows. No televisions flickering blue against the curtains. No dogs barking. It is as if the entire population has been erased, leaving only the shell of a town for us to play out our tragedy.

Behind me, the rhythm continues. Click. Click. Unhurried. Inevitable.

He is not running. He doesn't have to. Every time I turn a corner, the sound of his approach is there, steady as a heartbeat. He is cutting the angles. Or perhaps the town is shifting for him, opening paths while it closes them for me.

My chest heaves, each breath a jagged shard of glass. I stop for a second, bracing my hands against a low stone wall to keep from collapsing. The stitch in my side is a hot knife.

A cold wind rushes down the narrow street, swirling the fallen leaves around my ankles. It caresses my neck, a touch that is almost tender.

"He grows stronger," a voice sighs in my ear.

I jerk my head up. "Lachlan?"

"He grows stronger with distance from the castle," the voice whispers, sounding thin, stretched to breaking. It comes from the wind, from the stones. "I grow weaker. I am bound to the ruin, Fi. I am fading."

"Don't fade," I gasp, pushing myself off the wall. "Don't you dare fade on me."

"I cannae hold him back here," Lachlan mourns. "Down here, in the shadow of the living, he is the master of flesh. I am but a memory of pain."

I stumble forward, my legs heavy as lead. "Guide me," I beg. " tell me which way."

But the voice is silent. The wind dies.

The silence that follows is broken by the scrape of a shoe on stone. Close. Too close.

I look back. At the far end of the crooked street, a shadow detaches itself from the darkness. It stretches across the cobblestones, long and distorted, reaching for me like a claw. Murray steps into the pool of yellow light. He is not smiling anymore. His face is a mask of concentration, the hazel eyes black pits.

He sees me.

He does not run. He simply lengthens his stride, his movement blurring slightly, as if he is skipping frames of reality.

"Lachlan!" I scream.

The name tears out of my throat, raw and desperate. It echoes off the stone facades, bouncing back and forth—Lachlan, Lachlan, Lachlan—a summons that fills the empty street.

It is a mistake. I know it instantly.

Murray's head snaps up. The sound of my lover's name acts as a catalyst. The pretense of the slow hunt vanishes.

He breaks into a run.

It is terrifying. He moves with unnatural speed, covering ground that should take seconds in mere heartbeats. His coat flaps behind him like the wings of a great, dark bird.

I scramble backward, my feet slipping. I turn and sprint, lungs screaming, throwing myself blindly down a set of stairs that leads into the black maw of the lower town. The terror is absolute, a cold hand squeezing my heart until it stops. He is coming. The shadow is at my heels, and the castle is still just a silhouette against the indifferent stars.

I am not running toward safety. I am running toward the only place where the ghosts are strong enough to kill.

I burst from the suffocating warren of alleys into the open expanse of the town square. The space feels dangerously exposed, a vast stage lit by the sickly orange glow of sodium lamps. In the center stands the ancient mercat cross and a weathered war memorial, the names of the dead eroded by centuries of rain. Beyond them, the stone well sits like a black eye staring up at the clouds.

My eyes lock onto the road on the far side—the incline that leads up out of the bowl of the town, toward the cliffs, toward Sutherland Castle.

I surge forward, hope flaring in my chest.

A figure steps out from behind the war memorial.

I skid to a halt, my boots scraping sparks against the pavement. Murray stands directly in my path. He is not out of breath. He is not sweating. He stands with the stillness of a statue, blocking the only exit to the high road.

"Going somewhere?" he asks.

The voice is wrong. It is layered—Murray's smooth American accent twisting around the guttural, archaic vowels of the 17th century. It is a voice of two throats speaking in unison.

I back away, my eyes darting left and right. Shops line the square—a closed newsagent, a pub with dark windows, the shuttered post office. No help. No way out.

"You cannot outrun what's been chasing you for centuries, Isla," he says. He takes a step toward me, and the light above him flickers and dies. "You run in circles. You always have. From the tower to the ground. From the womb to the grave. It is the same circle."

"I am not her," I say, though the denial tastes like ash. I feel her inside me, trembling. I feel the phantom weight of a child that never took a breath. "I am Fi."

"Names," he scoffs. He spreads his hands, and I see the fingers are curled into claws. "You are the sin I must purge. You are the stain on my honor that will not wash out."

I retreat toward the center of the square, toward the well. My back is to the stone rim. I am trapped.

BONG.

The sound hits me like a physical blow. The bell in the church tower begins to toll the hour. A deep, resonant mournfulness that vibrates in the stones, in my teeth.

BONG.

In the resonance of the bell, the air beside the well shimmers. It is faint, barely a distortion of the mist, like heat rising from pavement. A flame flickers into existence—not fire, but spirit.

Lachlan.

He is translucent, a sketch of a man drawn in gray light. He looks down at his own hands, struggling to maintain his form against the overwhelming pull of the earth. He looks at me, his eyes pools of infinite sorrow.

"Lachlan," I whimper.

He lifts a hand, pointing a trembling finger past Murray, toward a narrow, dark gap between two buildings that I hadn't seen.

"The passage behind the baker's shop," he strains, his voice sounding like dry leaves skittering on stone. "It leads to the old pilgrim's path. Up the crag. To the castle."

Murray lunges.

He moves with the sudden violence of a striking snake. I throw myself sideways, away from the well, toward the gap Lachlan pointed out.

Murray's hand sweeps through the space where my neck was a fraction of a second ago. His fingertips brush against the heavy wool of my coat. The contact sends a shockwave of cold through my body, a necrotic chill that nearly buckles my knees.

"You will not leave me!" Murray roars, pivoting on his heel with impossible grace.

I scramble for footing on the wet stones, lungs heaving. I dive into the darkness of the baker's passage. It is narrow, smelling of yeast and damp rot, barely wide enough for two men to walk abreast.

I run.

"Run, Fi!" Lachlan's voice chases me, fading, dissolving into the tolling of the bell. "To the stones! I will meet you at the stones!"

I hear Murray crash into the entrance of the alley behind me, cursing in Gaelic, a stream of ancient hate.

The path begins to climb immediately. The cobblestones give way to dirt and bedrock—the old pilgrim's path, worn smooth by the knees and feet of penitents seeking salvation. I am seeking salvation too, but not from God.

I look up. Far above, rising against the bruising purple of the night sky, the silhouette of Sutherland Castle waits. It is a broken crown of jagged stone, dark and foreboding.

I run toward the ruin, toward the ghost, toward the only love that has ever mattered.

CHAPTER 19
The Attempted Claim

The pilgrim's path bites into the soles of my boots, an unforgiving ascent that burns the muscles of my calves. Sutherland Castle looms above, a jagged crown of black teeth tearing at the belly of the night sky. It is not the romantic ruin of the guidebooks tonight; it is a fortress of rot and memory, exhaling the damp breath of centuries.

I scramble over the crumbling perimeter wall, my hands scraping against rough granite, finding purchase where moss slicks the stone. The courtyard is a bowl of shadows, the wind whistling through the empty arrow loops like a choir of the damned.

"Lachlan!" I scream his name, the sound snatched away by the gale. "I am here! I am at the stones!"

The only answer is the rattle of dry bracken and the frantic pounding of my own heart against my ribs. The connection to him—that silver thread of presence I felt in town—is erratic here, pulsing like a dying nerve. The castle feels dormant, heavy, indifferent to my terror.

I run toward the Great Hall, or what remains of it. The roof is gone, open to the bruising clouds, but the walls stand high and oppressive. I stumble through the arched doorway, my breath hitching in my throat.

The silence here is profound, a physical weight that presses against my eardrums. It is the quiet of a tomb before the stone is rolled away.

"Lachlan?" I whisper, turning in a slow circle. "Please."

Shadows stretch from the corners, pooling like spilled ink. One shadow does not stay on the floor. It detaches itself from a darkened alcove near the remnants of the hearth, rising with a fluid, predatory grace that makes the hair on my arms stand rigid.

Murray steps into the faint moonlight filtering through the clouds.

He is not out of breath from the climb. His pea coat is buttoned wrong, missed by one hole, a frantic, human error that contrasts sharply with the inhuman stillness of his posture. His head is cocked to the side, listening to a frequency I cannot hear.

"You run with such spirit," he says.

The voice is wrong. It starts as Murray's smooth, practiced baritone but frays at the edges, revealing a rougher, darker substrate beneath. A voice of peat and blood.

I back away, my boots scuffing on the flagstones. "Stay back."

He smiles, and the expression splits his face like a wound. His eyes, usually a warm hazel, are swallowed by the dilation of his pupils, turning them into black pits reflecting the abyss.

"There is nowhere back to go, mo chridhe."

He moves. It is not a walk; it is a displacement of space. One moment he is by the hearth, the next he is gripping my wrist.

The pain is immediate and blinding. His fingers are clamps of iron, grinding the small bones of my wrist together. I cry out, twisting, digging my heels into the earth accumulated on the floor, but I might as well be fighting a landslide.

"Let go of me!" I strike at his face with my free hand, my nails raking across his cheek.

He doesn't flinch. He doesn't bleed. He merely looks at me with an expression of terrifying, hungry adoration.

"You mark me," he whispers, the dual voices layering over each other, creating a dissonance that vibrates in my teeth. "You always did have a fire in you, Isla. It is why I chose you. Why I keep choosing you."

He jerks my arm, pulling me off balance. I stumble forward, crashing into his chest. He smells of grave dirt, the scent of the storm wrapped in old wool.

"I am not Isla!" I spit the words at him, though I feel her waking in my blood, terrified and small.

"Hush," he croons. "We are going home."

He drags me toward the rear of the hall, toward a corridor that shouldn't be there. My research—my tidy, academic maps of the Sutherland estate—says this wall should be solid, leading only to the sheer drop of the cliffs. But the stones here are loose, shifting like teeth in a rotting gum line. A dark mouth opens in the masonry, exhaling a draft of air so cold it burns.

"No," I gasp, dragging my feet. "That's not... that doesn't exist."

"It exists because I remember it," Murray says. "Stone remembers its master."

He hauls me into the dark.

The transition is sickening. The air pressure drops, popping my ears. The sound of the wind outside vanishes, replaced by the wet, rhythmic drip of water in the distance. We are not outside anymore. We are inside, deep inside, in the arteries of the castle that time forgot.

I struggle, kicking at his shins, twisting my body. "Lachlan! Help me!"

"He cannot hear you here," Murray says, not looking back, dragging me effortlessly down the spiraling passage. "This is my domain. The roots. The dark."

But as he speaks, the temperature plummets further. My breath blooms in frantic white clouds.

Frost.

It races along the stone walls on either side of us, glittering, crystalline ferns growing with impossible speed. The damp on the floor turns to slick ice under my boots.

“I am here.”

The words aren't spoken; they are impressed directly onto the surface of my mind, cold and sharp. Lachlan.

A patch of shadow on the wall to my left writhes, twisting into the vague, agonizing shape of a man reaching out. A hand of mist and frost claws at the air, inches from my shoulder.

"Lachlan!" I reach for him with my free hand, desperation clawing at my throat.

Murray stops abruptly. He looks at the frost, at the shadow man flailing against the invisible barrier of the corridor. Murray laughs, a sound like grinding stones.

"Look at him," Murray sneers, tightening his grip on my wrist until I whimper. "Frozen. Impotent. He screams in the wall, Isla. Can you hear him? He bangs on the glass of the world, but he cannot break it."

The shadow-Lachlan surges, the frost thickening, snapping quietly as it expands, but he cannot cross the midpoint of the corridor. There is a line—a warding, a heaviness—that repels him. He is bound to the ruin above, and Murray is dragging me down into the earth, away from the sky, away from the light where Lachlan is strong.

"Let him go," I beg, tears freezing on my cheeks.

"I let nothing go," Murray says.

He yanks me forward again, pulling me away from the frost, away from the only thing keeping me sane. The corridor twists, the geometry wrong, sloping down at an angle that defies physics, leading us into the suffocating dark of the castle's forgotten heart.

The corridor ends in a heavy oak door, banded with iron that has rusted to the color of dried blood. Murray does not use a key; he places his palm against the wood, and the timber groans, the latch disengaging with a shriek of tortured metal.

He kicks the door open and flings me inside.

I stumble, my boots catching on a rug threadbare with age, and crash to my knees. The impact jars my spine, but adrenaline numbs the pain. I scramble upright, backing away until my shoulders hit cold stone.

The room is a mausoleum of intimacy.

It is circular, carved directly into the bedrock foundation of the tower. A single torch burns in a sconce on the far wall—impossible, for who lit it?—casting a greasy, erratic light that makes the shadows dance. The air is stagnant, devoid of oxygen, heavy with the scent of beeswax, mold, and a musk that makes my stomach churn.

Dominating the center of the room is a bed. It is massive, a four-poster monstrosity of dark wood carved with twisting serpents and thistles. The velvet curtains hang in tatters, moth-eaten and grey with dust.

"Do you remember this place?" Murray asks. He stands in the doorway, blocking the only exit. He runs a hand through his hair, smoothing it, a gesture of grooming that is grotesque in its normalcy.

I shake my head, though my body remembers. Isla remembers. My skin crawls with the phantom sensation of rough linen and the weight of a man I did not choose.

"No," I whisper. "It's a tomb."

"It is a bridal chamber," he corrects. His voice deepens, the Boston accent dissolving entirely into the guttural rolling R's of the 17th-century Highlands. Hamish is rising, wearing Murray's skin like a suit that is becoming too tight. "I built this for us. For when you would finally learn obedience."

He steps inside and closes the door. The sound of the latch clicking home echoes like a gunshot.

"Get on the bed," he commands.

I press myself harder against the wall. "Murray, please. You're sick. You need help."

"Murray is a vessel," he snaps, his face contorting. "A weak, pathetic shell who spent his life counting coins while I waited in the dark. But he serves his purpose." He stalks toward me, unbuttoning his pea coat with deliberate, slow fingers. The coat falls to the floor with a heavy thud. "You are Isla's soul. I smelled it the moment you stepped onto my land. You carry her essence like a perfume."

He lunges, grabbing my shoulders before I can dart sideways. He lifts me—literally lifts me off the floor—and throws me onto the bed.

Dust explodes in a choking grey cloud. The mattress beneath me is hard, lumpy with rot, and smells of old straw. I scramble backward, crabbing toward the headboard, my heart hammering a frantic rhythm against my ribs.

"Stay away from me!"

"I will take your body," he says, climbing onto the bed. The mattress groans under his weight. He crawls toward me on hands and knees, a beast stalking its meal. "I will plant my seed in you, Isla. A strong seed. Not the weakling bastard you tried to give my brother."

Terror, cold and absolute, washes over me. It is not just the threat of violence; it is the specific, historical weight of his intent. He wants to rewrite the history of my body. He wants to colonize my future to erase my past.

"You can't," I whimper, my eyes darting around the room, searching for anything—a loose stone, a shard of wood, anything.

The walls are carved with symbols. I recognize them from my textbooks, but here, carved deep into the granite, they vibrate with malice. Warding runes. Binding sigils. Knots that have no beginning and no end, designed to trap a spirit within a specific space.

"Lachlan!" I scream his name, a weapon and a prayer.

The room convulses.

The torch flame flares violently, turning from orange to a blinding, magnesium blue. The shadows on the wall contort, stretching and snapping, forming the silhouette of a man raging against invisible bars.

BOOM.

Dust rains from the ceiling as something strikes the rock from the outside. The stone floor trembles. Lachlan is there, just beyond the stone, beating his fists against the earth, tearing at the foundations of his prison.

"He hears you," Murray sneers, not breaking his gaze from my face. He reaches out, his hand hovering over my knee. "Let him hear. Let him listen as I claim what he stole."

The torch sputters, sparks showering down onto the stone floor. The shadows lash out, spectral claws raking the air, but they stop inches from the bed. The symbols on the walls glow with a faint, sickly red light, pulsing in time with Murray's heartbeat.

"He cannot cross the threshold," Murray whispers, his hand closing over my knee, squeezing until I cry out. "This room is bound in blood. My blood. Your blood."

He looms over me, blotting out the light, blotting out the world. I am trapped in the dark with a monster who has waited four hundred years to finish what he started.

My hands scrabble blindly behind me as I retreat against the headboard, tearing at the rotting fabric of the mattress. My fingernails scrape against rough ticking and dessicated straw. Murray is crawling closer, his eyes locked on mine, devouring my fear.

My fingers brush something cold.

Hard. Metallic. Hidden deep within the stuffing of the bed, tucked away centuries ago by a woman who knew she might one day need to defend her life. Or end it.

I wrap my fingers around the hilt. It is small, the leather grip eroded by time, but the metal of the pommel is solid against my palm. A dirk.

Murray lunges.

His weight hits me like a falling wall. He pins me to the mattress, his hips grinding down on mine, his hands clamping my wrists to the pillow. He is heavy with the density of two souls, crushing the breath from my lungs.

"Every lifetime," he hisses, his face inches from mine, his spittle flecking my cheek. "Every single time, you find him first. You look at him with those eyes. You give him the smiles that belong to me."

He releases my left wrist to tear at the collar of my flannel shirt. Buttons pop, pinging off the stone floor like hail. The sound of ripping fabric is loud in the small room, violent and final.

My right hand—my free hand—is buried beneath the pillow, gripping the dagger.

The terror that has been choking me shifts. It crystallizes. The trembling in my limbs stops, replaced by a cold, predatory stillness. The demarcation line between Fi MacPherson and Isla Sutherland dissolves. I am not possessed; I am integrated. I am the scholar who knows the history, and I am the woman who lived it. I remember the pain of the fall from the tower, and I remember the humiliation of the dungeon.

But mostly, I remember the hate.

"I never belonged to you," I whisper.

Murray freezes. He looks down at me, blinking, surprised by the change in my tone.

Outside the room, the world is ending. The walls shudder as if struck by a battering ram. Dust pours from the ceiling cracks, coating us in grey powder. Lachlan is screaming into the stone, a soundless vibration that rattles my teeth. The torch flares and dies, plunges us into darkness, then flares again—blue and violent.

"What did you say?" Murray growls.

"I said," I look directly into his black eyes, "I never belonged to you. Not then. Not now."

He roars, a sound of pure frustration, and rips the rest of my shirt open. The cold air of the dungeon hits my skin, but I do not shiver. I do not flinch.

I go limp beneath him.

It is the surrender of the trap door, not the victim.

He pauses, confused by my sudden lack of resistance. He shifts his weight, settling between my legs, his hand moving to his belt buckle. He thinks he has won. He thinks he has broken me.

"That is it," he breathes, his voice thick with lust and triumph. "Accept it. It is your destiny, Isla."

He leans down, his mouth seeking my throat, intending to mark me, to bite as he did in the dream.

He is heavy. He is close. He is vulnerable.

I tighten my grip on the dagger. The rusted metal bites into my palm, a grounding pain. I calculate the angle. Beneath the ribs. Upward. Into the heart that beats with a stolen rhythm.

"Come closer," I think, my eyes wide and dry in the flickering light.

Murray lowers his chest onto mine. I feel the frantic beat of his heart against my own ribs.

"Now." Lachlan whispers

I draw the blade.

CHAPTER 20
The Blade of Defiance

The blade is a sliver of ice in a room suffocating with heat. I hold it tight, the leather of the hilt crumbling against my sweat-slick palm, disintegration meeting desperation. Murray looks down at the rusted steel between us, and he doesn't recoil. He laughs.

It is a wet, dredging sound, like stones grinding in a riverbed. The vibration of it travels through his chest and into mine, claiming me even as I threaten to end him.

"A toy," he whispers, the dual timbre of his voice stroking my skin with sandpaper roughness. "You threaten a wolf with a splinter, Isla? You have forgotten what I am."

He shifts his weight, the heavy wool of his pea coat—no, the ghost-weight of a laird's plaid—scratching against my exposed collarbone. He does not try to wrestle the knife from me immediately. He wants me to have hope so he can strangle it. His hazel eyes, swallowed by the black pupils of the dead, bore into mine. They are ancient mirrors reflecting a thousand defeats, a thousand nights where I lost and he won.

"Get off me," I snarl, though the air in my lungs is thin, compressed by his mass.

"I am exactly where I belong." He lowers his head, his nose brushing the curve of my neck, inhaling the scent of my terror. "And you are finally where you belong. In the dark. Beneath me."

I thrust the dagger upward. It is a jagged, clumsy strike, born of panic rather than skill.

His hand snaps out, gripping my wrist with a force that bruises bone. He stops the blade an inch from his ribs. The rust flakes onto his shirt, orange dust settling on the fine gray wool. He holds me there, trembling, suspended in the stalemate of flesh against supernatural will.

"Predictable," he murmurs against my skin. "You always try to fight. It makes the breaking so much sweeter."

He squeezes.

Pain flares white and hot up my forearm, radiating into my shoulder. My fingers spasm, threatening to release the hilt, but I clamp them shut, refusing to drop the only thing standing between me and oblivion. I grit my teeth, a guttural sound of effort tearing from my throat.

Beyond the circle of our violence, the room screams.

The walls, carved with the spiral runes of binding, pulse with a sickly, arterial light. They thrum with the heartbeat of the castle, a rhythm of stone and blood. And beyond that stone, Lachlan rages.

I turn my head, fighting the pressure of Murray's grip, to look at the doorway. The oak is shut, barred by Hamish's will, but the spiritual veil is torn. I see through the wood, through the masonry.

Lachlan is a storm trapped in a bottle. His spectral form beats against the invisible barrier of the wards. His face is contorted in a rictus of pure, distilled agony—not for himself, but for me. He hammers his fists against the air, his mouth open in a silent roar that shakes the dust from the ceiling rafters. He throws his entire being against the prohibition, burning his essence to reach me.

Frost blooms on the inside of the door, sketching delicate, fern-like patterns that shatter and reform with every blow he lands on the other side.

"He is loud tonight," Murray says, noticing my gaze. He twists my wrist, forcing my arm down to the mattress, pinning it beside my head. The dagger points uselessly at the headboard. "He does not like to share. But he must learn his place. He is the past. I am the eternal present."

"He is worth ten of you," I spit, the words tasting of copper and ash.

Murray's face hardens. The veneer of the modern man slips entirely, revealing the jagged cliffs of Hamish's visage beneath. "He is nothing.

He is mist and memory. I am flesh. I am the one who fills your lungs with fear. I am the one who will fill your belly with heirs."

The threat lands like a physical blow. The damp, rotting smell of the bed seems to rise up to choke me. I can feel the history of this mattress—the women who wept here, the blood spilled here. It is an altar of submission, and he intends to make me the final sacrifice.

He releases my wrist only to slide his hand up my arm, his fingers trailing over my skin like cold worms. He explores the musculature, the pulse point, the vulnerability.

"You have his fire," he muses, looking at the dagger still clutched in my paralyzed hand. "Fi MacPherson. The scholar. The climber. You built a life of independence, didn't you? You thought you could study history without becoming it." He leans in, his breath rancid with the grave. "But history is a wheel, mo chridhe. And you are under the rim."

I struggle, arching my back, trying to buck him off. It is like trying to throw a mountain. He settles deeper into the cradle of my hips, his hardness pressing against my thigh, a terrifying promise of violation.

"Stop fighting," he commands, his voice dropping to a hypnotic, resonant frequency. "Yield. It is what you were made for."

"Never."

"Always," he corrects. "You yielded in the tower. You yielded in the village. You yielded in the snow. Why pretend this time is different?"

He grabs my chin, forcing me to look at him. His face blurs, the features shifting. I see Murray's hazel eyes, then Hamish's gray flint. I see Murray's straight nose, then Hamish's crooked break. The duality is nauseating.

"Because this time," I whisper, my eyes flickering to the frost-covered door, "I know the end of the story."

Lachlan throws himself against the barrier again. The stone groans. A crack appears in the lintel, a spiderweb fissure running down the rock. He is destroying himself to get to me. I can see his edges fading, his blue light dimming with every strike. He is pouring his soul into the stone, eroding the wards with the sheer acid of his love.

If he breaks through, Hamish will destroy him. Lachlan is weak, tethered to the ruin, while Hamish is engorged with the stolen vitality of a living vessel. If they fight now, Lachlan will be obliterated. He will not just fade; he will be unmade.

I cannot let that happen.

"I won't let you hurt him," I say, the realization settling over me like a shroud.

Murray smirks. "You have no choice. I will finish him after I am done with you. I will let him watch. I will let him see you cry out my name."

He reaches for the waistband of my jeans, his fingers fumbling with the metal button. The sound of the zipper rasping down is louder than the storm outside. It is the sound of a seal breaking.

My hand tightens on the dagger. My knuckles turn white. The rust bites into my palm, grounding me.

I look at Lachlan one last time. He stops hitting the wall. He presses his forehead against the barrier, his eyes locking onto mine through the stone. He sees the shift in me. He sees the resolve.

His eyes widen. He shakes his head—a frantic, desperate denial. No. Fi, no.

But there is no other way. The cycle requires blood. It always ends in blood. Hamish wants murder? He wants a tragedy? I will give him one, but it will be a tragedy he cannot control. It will be an ending he didn't write.

I stop struggling against Murray's weight. I let my muscles go lax.

Murray pauses, sensing the change. He pulls back slightly, suspicion narrowing his eyes. "Finally," he breathes, mistaking resignation for submission. "Finally, you understand."

He leans down to claim my mouth, to seal the pact of my defeat.

I pull my arm free from the mattress. The movement is smooth, unhindered by fear. I rotate my wrist. The point of the dirk hovers over my heart—over the center of the web that binds us all.

"I understand," I whisper, staring into the abyss of his eyes. "I understand that the only way to win is to leave the game."

Murray's eyes widen. He sees the angle of the blade. He sees the target.

"No!" he roars, lunging to stop me.

But he is too late. I am already falling into the dark.

The steel bites.

It is a sensation of cold fire, a precise and absolute violation of the self. I drive the rusted point through the fabric of my flannel shirt, through the skin, grating between the ribs to find the frantic, drumming bird of my heart. The pain is not a sound; it is a color, a blinding flash of white that obliterates the dungeon, the dark, and the man on top of me.

My breath leaves me in a rush, carrying with it the name I have whispered for centuries. Lachlan.

Murray flinches as if struck by lightning. He rears back, his hands hovering over me, coated in the blood that blooms instantly from my chest—a dark, wet poppy expanding across the gray wool. His face is a mask of shattered glass, the arrogance splintering into incomprehension.

"What have you done?" he gasps, the voice fracturing, the ancient laird and the modern man screaming in dissonance. "Isla, what have you done?"

He stares at the hilt protruding from my sternum, at his own hands slick with my life. He cannot comprehend it. He knows murder; he knows martyrdom; he knows defeat. But he does not know this. He does not know a woman who would burn down the house rather than let him own the key.

The shock freezes him. He is anchored to me by the horror of his loss, by the sudden, terrifying realization that the object of his obsession is slipping through his fingers like water.

"I..." I cough, blood bubbling hot and metallic in my throat. The pain is a rising tide, drowning my vision in red vignette. "I belong... only... to him."

And I am not done.

The curse demands a life for a life. It demands a circle. I will give it a straight line. I will give it a spear.

My fingers are slick on the leather hilt. My strength is bleeding out of me, flowing onto the rotting mattress, soaking into the memories of the dead. But there is one spark left. One final ember of the fire that Isla carried, that Fi protected.

I grip the dagger. The pain of moving it is a universe of agony. I cry out, a wet, ragged sound, and wrench the blade from my own flesh.

A fountain of heat follows it. My vision goes gray.

Murray screams—a sound of denial, reaching for me, trying to plug the wound, trying to keep his vessel of torment intact. He leans forward, his chest exposed, his guard down in the face of my suicide.

"You cannot leave me!" he howls.

"Watch me," I whisper.

I twist my body, summoning the last kinetic energy in my dying muscles. I drive the blade upward.

It sinks into his side, sliding easily through the expensive pea coat, through the shirt, through the flesh of the man who thought he could own a soul. I push it to the hilt, burying four hundred years of rage into his liver, into his gut.

Murray stiffens. His eyes bulge, the black pupils constricting to pinpricks. He makes a small, choked sound—huk—and slumps forward. His weight crushes me, pressing the air from my ruined chest, mingling his blood with mine.

We lie there, lovers in death, enemies in spirit. The heat of his blood washes over my cold hands.

The room convulses. The stone screams.

The binding runes on the walls flare with a blinding intensity and then shatter. The light explodes outward, no longer red but a purifying, searing gold. The air pressure drops to zero. The silence rushes back in, heavy and absolute.

I feel Hamish leaving.

It is a tearing sensation, a violent eviction. A shadow rips itself free from Murray's body, howling a soundless frequency of hate. It claws at the air, a black smoke trying to find purchase, trying to find a new host. But there is nowhere to go. The vessel is broken. The anchor is cut.

The shadow dissipates, shredded by the light of my sacrifice, dissolved into the ether like smoke in a gale.

Murray's body goes heavy, dead weight. The hazel eyes stare blankly at the pillow next to my head, empty of malice, empty of life.

I am cold. So cold.

The darkness at the edges of my vision rushes in to claim the center. The pain begins to recede, replaced by a numbness that feels like mercy. I can't feel my hands. I can't feel the mattress. I am floating.

The door bursts open.

It is not opened by a hand; it is obliterated by a force of nature. Splinters of oak rain down like confetti.

Lachlan falls into the room. He is solid now, or maybe I am becoming spirit. He shines with a blue brilliance, a star descended to earth. He rushes to the bed, falling to his knees in the dust and the blood.

"Fi!" He reaches for me, and this time, his hands do not pass through. I feel the cold shock of his touch on my face. "Isla! No, no, God, no!"

He tries to pull Murray off me, shoving the corpse aside with a roar of grief that shakes the foundations of the tower. He gathers me into his arms, pulling my broken body against his chest, heedless of the blood soaking his spectral plaid.

"Look at me," he begs, his tears falling onto my face, cold as rain. "Stay with me. You broke it. You broke the wards. Just stay!"

I try to lift my hand to his cheek, but my arm refuses to obey. I can only look at him. He is beautiful. He is the storm and the shelter. The scars on his face are gone, smoothed away by the breaking of the curse. He looks young. He looks free.

"It is... done," I whisper, though I don't know if the words make sound.

"Do not close your eyes," he commands, rocking me, his voice breaking. "I will not lose you again. Not like this."

But the light is growing brighter. It is not the torchlight. It is a dawn rising from within me. The tether that bound us to the tragedy is severed. The knot is untied.

"I'm not... losing," I think at him, projecting the thought with my fading mind. "I'm... waking up."

The walls of the dungeon dissolve into mist. The pain vanishes. The weight of centuries lifts from my shoulders. I am light as air. I am rising.

Lachlan holds me, and as the world fades to white, I feel him rising with me. We are not ending. We are finally, truly, beginning.

"I have you," his voice whispers, echoing in the infinite brightness. "I have you."

And then, there is only the light.

CHAPTER 21
Awakening to the Past

I expect fire. I expect the crushing weight of earth or the nothingness of the void. I do not expect the wet, freezing kiss of dew against my cheek.

My eyes snap open, but they do not find the dark. They find green, a verdant, aggressive green that sears the retina. I am lying on my side, my body curled into a shape of defense, cheek pressed against blades of grass that feel too thick, too waxen. The smell of damp earth fills my nose, rich and loamy, but it lacks the metallic tang of blood that was the last thing I tasted.

I push myself up. The movement is sluggish, my limbs heavy as if I am moving through water. My hands sink into the soil, grounding me, and for a moment, I am just Fi. I am a doctoral student who fell. I am a woman who made a terrible choice in a dark room.

Then I look up.

The breath leaves my lungs in a sharp, pained hiss.

Sutherland Castle stands before me. But it is not the jagged, broken tooth of rock I have spent weeks studying. It is not the ruin where tourists take selfies and buy overpriced shortbread. It is whole.

The towers scrape the sky, their stone facing smooth and unweathered. The roof of the Great Hall is intact, slate tiles gleaming with a dull, pewter sheen under a light that has no source. There are no gaps in the masonry, no creeping ivy choking the life from the walls. It is magnificent. It is impossible.

And I know it.

A second set of memories crashes into me, a tidal wave of recognition that nearly knocks me back into the grass. I know the mason who laid those cornerstones. I know the draft in the east corridor that never warms. I know the sound of Hamish's boots echoing in the courtyard.

Isla.

She is not a ghost haunting me anymore. She is the marrow in my bones. I am her. We are one thing, stitched together by trauma and time, waking up in a place that should be dust.

I bring a hand to my chest. I expect to feel the rough flannel of my shirt, sticky with the mess I made of myself. Instead, my fingers brush against coarse, unbleached linen. I look down. I am wearing a shift, simple and pale, the kind of garment from my dreams and memories.

My fingers trace the line of my sternum. The skin is smooth. Unbroken.

Phantom pain flares, a white-hot recollection of the steel sliding between my ribs, but there is no wound. No blood. No scar. The dissonance makes my head spin. I remember the crunch of cartilage. I remember the heat of Murray's blood mixing with mine. I remember the look on Lachlan's face as the light took us.

"Where am I?" I whisper.

My voice sounds wrong. It is too thin, snatched away by a wind that doesn't seem to move the trees.

I stand, my legs trembling. The world around me wavers. The edges of the horizon are not sharp; they blur and bleed like ink on wet paper. The colors are wrong—the purple of the heather on the distant hills is too vibrant, bruising the eye, while the sky is a washed-out, static gray that hangs low and oppressive. It looks like a memory that has been played too many times, the tape degrading, the image losing its fidelity.

I turn in a slow circle. The copse of trees to my left flickers. One moment it is a dense thicket of birch; the next, it is a smudge of charcoal shadow, then birch again. The reality here is thin. Unstable.

This is not the past. Isla remembers the past, and it was gritty, dirty, real. This is something else. A holding pen? A purgatory constructed from our shared grief?

The silence is absolute. No birdsong. No distant hum of traffic from the village below. Just the thudding of my own heart, which seems to beat in a rhythm that isn't quite human—too slow, too heavy.

Then, a sound cuts through the stillness.

Water.

It is a faint, melodic gurgle, the sound of a creek running over stones. It comes from beyond the glitching line of trees. It shouldn't be terrifying, but the hair on my arms stands up. The sound is familiar. It calls to a part of me that remembers washing clothes in the icy burn, remembers cooling a fevered forehead, remembers meeting a lover by the bank when the moon was hidden.

"Lachlan?" I ask the empty air.

The name hangs there, unanswered. But the water calls again, louder this time, urgent.

I take a step. The grass feels cold and real under my bare feet, the only solid thing in a world of shifting optics. My mind—Fi's mind, the rational, skeptical part that demands footnotes and sources—screams that this is a hallucination, a firing of synapses in a dying brain. But Isla's instinct overrides it. Isla knows that the land speaks, even when the land is a ghost.

I walk toward the trees. My movement feels predetermined, as if I am a piece on a board being slid forward by a giant hand. The closer I get to the copse, the more the trees seem to lean away from me, their trunks twisting in unnatural spirals.

The sound of the water grows. It is not just the sound of a creek anymore; it is a whispering chorus, a liquid language I almost understand. It promises answers. It promises him.

I push through the branches, which dissolve into mist against my skin rather than scratching, and step out onto the bank.

The water does not reflect the gray, dead sky. It generates its own light, a pale, bioluminescent hum that rises from the depths like the glow of submerged stars. It is impossibly clear, running over stones that look less like granite and more like polished bone.

I drop to my knees on the bank, the damp soaking into the linen of my shift. The cold here is different—sharp, intellectual, a clarity that slices through the fog in my mind.

I lean over the surface.

The face that stares back is not the one I see in the mirror every morning. It is not Fi MacPherson, the tired academic with the Boston accent and the dark circles under her eyes. Nor is it purely Isla, the healer's daughter with the wild hair and the doomed destiny.

It is a composite. A violent oscillation.

For a second, I see my own short, practical cut, the scar above my eyebrow from a childhood fall in Massachusetts. Then the water ripples without wind, and the reflection stretches. The hair lengthens, turning a deeper, bloodier red. The features soften, becoming archaic, the eyes widening with a terror that belongs to the sixteenth century.

We flicker. Fi. Isla. Fi. Isla. Two exposures on the same strip of film, fighting for dominance.

"Who are we now?" I whisper to the water.

The reflection mouths the words back, but the timing is off. The delay sends a spike of nausea through my gut.

I reach out. I have to know if it is real. My hand trembles as it hovers over the surface, the glowing water illuminating the dirt beneath my fingernails—dirt from a grave I haven't dug yet.

I plunge my fingers in.

The shock is not cold; it is data. Pure, unadulterated memory rushes up my arm and detonates in my skull.

I am five years old, running through the heather, scraping my knee on the rough stone of the castle wall. I am twenty-two, stepping off the train in the rain, pulling my suitcase toward a rental car, escaping a man named Murray. I am standing in the shadows of the solar, Lachlan's hand hot on my waist, knowing that this touch is a death sentence. I am watching Hamish's face contort as the dagger slides home.

The images cycle rapidly, a strobe light of joy and horror. Lachlan's smile. Hamish's fist. The way the light caught the dust motes in the library. The smell of burning tallow in the dungeon.

The water swirls around my wrist, grasping, tactile. It whispers. The sound bypasses my ears and resonates directly in the fluid of my brain.

Folded, the creek murmurs. The time is folded. The knot is tight.

I snatch my hand back, gasping. The connection severs, leaving me panting on the bank. The water settles instantly, the ripples smoothing out into glass.

Trapped, the water adds, a final, fading sibilance.

I scramble to my feet. The urge to flee is overwhelming, but there is nowhere to go but forward. The creek winds its way uphill, defying gravity, snaking toward the black maw of the castle entrance. It is a tether. A fuse burning toward the powder keg.

I follow it. I have to.

The landscape begins to rebel as I walk. To my right, a boulder flickers out of existence, leaving a hole in the world that shows only static gray before popping back into solidity. Above, the clouds are moving too fast, racing across the sky in a time-lapse frenzy, while the air around me remains dead still. Shadows detach themselves from the trees and stretch toward me at impossible angles, long black fingers trying to graze the hem of my shift.

I am alone in this distortion, yet I am the center of attention.

I feel it on the back of my neck—the weight of a thousand eyes. I look up at the castle looming ahead. The windows are dark slits, empty sockets in a skull, but I know something is watching. The stones themselves seem to observe my approach, hungry and patient. Sutherland Castle does not just house history; it eats it.

I crest the final rise. The main gates stand before me, monstrous slabs of oak bound in iron, rising twenty feet high. They are shut tight, a barrier meant to keep armies out, or monsters in.

I stop. The silence returns, heavier now, pregnant with expectation. The castle towers over me, blocking out the frantic sky. I feel small. I feel like an insect on a dissection table.

"Where am I?" I ask the stone. My voice is steady, hardened by the memories of two lifetimes of survival.

The wind does not answer. The water does not answer.

Instead, a deep, grinding groan emanates from the earth. The iron hinges shriek—a sound like a woman screaming in the distance.

Slowly, impossibly, the great doors begin to swing inward.

They open onto darkness. A thick, velvet blackness that smells of beeswax and old blood. It is an invitation. It is a mouth opening to swallow me whole.

I do not hesitate. I know this dark. I was born in it. I died in it. And somewhere inside, he is waiting.

I step across the threshold.

CHAPTER 22

The First Breath of Lachlan

The air is heavy, pressing against my skin with the weight of unspilled rain. I turn in a slow, drunken circle.

Sutherland Castle rises above me. It is not the jagged, black-toothed ruin that has haunted my research for a decade. It is whole. It is a lie constructed of stone and memory. The slate roof gleams with a dull, pewter shine that hurts my eyes. The banners snapping from the turret poles are too blue, a violent, chemical azure that doesn't exist in nature. It looks like a film reel stuck in the projector, vibrating with a manic, artificial intensity.

I stumble forward. My bare feet sink into the earth, but it doesn't feel like mud. It feels like flesh yielding under pressure.

"Where is this?" I whisper, my voice swallowed instantly by the vast, silent twilight.

My vision blurs at the edges, a vignette of gray fog creeping in to obscure the periphery. I rub my eyes, trying to clear the film, but the distortion remains. It is as if the world is rendering itself only where I look, leaving the rest in chaos. I am Fi, the historian who knows this castle fell hundreds of years ago. I am Isla, the woman who remembers the mason's chisel marks on the gatehouse. The two minds grind against each other, striking sparks of panic.

A movement snaps my head to the right.

At the edge of the tree line, where the forest bleeds into the meadow, a figure stands.

He is still. So still he might be a statue carved from the twilight itself. But statues do not breathe. I see the rise and fall of his chest, the white plumes of vapor escaping his lips in the cooling air.

Lachlan.

He is not blue light. He is not a shadow on a wall or a chill in the room. He is solid. He wears the Sutherland tartan, the colors rich and dark—green and navy and black—dyed with plants from a world that died centuries ago. His hair is loose, a dark curtain framing a face that I have sketched a thousand times in the margins of my notebooks.

He stares at me. His body is rigid, coiled tight with disbelief. He looks at me as if I am a ghost, as if he is the one haunting the living and I am the spectre he cannot quite believe is real.

"Lachlan," I say. The name falls from my lips like a stone.

He flinches. The sound of his name breaks the spell of his paralysis.

He takes a step. Then another. And then he is running.

He tears across the field, his boots destroying the perfect, waxen grass. He runs with a desperation that terrifies me, a hunger that eats the distance between us in heartbeats. I cannot move. I am rooted to this impossible earth, trembling, my hands half-raised in a gesture of defense or welcome, I do not know which.

He collides with me.

It is not a gentle meeting. It is a crash of bodies, a violent reclamation. The impact knocks the breath from my lungs. His arms wrap around me, iron bands that threaten to crack my ribs, and he lifts me off the ground.

The shock of it burns. Heat. Solid, undeniable heat transfers from his chest to mine through the thin linen of my shift. I gasp, a jagged sound of pure sensation. For four hundred years, my love has been cold—a chill in the spine, a drop in temperature, a frost on the window. Now, he is a furnace.

"Isla," he groans, burying his face in the crook of my neck. His beard scratches my skin—rough, abrasive, real. "Isla, God, you are here. You are warm."

I cling to him. My fingers dig into the wool of his plaid, feeling the coarse weave, the dampness of the mist clinging to the fibers. I inhale, dragging the scent of him deep into my lungs. He smells of peat fires and rain, of sweating horses and the metallic tang of sharpened steel. He smells of the sixteenth century. He smells like home.

"I'm here," I sob, the tears coming hot and fast. "I'm real. We're real."

He drops me to my feet but doesn't let go. He frames my face with his hands. His palms are rough, calloused from the sword and the reins, rasping against my skin. His thumbs wipe away my tears, rough pads dragging over my cheeks.

We stare at each other. His eyes are the blue of the loch in winter—piercing, bottomless. There is no madness in them now, no spectral rage. Only a raw, terrified hope.

"Ye died," he whispers, his voice breaking. "I saw the knife. I felt ye leave."

"I came back," I answer, tracing the line of his jaw with trembling fingers. I need to map him. I need to verify every inch of him. "The circle broke, Lachlan. We fell out of the story."

He closes his eyes and leans his forehead against mine. His breath mingles with mine, sharing the same air, the same rhythm. He shudders, a tremor running through his massive frame that transfers into my own bones.

“Thought I had lost ye tae the void,” he murmurs against my skin. “I thought the light had eaten ye.”

"You have me," I promise, pressing my body closer to his, needing the friction to prove I exist. "You have all of me."

He pulls back just enough to look at my mouth. The hunger in his gaze shifts, darkening, becoming something ancient and starving. It is not just relief anymore. It is a need that has been denied for lifetimes.

"Then show me," he growls.

He takes my hand. His grip is tight, possessive, the bones of his fingers pressing hard against mine. We do not speak. There is no language for this urgency, no words that can bridge the gap between the grave and this frantic, living moment.

He pulls me toward the tree line, away from the manic perfection of the castle. We move toward the sound of the water, that strange, liquid song that seems to vibrate in the marrow of my bones. The ground slopes downward into a hollow sheltered by the roots of massive oaks—trees that should have been felled for timber three hundred years ago but stand here, ancient guardians of our limbo.

The creek cuts through the hollow, the water running clear and impossibly bright over stones that gleam like polished teeth. The light from the water casts dancing, liquid shadows on the underside of the leaves, painting our skin in shifting patterns of silver and blue.

Lachlan stops. He turns to me, and the ferocity in his face stops my heart.

He reaches for the neck of my shift. There is no hesitation, no coy fumbling. He grips the linen in two fists and tears it.

The sound of ripping fabric is loud, violent in the quiet hollow. The cool air hits my skin, but I do not shiver. I am burning. He strips the ruined garment from my shoulders, pushing it down over my arms, leaving me standing naked in the strange grass.

He looks at me. His gaze is a physical touch, heavy and scorching. He tracks the curve of my waist, the swell of my breasts, the flare of my hips. He drops to his knees, his hands spanning my waist, his face pressing against my stomach.

"Mine," he breathes against my skin. "Flesh and blood. Mine."

I tangle my fingers in his hair, gripping the dark strands, pulling him closer. "Take it off," I command, my voice a stranger's rasp. "I need to see you. All of you."

He stands, his movements a blur of efficiency. He unbuckles the belt at his waist, the heavy leather dropping to the grass. The plaid follows, unraveling from his shoulder, revealing the broad expanse of his chest, the muscles corded and jumping under the skin. He kicks off his boots. He shoves down his breeches.

He is magnificent. He is a map of violence.

Silver scars crisscross his torso—souvenirs of clan skirmishes, of knife fights in the dark, of a life lived by the blade. But my eyes are drawn to the jagged, puckered ridge of white flesh just above his heart. The killing blow. The mark Hamish left on his soul.

I reach out to touch it, but he catches my hand. He pulls me into him, skin crashing against skin. The texture of him is overwhelming—the coarse hair on his chest, the slick sweat on his shoulders, the hard, unyielding wall of his thighs.

He kisses me. It is not a kiss; it is an invasion. His tongue sweeps into my mouth, tasting of the wild, of iron and salt. I taste him back, drinking him in, desperate to replace the taste of dust and death that has coated my tongue for so long.

He lifts me. My legs wrap around his waist, a muscle memory that predates my birth. He carries me down to the mossy bank of the creek, sinking down until my back presses against the cool, damp earth.

He settles between my thighs, his weight heavy and wonderful. He is hard, pressing against my entrance, demanding and desperate.

"Look at me," he grates out, his pupils blown wide, swallowing the blue. "I want ye to ken who takes ye."

"Lachlan," I gasp, arching my hips, seeking him. "Now. Please, now."

He thrusts.

He fills me in a single, devastating stroke.

I cry out, my head falling back into the moss. The sensation is blinding. It is too much and not enough. I am stretched, filled, claimed. The friction is a spark in dry tinder. After centuries of being nothing but a watcher, nothing but a vessel for memories, I am entirely, painfully present.

He moves with a rhythm that has no music. It is the rhythm of survival. He pounds into me, his hips grinding against mine, seeking to erase the distance, to merge our bodies until we are one creature with two heads. I claw at his shoulders, my nails digging deep, drawing beads of bright red blood that look black in the silver light of the water.

"Isla," he groans, each thrust accompanied by my name, a litany, a prayer.

I am Fi. I am the woman who worries about infection, about birth control, about the damp ground. But those thoughts are fleeting sparks, extinguished by the ocean of Isla's need. I wrap my legs tighter around him, pulling him deeper. I match his pace, bucking against him, meeting his violence with my own.

We are animals. We are gods. We are star-crossed lovers breaking the stars.

The pleasure builds, a dark wave rising inside me. It coils tight in my belly, a tension that borders on pain. I bite his shoulder, tasting the metallic tang of his blood.

"Yes," I hiss. "Yes, break it. Break the curse."

He drives into me, harder, faster. I feel him unraveling. His control snaps. He buries his face in my neck, a guttural roar tearing from his throat as he spills himself into me. I shatter beneath him, my body clenching around him, milking the life from him, convulsions racking me from head to toe.

We collapse.

Lungs heaving. Hearts hammering a frantic, synchronized beat against our ribs. The silence rushes back into the hollow, heavy and stunned.

He does not withdraw. He stays inside me, heavy and grounding, his forehead resting against mine. We breathe each other's air.

"Alive," he whispers, the word trembling. "We are alive."

I stroke the damp hair back from his forehead. "For now."

We lie there until our breathing slows, until the sweat on our skin begins to cool in the strange twilight. Then, slowly, with infinite care, he begins to move again.

This time is different.

This time is worship.

He withdraws almost fully, then slides back in, slow and deliberate, mapping every inch of friction. He kisses my eyelids, my nose, the scar above my brow. His hands roam my body, not to grasp and bruise, but to memorize. He traces the curve of my hip bone, the softness of my breast, the line of my throat.

"Yer different," he murmurs, his eyes searching mine. "Yer skin is softer. Yer hands... they have no worked the fields."

"I am from a different time," I whisper, turning my head to kiss his palm. "A softer time. But my heart is the same."

He smiles, a soft, heartbreaking expression that smooths away the centuries of rage. "Aye. The heart is the same."

He makes love to me with a reverence that makes me weep. He moves with a liquid grace, coaxing pleasure from me that is deep and rolling and golden. I watch him above me, silhouetted against the impossible leaves. I see the dirt under his fingernails—soil from a grave, perhaps, or just the earth of this realm. I see the fine lines around his eyes. He is so real it hurts.

When the end comes this time, it is a quiet shudder, a shared sigh that leaves us drifting.

He rolls to his side, pulling me with him, keeping us tangled together. My back is pressed against his chest, his arm draped heavy over my waist, his hand cupping my breast possessively. I listen to the steady, thumping rhythm of his heart against my shoulder blades.

Thump-thump. Thump-thump.

A sound I have chased through many lifetimes. A sound I was never supposed to hear again.

I close my eyes, trying to ignore the way the edges of the hollow flicker like a bad signal. I try to be just a woman in her lover's arms. But Fi is awake now. Fi sees the way the light from the creek doesn't cast the right shadows. Fi knows that biology doesn't work this way in the afterlife.

"It's perfect," I lie to the darkness.

"It is a memory," he corrects softly, his breath stirring the hair at my ear. "But it is a good one."

I turn in his arms, shifting so I can face him. The grass beneath us is flattened, a nest made of impossible greenery. I run my fingertips down the center of his chest, parting the dark hair to find the skin beneath.

There it is. The mark.

It is a raised, white keloid, jagged and ugly. It sits directly over his heart, a permanent record of brotherly betrayal. I trace the shape of it. It feels smooth, waxy, dead.

"He struck true," I whisper. The memory of the dungeon flashes in my mind—the smell of the torch, the sound of the blade entering meat.

Lachlan catches my hand, stopping my exploration. His grip is not as strong as it was moments ago. A tremor runs through his fingers, a subtle vibration like a wire under tension.

"He struck with hate," Lachlan says, his voice rough. "That is why it lingers. Love heals, Isla. Hate leaves scars."

I look up at his face. The shadows under his eyes are deepening, turning the color of bruised plums. His skin, which had been so warm, so vibrant, now has a pallor to it, a subtle translucence that catches the eerie light of the creek.

Around us, the world stutters.

A tree to my left elongates, stretching upward like taffy before snapping back to its original shape. The glowing water of the creek pulses, dimming to a dull mud-brown before flaring bright neon again. The sky above is no longer a static gray; it is boiling, clouds rolling in fast-forward, looping the same storm pattern over and over.

"We can stay here," I say. The words rush out, fierce and desperate. I sit up, ignoring my nakedness, grabbing his shoulders. "Lachlan, we can stay. It's quiet. It's safe. Murray is gone. Hamish is gone."

Lachlan looks at me with a sorrow so profound it threatens to stop my heart. He sits up slowly, his movements heavy, as if the air around him has turned to syrup. He reaches out and touches my cheek. His hand is cooler now.

"Look at the horizon, mo chridhe," he says softly.

I look.

Beyond the tree line, where the castle stands, the world is unraveling. The stone walls of Sutherland Castle are not solid. They are wavering like heat haze on a highway. The towers detach from the main keep, floating inches in the air before slamming back down. The mountains in the distance are missing pixels, chunks of purple heather simply absent, replaced by a void of static.

"It's just... it's just settling," I lie, my voice rising in pitch. "I created this. Or you did. We can fix it. We can stabilize it."

"We created nothing," Lachlan corrects me. He takes my hands in his. His skin feels thin, papery. "This place... it is the residue of the curse. It is the energy of our binding, spun into a dream by the violence of the breaking."

He gestures to the flickering trees. "This is wha's betwixt life an' death. Between the past an' the present. It is a bridge, Isla. An' bridges aren't meant tae be lived on.

"I don't care," I cry, clutching his hands tighter, trying to transfer my own vitality into him. "I don't care if it's fake. You're here. I can touch you. I can't go back to a world where you're just a cold spot in the room. I can't go back to being alone."

"You willna be alone," he says, but he doesn't promise that he will be there.

The evasion strikes me like a slap.

"No," I whisper. "Don't you say it. Don't you dare tell me you're leaving."

"I am tired, Isla," he confesses. The admission seems to cost him everything. His shoulders slump. The blue light of his eyes dims, flickering like a dying bulb. "Holding this form... holding this memory... it takes more than I have. I am a soul that has been screaming for four hundred years. I need to rest."

"Rest here!" I beg. "Sleep. I'll watch over you. Just don't fade. Please, Lachlan, don't fade."

He pulls me into his lap, cradling me against his chest. I can feel his ribs now, sharp against my skin, as if he is hollowing out from the inside.

"The realm is collapsing," he murmurs into my hair. "Can ye feel it?"

I can. The ground beneath us vibrates, a low-frequency hum that rattles my teeth. The light from the creek is strobing now, flashes of blinding white interspersed with absolute darkness. The air pressure fluctuates, popping my ears.

"I don't care," I sob, burying my face in his neck. "Let it collapse. Let it fall into the void. As long as we fall together."

"That is the tragedy of it," he says, his voice sounding distant, as if he is speaking from the bottom of a well. "We cannot fall together. You belong to the living, Fi. Your heart beats with blood that flows. Mine..." He takes my hand and places it over his heart.

The rhythm is erratic. Thump... thump... pause. Thump.

It is slowing.

"You are a ghost," I whisper, the realization shattering me. "You're still a ghost."

"And you are a woman with a life waiting for her, yer heart yet beats," he says. "A life you fought for. A life you killed for."

"I killed for us!" I scream at the dissolving sky. "I killed him so we could be together!"

"And we are," he soothes, rocking me back and forth as the trees around us turn into pillars of gray smoke. "We are together in the only way that matters. We broke the wheel. Hamish is gone. The cycle is ended."

"It's not enough," I weep. "It's not fair."

"It is never fair," he agrees. "But it is free."

The castle in the distance explodes silently. One moment it is there, the next it bursts into a cloud of birds—crows, thousands of them, erupting from the stone and spiraling up into the white void of the sky. The ground beneath the creek vanishes, the water falling into nothingness.

The darkness creeps in from the edges of my vision, a vignetting tunnel that forces me to look only at him.

He is fading. I can see the trees through his chest. I can see the darkness through his arm.

"Lachlan!" I grab him, my fingers passing slightly into his flesh before hitting resistance. "Stay! Fight it!"

“Love ye,” he says. The words are solid, even if he is not. “I hae loved ye through stone and fire and death. I will love ye until the stars burn.”

"Then stay!"

He shakes his head, a sad, weary motion. "I cannae. The morning comes, my love. And ghosts cannae abide the sun."

The ground beneath us dissolves. We are floating in the gray. He is transparent now, a sketch of a man made of blue light and sorrow. I am solid, heavy, real. The contrast is unbearable.

"Wait for me," I beg, clawing at the light that was his arm. "If you go, wait for me. I'll find you. I always find you."

He smiles, and it is the smile from the coffee shop reflection, the smile from the dungeon, the smile of the man who married me in secret four centuries ago.

"I ken," he whispers.

And then the light takes him. Not the white light of the crossover, but the blinding, golden, terrible light of the sun.

I squeeze my eyes shut and scream his name into the void.

CHAPTER 23
The Shadow World Explained

The white void does not promise heaven. It spits me out onto a floor of damp, gray slate that smells of ozone and forgotten rain.

I gasp, the air entering my lungs like swallowed glass. My hand flies to my chest, fingers clawing at the linen shift I wear. The fabric is whole, the skin beneath it unbroken, but the memory of the blade is a living thing. It pulses in time with a heart that shouldn't be beating—a hot, rhythmic echo of the steel grating against the sternum, the terrifying liberation of the puncture. I am not bleeding, yet I am drowning in the sensation of blood loss.

"Lachlan," I croak.

The name falls dead in the air, swallowed by a silence so absolute it presses against my eardrums.

I push myself up. My limbs feel heavy, filled with lead instead of marrow. I turn, expecting the dungeon, expecting Murray's corpse, expecting the impossible green meadow where I just held my lover.

I find only the fragment.

I am standing in a corridor that has no ceiling. Above, the sky is a bruised smear of charcoal and violet, moving too fast, clouds roiling in a silent storm. To my left, the wall is rough-hewn granite, weeping moisture, hung with iron sconces that hold cold, unlit torches. To my right, the wall is drywall, painted the sterile beige of my university office in Boston, adorned with a framed degree that is slowly melting, the ink dripping down the glass like black tears.

I stumble forward. My bare foot lands on a flagstone, cold and biting. The next step sinks into plush, synthetic carpet.

"Focus," I whisper. Fi's voice. The historian. The rationalist. "It's a construct. Synapses firing in a dying brain."

It is the veil, Isla whispers back, her voice rising from the blood in my veins. It is the place where the ghosts wait.

We are two minds trapped in a single vessel, grinding against each other like tectonic plates. I look at my hand. It flickers—one moment the pale, manicured hand of a doctoral student, the next the calloused, red-knuckled hand of a healer who grinds herbs and washes linens in the burn. The dissonance makes me retch, my stomach heaving with nothing to expel.

I walk. I have no choice. The corridor stretches and warps, breathing around me.

A door appears ahead. It is red, peeling, familiar. The door to my grandmother's house in Massachusetts. I reach for the knob, desperate for the smell of baking bread and safety.

The wood dissolves under my fingers, turning into a swarm of moths that scatter into the dark. Behind where the door stood is a window—an arrow loop cut into thick stone. I look through it.

I see the moors of the 1600s. I see the heather stained brown with winter kill. And I see a woman falling from a tower, her skirts billowing like a shroud, hitting the stones with a sound that never ends. Thud. Thud. Thud.

I recoil, backing away until my shoulders hit the beige wall. "Stop it," I hiss at the realm. "Stop showing me."

The realm does not care. It is a tapestry woven from our trauma, and the thread is pulled tight.

Through the oppressive quiet, a sound threads its way to me. Liquid. Rhythmic. The sound of water moving over stones.

Isla...

It is not a voice. It is the vibration of the water itself, translating into a syllable I know better than my own name.

I push off the wall. The ache in my chest throbs, a compass needle pulling me north. I follow the sound. The floor beneath me ripples, turning into wet grass, then cobblestones, then grass again. The air grows colder, carrying the scent of peat smoke and longing—a desire so old it has calcified into the atmosphere.

I round a corner that shouldn't exist, the geometry bending impossibly, and find the source.

The creek does not run through a forest this time. It cuts through the center of a library, winding between stacks of rotting books. The water glows with a sickly, bioluminescent pulse. It flows over the books that have fallen into its bed, washing away the ink, erasing the stories to make room for ours.

I kneel by the edge on the sodden carpet. The water calls. It sings with a baritone warmth that vibrates in my hollow bones.

Come to me, the water whispers in Lachlan's cadence. The knot is loose, but the rope remains.

I stare into the depths. My reflection is there, but it is not me. It is a blur of faces—Fi screaming in a hotel room, Isla laughing by a fire, Fi crying over a dissertation, Isla weeping over a grave. We are a mosaic of grief.

"I am here," I say to the water. "Where are you?"

The library dissolves. The books turn to ash, the shelves to dead trees. The world spins, sickening and gray, and I am falling again, not down, but in, drawn toward the center of the web where the spider waits.

The spinning stops with a jarring suddenness that nearly throws me to my knees. The library is gone. The corridor is gone. I am standing on a patch of heather that floats in a sea of gray mist, an island of memory anchored in the void.

And he is there.

Lachlan steps from the vapor as if he is woven from it. First the outline of his broad shoulders, then the sweep of his plaid, and finally the stark, beloved geography of his face. He is not the translucent shade who haunted my hotel room, nor the fading dream from the hollow. He is solid. He is high-definition heartbreak.

"Fi," he breathes.

I collide with him. There is no grace in it, only the collision of two celestial bodies drawn by an inescapable gravity. My hands slap against his chest, gripping the rough wool of his Sutherland tartan. His arms wrap around me, crushing the air from my lungs, and the pain in my chest flares and vanishes, eclipsed by the heat of him.

"You're here," I sob into his neck, tasting the salt on his skin. "You're real."

He cups my face in his hands, his thumbs dragging over my cheekbones, rough and trembling. He tilts my head back, forcing me to look at him. His blue eyes are wide, frantic, searching my features for any sign of the fading.

"I could not hold on," he says, his voice a raw rasp. "The light... it tried to scour me away. But you pulled me back. You are the anchor, Isla. You are the stone."

He kisses me. It is not a gentle greeting. It is a desperate, devouring thing. His mouth crashes against mine, hungry and terrified, trying to breathe his own life into my lungs. I open to him, drinking him in, my fingers tangling in the dark hair at the nape of his neck, pulling him closer until there is no space left between us for the ghosts to slip in.

We cling to each other, swaying on the patch of heather while the gray nothingness swirls around us. My body responds to him with a violent, cellular recognition. My pulse hammers against his wrist where it rests on my neck. The heat pooling in my belly is not just desire; it is the affirmation of life in a place of death.

"Where is this?" I ask against his mouth, breathless. "Why didn't we pass on?"

Lachlan pulls back slightly, resting his forehead against mine. He closes his eyes, and I see the exhaustion etched into the corners, the weight of centuries pressing down on him.

"We are in the knot, yer heart beats it's last," he whispers. "Between the tick and the tock. We destroyed the vessel—Murray is gone, the physical binding is broken—but the spirit..." He shudders. "The spirit remains."

I pull back, looking at him. "Hamish."

"He is the third strand," Lachlan says, opening his eyes. The blue is dark, turbulent. "He bound us in blood, Fi. He cursed us to a cycle. We broke the cycle of rebirth, aye, but we are trapped in the residue of his hate. This realm... it is built from us. My grief. Your fear. His jealousy."

He runs his hands down my arms to my hips, grounding me, holding me as the ground beneath our feet trembles.

"We cannae stay here," he continues, urgency sharpening his tone. "This place is temporary. It is a dream dying in the morning light. If we stay, we fade. We become nothing more than echoes in the stone."

"How do we leave?" I ask, gripping his forearms. "How do we finish it?"

“Must face him, then,” Lachlan turns, looking out into the swirling mist. “We hae to find the center. The place where the memory's strongest. We hae to tell the story one last time, and we must change the end.”

He looks back at me, and the vulnerability in his warrior's face breaks my heart. "I cannae do it alone, mo chridhe. In this place, he is strong. He feeds on the dark. I need... I need ye tae choose."

"I already chose," I say fiercely, placing my hand over his heart. I feel the beat of it—slow, heavy, but there. "I drove a knife into my own heart to choose you."

“Ye chose death tae escape him,” Lachlan corrects gently, covering my hand with his. “Now, ye must choose life tae keep me.”

The mist around us begins to darken, curdling from gray to a bruised purple. The air grows cold, the kind of cold that starts in the marrow and works its way out.

"He kens we are here," Lachlan says, drawing his sword—a blade of spectral steel that manifests in his grip. "Come, Fi. The hunt begins."

The heather dissolves into cobblestones slick with slime. The open air vanishes, replaced by walls of weeping stone that close in like the ribs of a leviathan. We are no longer walking; we are being digested.

Lachlan grips my hand so tight his knuckles are white, pulling me through the labyrinth of our own damnation. The air here is foul, tasting of stagnant water and old iron.

"Don't listen," Lachlan warns, his voice tight. "Whatever he says, dinnae listen."

A laugh echoes through the corridor. It bounces off the wet stones, coming from everywhere and nowhere. It is a sophisticated, cultured laugh, stripped of Murray’s hesitation and filled with Hamish’s ancient arrogance.

"Listening was never her strong suit, was it, brother?"

The shadows ahead of us coalesce, twisting into vaguely human shapes that dissolve as we approach. The temperature plummets. My breath blooms in white clouds before my face. I look down at our joined hands. Where Lachlan's skin touches the air, faint, spectral sprigs of purple heather sprout from the stone floor, struggling to live for a heartbeat before the frost claims them.

"You lead her through the dark," Hamish's voice croons, sliding along the walls like oil. "Just as you did then. Leading her to ruin. Leading her to the slaughter."

"Shut up!" I scream, the sound scratching my throat.

We burst through an archway into a vast, circular chamber. I stumble, my feet slipping on the icy floor.

I know this place. It is the Great Hall, but it is wrong. The tables are set for a wedding feast, but the food is rotting, covered in gray mold. The banners hanging from the rafters are tattered, dripping black sludge that pools on the floor.

And in the center, a memory plays out.

Shadow figures—static and jerky, like a bad film—enact a scene. A woman with my hair stands before a priest. A man with Hamish's silhouette holds her hand. She is weeping. He is smiling.

"Did you ever truly belong to him, Isla?" Hamish whispers. The voice is right in my ear, cold breath stirring my hair. I spin around, but there is no one there. "Or was it always me? I was the one who claimed you. I was the one who put the ring on your finger. I was the one who killed for you."

"You killed us," Lachlan roars. He slashes his sword at a banner, slicing the fabric. The black sludge sprays outward, sizzling where it hits the floor. "You owned nothing but a corpse!"

"I owned her fear," Hamish counters. The walls begin to crack. Fissures race across the stone, bleeding a thick, ink-like shadow. "And fear lasts longer than love. Fear is eternal."

We run. Lachlan drags me toward the far door, away from the rotting feast. The floor tilts, throwing us off balance. Black ice skitters across the stones, chasing our heels, freezing the rot where it lies.

We crash through the door into a narrow alcove. The air here is suffocatingly hot, smelling of musk and sweat.

"Here," Hamish whispers. "Do you remember? You thought you were hidden. You thought you were free."

The shadows on the wall writhe, forming the shapes of two lovers pressed against the stone. It is a grotesque parody of our passion, distorted and ugly. The shadow-Isla looks not rapturous, but trapped. The shadow-Lachlan looks predatory.

"He creates his own truth," I gasp, pressing my hands to my temples. "He's twisting it."

"He cannae twist what is real," Lachlan says. He drops the sword and grabs my shoulders, turning me to face him. "Look at me, Fi. Not at the shadows. Look at me."

I lock eyes with him. The blue is the only true color in this world of gray and black.

"I chose you," I say, fighting the insinuation of the realm. "I wanted you."

“Aye,” Lachlan says.

Where we stand, the ice recedes. A circle of warmth expands from our bodies. The black slime on the walls hisses and retreats. We are the burning coal in the snowbank.

"How touching," Hamish sneers. The alcove begins to elongate, stretching into a tunnel that leads upward. "Come then. Come to the end of the road. Let us see if yer love can fly."

The tunnel pulls us upward, defying gravity, sucking us toward the place where the story began and ended. The darkness pulses, a giant heart beating with anticipation. We are not running anymore; we are being summoned.

We burst from the suffocating tunnel into the open air, but there is no relief. The sky is a vortex of white noise, a screaming nothingness that swirls above the battlements.

We are standing on the precipice. It is the tower where I fell. It is the courtyard where they dragged Lachlan in chains. It is the dungeon where he died. It is all of them at once, layered like transparencies over a single moment of trauma.

And he is waiting.

Hamish stands at the edge of the abyss. He is a nightmare given form. He wears Murray's slate-gray pea coat, but it is tattered, blowing in a wind that screams like a banshee. Beneath the coat, he wears the Campbell plaid, stained dark with blood. His face shifts—now Murray's soft features, now Hamish's sharp, cruel lines, now a faceless void of swirling shadow.

"Welcome home," he says. His voice is a landslide, heavy and crushing.

"End this, Hamish!" Lachlan steps in front of me, raising his spectral sword. "Let her go!"

"Never!" Hamish roars. He raises a hand, and the shadows of the battlements surge forward like black water. They crash against Lachlan, driving him back. Lachlan grunts, his blue light flickering, dimming under the assault.

"You think you can break what I forged in blood?" Hamish screams, striding forward. The stones beneath his feet crack and bleed. "I bound us! I tied the knot! You cannot cut it! The etchings are carved into the walls by the wicked women who would ensure it," he sneers

Lachlan pauses, "What did ye do, brother?"

"I long heard the whispers. I suspected. I had the women people talked about, the ones called witches, come and etch a binding into the stone! It was meant to bind her to me forever. I didna know you had already spread her legs, ruining it all!" Hamish yells, moving toward us.

He swings a sword that is made of pure darkness. Lachlan parries, steel meeting shadow with a sound like a thunderclap. Sparks shower down —blue and black—burning the stone.

They fight. It is a dance of brothers, of hate and love twisted into a singular violence. But Lachlan is tired. I can see it. With every blow he blocks, he becomes more translucent. The realm is eating him to feed Hamish's rage.

Hamish lands a blow that sends Lachlan sprawling. The sword skitters away across the stones.

"Lachlan!" I scream, lunging for him.

Hamish catches me. He doesn't touch me; he hits me with a wall of force that pins me against the parapet. I hang there, suspended over the drop, the wind tearing at my clothes.

"Look at him," Hamish commands, pointing at Lachlan, who struggles to rise. "He is weak. He is the past. I am the force that keeps you here, Isla. I am the reason you exist. Without my hate, you would have faded centuries ago."

"I am not Isla!" I shout, the wind snatching the words from my mouth. "I am Fiona MacPherson! And I am done with you!"

Hamish laughs, stepping closer. "Names. You are the prize. And the prize does not speak."

Lachlan roars, throwing himself at Hamish's legs, tackling him. They roll across the stones, a tangle of limbs and shadows. But Hamish is stronger. He rises, lifting Lachlan by the throat, holding him up like a doll.

"Say goodbye, brother," Hamish hisses. "I will dissolve you. I will scatter your soul so wide not even God will find the pieces."

Lachlan kicks, his hands clawing at Hamish's grip, but his light is failing. He looks at me, his eyes filled with a terrible, accepting love.

No.

The word detonates in my mind.

I push off the parapet, fighting the pressure of Hamish's will. I do not run to Lachlan. I run to the center. I run to the crossroads.

"Hamish!" I scream.

He turns, startled by the force of my voice.

I stand tall. I am shaking, but my soul is granite. I strip away the fear. I strip away the guilt. I strip away the memory of the fall.

"You didn't bind us," I say, my voice steady, resonating with the power of the stone beneath my feet. "I held on. I held on because I was afraid to let go. I kept you alive because I hated you."

Hamish freezes. "What are you doing?"

"I am letting go," I whisper.

I look at Lachlan. I pour every ounce of my will, every drop of my love, into the space between us.

"I choose him," I declare to the void. "Not because of the curse. Not because of the past. I choose Lachlan. Fully. Consciously. Without regret."

I turn my gaze to Hamish. "And I release you."

Hamish's eyes widen. "You cannae—"

"You are nothing," I say. "You are a memory of a bad man. And I am forgetting you."

The effect is instantaneous. Hamish screams—a sound of pure ego being dismantled. His form begins to unravel. The pea coat dissolves into smoke. The plaid turns to ash. The shadow boils away, revealing nothing beneath but emptiness.

"No! I am—I am—"

He bursts apart. There is no explosion, just a sudden, violent cessation of existence. He is deleted.

The realm screams. The sky cracks open. The stones beneath our feet turn to white sand, then to light.

Lachlan falls as the hand holding him vanishes. He hits the ground, gasping.

I run to him. The world is ending. The castle is dissolving into brilliance. The ground is falling away.

"Fi!" He reaches for me.

I grab him. We wrap our arms around each other, tangling our legs, pressing our bodies together into a single entity.

"I have ye!" he cries, his voice echoing in the rising white tide.

"I know!" I sob, burying my face in his chest.

The darkness is gone. The gray is gone. There is only the blinding, searing white of absolute morning. We fall into it together, not down, but through. The curse is broken. The story is over.

And we are finally, terrifyingly, free.

CHAPTER 24
The Hunting of Hamish

The white light does not bring heaven. It brings the damp.

It settles on my skin like a second layer of sweat, cold and clinging. I blink, expecting angels or the void or perhaps just the ceiling of a hospital room in Boston. I find none of these. The blinding brilliance that swallowed us fades, peeling away like paint stripped from a rotting wall, revealing the gray bones of a world that shouldn't exist.

I am standing on stone. No, I am standing on mist that pretends to be stone. It shifts under the soles of my boots—boots I don't remember putting back on—and coils around my ankles with the familiarity of a shackle.

"Lachlan?"

My voice is a small thing here. It drops from my lips and is instantly devoured by the gloom.

"Hold to me."

The command comes from beside me. Lachlan is there. He is solid, or at least he convinces my eyes that he is. The tartan wrapped around his shoulder is vibrant against the desaturated gray of the corridor, the greens and blues of the Sutherland plaid screaming of life. But when I reach for him, my fingers pass through the wool for a fraction of a second before hitting resistance. We are substance, but we are negotiation.

I grip his hand. His skin is cool, lacking the fever-heat of the meadow. He looks at me, and the centuries of fatigue are etched into the lines around his eyes.

"I thought we were free," I whisper. The hope tastes bitter on my tongue, like aspirin crushed between teeth. "We broke him. I saw him dissolve."

"We broke the vessel," Lachlan corrects, pulling me forward. We walk, though there is no distance here, only the sensation of movement. "We destroyed the anchor in the mortal world. But the stain remains, Fi. A man like Hamish... a hate like that... it does not leave a room just because ye blow out the candle. The smoke lingers."

We are in a corridor that mimics the castle, but it is a castle drawn by a madman. The walls to my left are granite, weeping moisture that smells of old pennies. The walls to my right are not walls at all, but a falling curtain of rain that hangs motionless in the air.

We step through the quiet. It is a predatory silence. It watches.

"Stay close," Lachlan murmurs, his gaze darting to the darkness stretching ahead. "This realm... it is the In-Between. It is built of our memories, twisted by his jealousy. It wants to separate us. It wants us lost in the labyrinth of our own history."

I squeeze his hand until my knuckles ache. "I know the history. I wrote a dissertation on it. I lived it."

"Ye lived the truth," he says, tightening his grip. "This place tells lies."

The corridor stretches out, impossibly long, the perspective forced and unnatural like a Renaissance painting gone wrong. Torches line the walls, but they do not burn with fire. They burn with a cold, blue luminescence that offers no warmth.

The floor beneath us ripples. Stone turns to mud, sucking at my heels, then snaps back to slate. I stumble, lurching into Lachlan. He steadies me, his arm a band of iron across my chest.

"Careful," he breathes against my ear. "The ground remembers ye falling. It wants to repeat the sensation."

I shudder, the phantom impact of the tower drop jarring my spine. "Hamish did this? Even now?"

“Now. He’s stripped o’ form, Fi. He’s naught but will and malice. He’s the draft in the room.”

As he speaks, the air changes. The temperature plummets, slicing through my flannel shirt, through the linen shift of memory, biting into the bone. It is not a natural cold. It is the vacuum of a soul that starves.

Pop.

The torch furthest from us extinguishes.

Pop. Pop.

The darkness rushes toward us, eating the blue light. The shadows detach themselves from the corners, sliding along the floor like oil.

"He is here," Lachlan hisses. He drags me back, pressing us into a shallow alcove where the stone feels slimy and organic. "Dinnae look at him."

But I look. I am Fi MacPherson. I look at the car crash. I look at the ruins. I cannot help but witness.

At the far end of the dying corridor, a shadow condenses. It does not obey the light source. It stands tall—too tall. It stretches upward, the proportions wrong, the limbs elongated and spindly like a spider's. It has the silhouette of a man in a greatcoat, but the angles are sharp, jagged.

It is Hamish. It is the monster Isla saw in her nightmares, stripped of the handsome mask Murray wore.

The shadow glides forward. It doesn't walk; it flows, erasing the floor as it comes.

"My brother," Lachlan growls, a vibration in his chest that I feel against my shoulder. "Even in hell, he is a peacock."

The shadow pauses. The head, a shapeless void of blacker dark, tilts to the side. It is listening. It is sniffing the air for the scent of our fear.

I hold my breath. My heart hammers a frantic rhythm against my ribs—traitor, traitor, traitor.

The shadow turns. It faces the alcove.

It has no eyes, but I feel the weight of its attention. It is a physical pressure, a gravity that pulls at the lining of my stomach. The darkness of its face splits, a tear in the fabric of the shade, revealing a mouth that is nothing but a vertical gash of gray static.

It smiles.

"Found," the corridor whispers. The word doesn't come from the shadow; it comes from the walls, from the floor, from the blood in my ears.

The shadow lunges.

It expands, rushing toward us like a tsunami of ink. Lachlan shouts, throwing his body in front of mine, shielding me with his spectral form.

The darkness hits us.

It is cold, so cold it burns. The world dissolves. The corridor shatters into fragments of gray slate and blue light. We are falling again, not down, but through. The sensation of the stone alcove vanishes, replaced by the smell of roasting meat and stale wine.

The floor slams into my feet. Hard. Solid.

I gasp, stumbling forward, catching myself on a heavy wooden table. The air is still. The mist is gone.

We are not in the corridor. We are in the Great Hall. But the tables are set for a feast that ended three hundred years ago.

The table under my hand feels greasy. I pull my fingers back, stained with the residue of a feast that has been rotting since the seventeenth century. The Great Hall is vast, the ceiling lost in shadow, but the walls are closing in. They breathe. The stone expands and contracts with the wet, rattling sound of a dying lung.

"Keep moving," Lachlan commands. He grabs my wrist, his touch the only anchor in the drift. "The memory is trying to solidify. If it hardens, we are trapped in the moment."

We run past the high table, past the empty thrones of the Sutherland lairds. The air grows heavy with moisture. The smell of roasted meat curdles, turning into the sharp, green scent of pine needles and damp earth.

The flagstones beneath my boots soften. The echo of our footsteps dulls, replaced by a wet crunch.

I look down. The stone is gone. I am stepping on a carpet of dead leaves, brown and slick with rot.

" The woods," I breathe. My voice shakes. "Why here?"

"Because we were happy here," Lachlan says, his voice grim. He draws his sword, the spectral steel glimmering in the twilight that filters through the canopy. "And he corrupts everything we loved."

The forest has evaporated. We are standing in the hollow below the castle, the place where the burn runs deep, and the oaks grow thick. But the trees are not right. Their bark is black, oozing a dark sap that looks like coagulated blood. The mist that curls around their roots is not the gentle breath of the Highlands; it is a choking, yellow fog.

I stumble as a root writhes up from the earth to snag my ankle. I pitch forward, hands splaying to catch myself on the rough bark of an oak. The wood feels warm. Pulsing.

Lachlan is there instantly, hauling me upright. "Stand, Fi. Do not touch them."

Snap.

The sound is loud as a gunshot in the muffled quiet.

We freeze. We stand back to back, a defensive circle of two. My eyes scan the gaps between the trees, searching for motion in the gloom.

"Come out," Lachlan roars at the forest. "Face me, you coward!"

A laugh answers him. It doesn't come from one throat. It drips from the canopy. It rises from the mulch. It is a stereo surround of mockery.

"Face you?" The voice is Hamish's, cultured and cruel. "I am all around you, brother. I am the root and the branch. I am the very air you try to breathe."

The light dims. The yellow fog thickens, swirling into shapes that look like reaching hands.

"Did you think death would free you from me?" The voice drops an octave, resonating in my chest. "You broke the vessel, yes. But you cannot break the claim. The claim is written in the blood."

"There is no claim!" I shout, spinning toward the sound. "I annulled it!"

"You?" The laughter turns sharp. "You are property, Isla. Property does not speak."

Between two ancient, weeping oaks, the mist parts.

He is there.

Hamish stands in the clearing. He wears the Sutherland plaid, but the colors are bled out, gray and black. He looks... wrong. Like a video file that hasn't buffered correctly. His face flickers. One moment he is the handsome, arrogant man who courted me in the village square; the next, he is a corpse, the skin sloughing off his cheekbones to reveal the white grin of the skull beneath.

His eyes are pits of blue fire, burning with a cold, nuclear hate.

"Look at you," he croons, stepping forward. His boot hits the ground, but there is no sound. "Running through the woods like naughty children. Did you think you could hide?"

He takes another step. The decay spreads from his footprint, the grass turning black and withering instantly.

Lachlan steps in front of me, raising the sword. "Stay back, Hamish. We have killed you once today. I will enjoy doing it again."

Hamish smiles, and his lip splits, weeping black ichor. "You killed a suit of clothes, Lachlan. I am the man inside."

He raises his hand and snaps his fingers.

The forest vanishes.

The sensation of open air is sucked away, replaced by the crushing intimacy of four stone walls. The smell of pine is obliterated by the scent of beeswax and lavender—stale, cloying, suffocating.

I gasp, backing away until I hit a heavy wooden post. I grab it for support. Velvet curtains brush my cheek, dusty and motheaten.

We are in the bedchamber. His bedchamber.

The bed dominates the room, a massive altar to a marriage that was a prison sentence. Hamish stands at the foot of it, the flickering horror of the forest gone. He looks whole now. Solid. Commanding. He runs a hand along the carved footboard, his eyes locking onto mine.

"She was mine," he whispers, the acoustics of the room amplifying the possessiveness. "My wife. My vow. My claim."

I tremble. I can't help it. The room remembers me. My wrists ache with the phantom sensation of bruises where he dragged me. My finger burns where the heavy gold ring used to sit—a circle of metal that felt like a collar.

"I never said the words," I whisper, the memory of the wedding rushing back. The silence. The priest hurrying through the Latin.

"Your father said them," Hamish says, circling the bed. He moves with a jerky, stop-motion quality, missing frames of reality. "And you obeyed. You always obey in the end, Isla."

He reaches for me. His hand is a claw, the fingers too long, the nails dark.

Lachlan lunges across the room, but the air thickens, turning to molasses. He moves in slow motion, shouting a warning that drags out into a low, distorted groan.

Hamish is fast. He is right in front of me. I smell the grave dirt on his clothes.

"Welcome home," he hisses.

I recoil from his touch, squeezing my eyes shut. I expect the bedpost against my back, the velvet curtains.

I feel cold, slime-slicked stone.

The smell of lavender rots instantly, replaced by the ammonia reek of urine and the copper tang of old blood. The air pressure drops, popping my ears.

I open my eyes. The bed is gone. The windows are gone. There is no light but a sickly, greenish glow filtering through a grate high above.

We are in the hole. The oubliette. The place where hope goes to starve.

"Lachlan!"

I spin around. He is not beside me. He is across the small, circular chamber, thrown against the far wall. And he is not free.

Iron manacles rust-red and heavy clamp his wrists, bolting him to the stone. Chains rattle as he pulls against them, the sound sharp and biting in the damp acoustic. He is on his knees, his plaid torn, his chest heaving. He looks at me, and the anguish in his eyes is not for his own captivity, but for mine.

I rush forward, my hands outstretched.

Clang.

My palms hit cold iron. Bars. A gate separates us, thick and immovable. I am on the outside, in the guard's corridor. He is inside, the prisoner.

"No," I whimper, shaking the bars. They are freezing, biting into my skin. "Not this. We passed this."

"History is a wheel, my love," a voice says from the shadows. "It turns, and the same spoke hits the mud."

Hamish steps out of the gloom. He stands in the corridor with me, between the bars and freedom. He is solid now, more real than the stone walls. He glows with a faint, necrotic luminescence. He looks at Lachlan through the bars with the satisfied expression of a man studying a bug pinned to a board.

"Look at him," Hamish says softly. "The warrior. The lover. Reduced to meat in a cage."

"Let him go!" I lunge at Hamish, my fingers forming claws.

He doesn't move. He simply looks at me, and a wall of force slams into my chest, knocking me backward. I stumble, hitting the opposite wall. Rats scatter at my feet, their claws clicking on the wet stone, their eyes red beads in the dark.

"Every time you find him, I find you," Hamish says. He walks toward me. He is calm. He has all the time in the afterlife. "It is the geometry of us, Isla. A triangle is the strongest shape in nature. It cannot be broken."

He reaches out. This time, I cannot dodge. His finger traces the line of my jaw, down to my throat.

It burns. Not like fire, but like absolute zero. Frost blooms on my skin where he touches, a spiderweb of white ice spreading across my neck. The cold paralyzes my vocal cords, choking off my scream.

"Get your hands off her!" Lachlan roars.

He throws his weight against the chains. The bolts in the wall groan. Dust showers down from the ceiling. His spectral form flares blue, fighting the suppression of the dungeon. He is a storm trapped in a bottle, raging against the glass.

Hamish laughs. It is a dry, rattling sound. He turns his head to look at his brother.

"Scream all you want, Lachlan. It is the only music I enjoy." Hamish leans closer to me, his breath smelling of the void. "You think you love him? You love the defiance. You love the tragedy. Without me to forbid it, your little romance is common. Boring. I make you legendary."

"We don't want legends," I manage to gasp, the frost cracking on my skin. "We want peace."

"Peace is for the dead," Hamish sneers. "And we are something else entirely. Three souls, braided together in the dark. One pulls, the others follow."

He steps back, spreading his arms. The dungeon shudders.

A crack appears in the ceiling, running through the grate. Water pours in, black and oily. The stone floor beneath my feet lurches. The reality of the memory is failing under the weight of the conflict.

"The knot is fraying," Hamish observes, sounding almost disappointed. "The stage cannae hold the actors."

The walls begin to dissolve. Stones turn to gray smoke. The iron bars of Lachlan's cage waver, turning liquid for a second before hardening again.

"Isla!" Lachlan shouts. "Run!"

"Not without you!"

I throw myself at the bars again. The metal is hot now, vibrating with the instability of the realm. I reach through the gap. Lachlan strains against his chains, stretching his arm out. His fingers are inches from mine.

"You cannot escape what we are!" Hamish's voice rises, booming, no longer coming from his mouth but from the collapsing architecture. "We are the tower! We are the fall! We are the ruin!"

Hamish's form begins to blur. He is becoming the storm. The dungeon spins, a kaleidoscope of gray stone and black water.

Lachlan's fingertips brush mine. A spark jumps between us—blue fire.

"Hold on!" he screams.

The floor drops out from under us. The dungeon explodes into mist. We are falling again, tumbling through the chaotic debris of our own souls, with the laughter of the third strand chasing us down into the dark.

CHAPTER 25
Confrontation

The fall does not end in a thud. It ends in a slide, a sickening lurch of gravity that deposits us onto a surface that feels like wet lung tissue.

I scramble for purchase, my fingers sinking into a floor that ripples and groans beneath my touch. It is not stone. It is not earth. It is a membrane stretched over a void, pulsating with the erratic rhythm of a dying heart.

"Stand up, Fi."

Lachlan hauls me to my feet. His grip is the only solid thing in a universe of fluid terror. We are back-to-back instantly, a posture carved into our muscle memory by four centuries of running. I feel the ridge of his spine against mine, the tension in his shoulder blades vibrating through the thin linen of my shift. He is a wall of heat in a world that smells of cold ash.

"Where is he?" I whisper. The air tastes metallic, like licking a battery.

"Everywhere," Lachlan grates out.

The realm is screaming. The dungeon walls that surrounded us moments ago have fractured, splitting open like rotten fruit to reveal glimpses of other horrors. To my left, a section of the Great Hall hangs suspended in the grey mist, the long tables set for a feast of maggots. To my right, the dense, weeping forest of the hollow grows out of the masonry, the black trees twisting their roots into the mortar.

A fissure races across the ground between my feet, leaking a darkness that smokes when it touches the air.

"Isla..."

The voice comes from the crack in the floor. It comes from the ceiling that isn't there. It comes from the hollow space behind my own eardrums.

Hamish.

He does not step out of the shadows this time. He erupts from them.

A figure flickers into existence ten yards away—a tall, imposing silhouette wearing the tattered remains of a pea coat. But before my brain can process the image, another figure blinks into view on the opposite side. And another. And another.

They circle us. Five Hamishes. Ten. A legion of spite wearing the same face.

"You look tired, my love," the nearest Hamish croons. His face is a glitch, sliding between Murray's handsome, predatory sneer and a skeletal visage stripped of flesh. "Is the afterlife not the paradise you were promised?"

"He is nae real," Lachlan says, his voice a low rumble against my back. "Dinnae give him yer fear. He eats it."

"I am the only thing that is real," the Hamishes speak in unison. The sound is nauseating, a chorus of damp distortion. "I am the wall you cannot climb. I am the water filling your lungs."

The circle tightens. The Hamish to my left steps forward, and the ground beneath his boot turns to black sludge. He reaches out, and his hand is not a hand, but a claw of gray mist.

"You tried to leave," he accuses, his eyes burning with blue malice. "You tried to cut the rope. But the rope is woven into your marrow, Isla. You cannae cut what ye are."

"I am not yours!" I shout. My voice cracks, thin and reedy against the overwhelming pressure of the atmosphere. "I never was!"

"Lies," the chorus whispers.

The realm convulses. The forest section to my right violently intrudes, branches whipping out like lashes. They strike the invisible barrier of Lachlan's will, sparking blue fire where they connect.

"Hold fast," Lachlan commands. He shifts his weight, pressing harder against me. I dig my heels into the unstable floor, clutching his hands where they meet at our hips. We are a singular entity, a totem of defiance planted in the shifting sands of purgatory.

"Do you remember the tower?" Hamish asks. One of the figures grows taller, stretching upward until he looms over us like a gargoyle. "Do you remember the wind in your skirts? The sudden, terrible clarity of gravity?"

The floor beneath us liquefies.

I gasp as my feet sink to the ankles in cold, viscous water. The sensation of falling rushes through me—the vertigo, the stomach-dropping terror of the descent. For a second, I am not standing in the In-Between; I am plummeting through the damp Highland air of 1610, the stones of the courtyard rushing up to meet me.

"No," I grit out, shaking my head. "That's a memory. Just a memory."

"It is your destiny," Hamish counters. The giant figure leans down, his face a landscape of shifting shadows. "You fall. You break. I collect the pieces. It is the only dance we know."

"We are changing the steps," Lachlan roars.

He releases my hand for a fraction of a second to summon his sword. The spectral blade flares into existence, a jagged bolt of blue lightning. He slashes wide, a horizontal arc that cuts through the knees of the approaching phantoms.

They do not bleed. They dissolve into smoke, only to reform instantly, closer this time.

"Useless," Hamish laughs. "You cannot kill a ghost with steel, brother. You taught me that."

The walls of the fractured corridor bleed. Thick, dark rivulets of crimson ooze from the stone, pooling around our sunken feet. The smell is overpowering—copper and rot, the scent of the slaughterhouse.

"He's destabilizing everything," I say, watching a window frame melt like wax nearby. "He's tearing the place down to get to us."

"He does not care if the house burns," Lachlan says, "as long as he locks the door."

A sudden violent tremor knocks us sideways. We stumble, turning in the sludge to stay upright, clutching at each other's clothes. The friction of Lachlan's wool plaid against my arm is rough, grounding.

Hamish lunges.

Not one figure, but all of them. They rush inward like a collapsing star, a tidal wave of gray coats and hate.

"Mine!" the voices scream.

Lachlan braces himself, turning to shield me, but the attack is coming from all sides. The air pressure drops so low my ears pop painfully. The darkness swallows the ambient light, leaving only the blue glow of Lachlan's spirit and the sickly, nuclear fire of Hamish's eyes.

We are alone in the dark with a monster who has had four hundred years to perfect his cruelty.

The darkness does not hit like a fist. It hits like a blizzard of razors.

Hamish does not strike us with his hands; he strikes us with history. He peels back the skin of the world and flings the trauma of our past lives at us, sharp and glittering.

I scream as something slices across my arm. There is no blade, no blood, yet the pain is absolute—a white-hot line of agony that mimics the bite of a serrated knife. I stagger, clutching my bicep, but before I can process the wound, the air changes.

It turns heavy. Wet.

My lungs seize. I try to inhale, but my mouth is filled with brackish, freezing water. I am drowning. I am back in the loch, weighed down by stones in my pockets, the light fading above me as I sink into the black. The pressure builds in my chest, a crushing weight that threatens to collapse my ribcage.

"Breathe, Fi!" Lachlan's voice reaches me through the phantom water. "It is not real! Breathe!"

He wraps his arms around me, pulling me into the shelter of his chest. His spectral form flares, pushing back the crushing sensation. I gasp, coughing violently, expelling air that feels dry and thin. The water vanishes, leaving only the ghost of salt on my lips.

"He's... he's inside my head," I choke out.

"He is using the connection," Lachlan growls, turning us so his back takes the brunt of the next wave. "He is pulling the threads of the knot."

The realm tilts. The floor beneath us slants at a forty-five-degree angle. We slide, boots scraping on slick stone, crashing against a wall that is suddenly scorching hot.

Fire.

I smell burning hair. I feel the blistering heat of flames licking at my skirts. I am bound to a stake in a village square, the mob chanting, the smoke choking me. The heat is unbearable, cooking the skin on my arms, boiling the marrow in my bones.

"I burned for you!" Hamish's voice booms from the ceiling. "I burned the world to keep ye, and ye threw yourself into the fire!"

Lachlan roars, a sound of pure defiance. He expands his energy, a blue dome of force that pushes the heat away. The sensation of burning recedes, leaving me shivering and raw, my skin prickling with phantom blisters.

"I have ye," Lachlan whispers, his lips against my temple. He is trembling. The effort of shielding me is costing him. His light is dimming, the vibrant sapphire fading to a pale, washed-out azure. "Dinnae look at the flames, Isla. Look at me."

I look up at him. His face is tight with strain, sweat—or something like it—sheening his forehead. His eyes are the only safe harbor in this storm. He interlaces his fingers with mine, squeezing until the bones grind together.

"Isla," he breathes. "Isla. Isla."

It is an incantation. A reminder of who I am underneath the trauma.

The shadows coalesce again. Hamish is growing. He is no longer a man; he is a titan of smoke and malice, his form stretching up to the nonexistent rafters. He fills the room, blotting out the gray light, blotting out hope. His face is a vast, shifting landscape of cruelty.

"You break," the giant Hamish rumbles. The sound vibrates in the floor, in my teeth. "That is what you do. You are fragile things, made of soft flesh and weak promises. I am the iron that outlasts the rust."

"We are not breaking," I whisper, though my knees are knocking together. I press my ear to Lachlan's chest.

Thump-thump. Thump-thump.

It is not a physical heart. It is the rhythm of his soul. Steady. Unyielding. It is the drumbeat I have followed through centuries of silence.

"You have failed every time," Hamish taunts. He reaches down with a hand the size of a carriage, fingers dripping with black sludge. "Why fight the inevitable? The grave is warm, Isla. Surrender to it. Surrender to me."

The temptation washes over me like a drug. To stop fighting. To stop running. To let the darkness take me and sleep for a thousand years without pain. The weight of the centuries presses down on my shoulders—the sheer, exhausting effort of loving a ghost.

Lachlan feels my sag. He feels the moment my will falters.

He grips my chin, forcing my head up. His eyes are fierce, blazing with a sudden renewal of blue fire.

"Dinnae listen to the sleep," he commands. "We are awake. Finally, mo chridhe, we are awake. Dinna Fash. Stay with me. We have never got this close."

"I'm trying," I sob, the tears hot on my cheeks. "It's so heavy."

"I will carry it," he vows.

He turns to face the giant shadow. He does not cower. He stands tall, a warrior king in a realm of monsters.

"Come then, brother!" Lachlan shouts. "Ye are iron, then I am the fire that melts it!"

Hamish laughs, and the sound brings the ceiling down. Stones rain around us, dissolving into ash before they hit the floor. The giant hand descends, not to crush, but to snatch.

"I do not want to melt you, Lachlan," Hamish hisses. "I want to watch you shatter when I take her."

The giant hand dissolves into a swarm of black vipers. They hit the floor with a wet slap and surge toward us, a writhing carpet of shadow.

"No!" I scream, kicking at them, but they are faster than thought.

Tendrils of darkness lash out, wrapping around my ankles like wet, cold ropes. They bite into my skin, unnaturally heavy, dragging me backward. I lose my footing on the slick floor and crash to my knees.

"Lachlan!"

He lunges for me, his hand catching my wrist just as the darkness pulls taut. The jolt nearly dislocates my shoulder. I cry out, digging my nails into his forearm, drawing blood that glimmers like mercury.

"Let her go!" Lachlan roars, hacking at the tendrils with his sword. The blade passes through them harmlessly. They are not made of magic he can cut; they are made of a claim he cannot break with violence.

"She belongs to the dark!" Hamish's voice is a hurricane wind, battering us. "She belongs to the debt!"

I am being dragged away. Inch by inch. My fingernails scrape furrows in Lachlan's skin. He is sliding with me, his boots carving grooves in the stone, but the pull is inexorable. He is losing purchase. I am slipping from his grip.

I look up at him. His face is contorted with panic—raw, naked terror. He thinks he is losing me again. He thinks this is the end of the story, the part where the hero fails and the maiden falls.

But I am not a maiden. And he is not just a hero.

We are survivors.

I stop fighting the pull. I stop trying to kick the shadows away. Instead, I focus entirely on him. On the blue of his eyes. On the heat of his hand gripping mine.

In the midst of the chaos, the screaming wind, and the writhing floor, a sudden, crystalline silence opens up in the center of my chest.

It is the silence of the decision.

For four hundred years, we have reacted. We have run. We have died. We have been victims of a curse, players in Hamish's game. I realized in the dungeon, when I drove the knife into my heart, that I could change the rules. But I didn't finish it. I tried to escape the game.

Now, I have to win it.

"I am not a debt," I say. The words are quiet, but they cut through the roar of the storm like a diamond through glass.

Lachlan's eyes lock with mine. He sees the shift. He sees the fear evaporate, replaced by a granite certainty.

"Fi?" he whispers.

I tighten my grip on his hand, pulling myself toward him against the drag of the darkness.

"I am not a prize," I say, louder this time. The tendrils around my ankles smoke and loosen. "And I am not a victim."

I look past Lachlan, directly into the void where Hamish waits.

"I choose," I declare. "I choose Lachlan. Not because I have to. Not because it's written. But because he is mine."

The air shimmers. A pulse of energy radiates from my chest—warm, golden, smelling of sunlight on heather.

"I choose him in the dark," I say, pulling myself closer, until our knees touch. "I choose him in the light. I choose him in this life, and I choose him in the death that follows."

Light erupts from our joined hands.

It is not the cold blue of a ghost. It is the blinding, molten gold of a sunrise. It flows up Lachlan's arm, chasing away the shadows, filling the spectral hollowness of his form with substance. He gasps, throwing his head back as the vitality hits him.

"Isla!" Hamish screams. It is a sound of pain. Real pain.

The giant shadow recoils. The light burns him. It is a frequency he cannot exist within. It is the frequency of a love that is no longer tragic.

"No!" Hamish lunges, reforming into a spear of absolute blackness, aiming for my heart. "Ye cannae!"

Lachlan pulls me into him. We collide, chest to chest, heart to heart.

We do not brace for impact. We embrace.

The golden light expands. It explodes outward from our bodies, a supernova of shared soul. It obliterates the dungeon walls. It incinerates the black tendrils.

It hits Hamish.

He does not explode. He unravels.

I watch over Lachlan's shoulder as the darkness hits the wall of light. Hamish shrieks—a sound that thins and warps, turning from a roar into a whine, and then into nothing. His form peels away layer by layer. The arrogance. The hate. The memory. It is all stripped violently from existence, bleached white by the power of our union.

He tries to hold on. He tries to find a hook in my soul, a scar he can leverage.

But I am healed.

"Gone," I whisper into Lachlan's neck.

Hamish Campbell vanishes. There is no smoke. No ash. Just an empty space where a monster used to be.

The realm collapses.

The floor drops away. The ceiling turns to stardust. Gravity releases us.

We are floating in a sea of blinding, perfect white. The cold is gone. The rot is gone. There is only the warmth of Lachlan's arms around me, the solid beat of a heart that has finally found its rhythm.

I close my eyes and bury my face in his shoulder.

"Are we free?" he sobs, the vibration traveling through my entire being. "God, Fi, are we free?"

And then, the white light swallows us whole, carrying us away from the ruin, away from the ghost story, and into something new.

CHAPTER 26
The End

I stand in the center of the sun. It is a violent, churning brilliance that should incinerate bone, yet I am not burning. I am forging. Lachlan is the steel against my spine, his arm a band of absolute solidity across my chest, anchoring me as the universe screams.

And it is screaming.

Hamish is not gone. Not yet. He hangs suspended in the gold-white torrent, impaled on the rejection we just hurled at him. He is no longer the giant of shadow or the handsome laird in the pea coat. He is a tear in the fabric of the light, a jagged wound trying desperately to stitch itself back together.

"You cannae!" he howls. The sound does not come from a throat. It vibrates through the ether, a discordant frequency that rattles the fillings in my teeth. "I am the architect! I built this hell for you!"

"The lease is up," I whisper, though in this place, a whisper carries the weight of a gavel strike.

I press my hand over Lachlan's on my heart. We push. It is not a physical shove, but a psychic expulsion. We shove the memory of him, the history of him, the very concept of him, out of the circle of our existence.

Hamish's form distorts. It is sickening to watch—a biological glitch. His torso elongates, stretching upward like taffy pulled by a cruel child. His face, that mask of arrogant entitlement, slides sideways. The jaw disconnects from the skull. The eyes, burning with that nuclear, necrotic hate, widen until they are nothing but white panic.

He realizes, finally, that he is not the protagonist. He is the cancer, and we are the knife.

"Lachlan!" he shrieks, reaching out with a hand that is already turning to gray ash. "Brother! You cannae destroy me! I am yer blood!"

"Yer naught," Lachlan answers. His voice is deep, resonant, vibrating through my own chest wall. "Yer the winter that went on too long. And I am bringing the thaw."

Lachlan tightens his grip on me. I feel the surge of his will, a blue tidal wave crashing into the gold. It hits Hamish with the force of a train wreck.

The scream shreds the air. It is the sound of metal shearing, of stone cracking, of a soul being ripped from the history books. Hamish's outstretched arm dissolves. It doesn't fall off; it simply ceases to be, turning into a cloud of black particles that are instantly bleached white by the light.

The disintegration travels up his shoulder, consuming the chest that harbored so much envy, the throat that spoke so many lies.

"I will return!" he gurgles, his mouth dissolving even as he speaks, the words slurring into nonsense. "I will... I... will..."

"No," I say. I look directly into the void where his eyes used to be. "You won't."

I feel it then. The Snap.

It happens deep inside me, behind the ribs, in the space where the dread has lived for four hundred years. A cable, pulled tight through centuries of reincarnations, through nightmares and murders and silences, suddenly gives way. The tension vanishes. The recoil nearly knocks me off my feet, leaving me breathless and light-headed.

The curse breaks.

It is not a poetic fading. It is a violent eviction.

Hamish's face contorts in a final rictus of disbelief. He sees the end. He sees the absolute zero of non-existence yawning beneath him. He tries to scream again, but he has no lungs. He tries to hate, but he has no heart.

He shatters.

Like a mirror dropped from a tower, he explodes into a billion jagged shards of gray light. There is no explosion of fire, only a implosion of silence. The shards spin for a heartbeat, caught in the turbulence of our power, and then they are gone. Erased.

The wind dies. The screaming stops.

There is only the empty space where a monster stood, and the echo of a promise that turned to dust on his tongue. I stare at the emptiness, my chest heaving, waiting for the trick. Waiting for the shadow to reform.

But the air is clean. It smells fresh.

"He is gone," Lachlan says against my hair. The wonder in his voice breaks me more than the battle. "Fi... he is truly gone."

I lean back against him, my legs trembling, watching the place where the darkness used to be, ensuring it stays empty.

"Good riddance," I breathe, and the silence rushes in to agree with me.

The silence holds for a single, terrifying second. Then, the world remembers it is dead.

It starts with the floor. The impossible membrane we stand on, that surface of wet lung tissue and slate, shudders violently. A low groan builds from the abyss below—the sound of tectonic plates grinding together without the lubrication of life.

"The construct," Lachlan warns, his arms tightening around my waist. "It cannae hold."

To my left, a wall of the spectral castle begins to bleed. It doesn't weep water or slime; it weeps shadow. Thick, ink-black tears run down the masonry, dissolving the stone as acid dissolves flesh. The granite softens, turning to gray smoke that swirls sluggishly around our knees.

I watch, mesmerized by the undoing.

A flagstone near my boot detaches itself from gravity. It floats upward, spinning lazily, turning from solid rock into a translucent smear of charcoal before vanishing into the white void above. Then another goes. And another. The ground is unravelling like a cheap sweater snagged on a nail.

"The dungeon," I whisper, pointing to a fragment of reality hovering in the mist.

The iron bars that separated us—the bars I scorched my hands on—are melting. They drip like wax candles, the metal pooling into puddles of quicksilver that evaporate instantly. The heavy oak door, the symbol of my captivity, splinters into dust. It creates a cloud of particles that tastes bitter on my tongue—the taste of ancient regrets and screams that went unheard.

The forest of the hollow, which had forced its way into the hall, is dying. The black, weeping oaks wither in fast-forward. Their branches turn brittle and gray, snapping off with the sound of breaking bone, turning to mist before they hit the ground. The moss shrivels. The damp, earthy smell is sucked away, replaced by the sterile scent of vacuum.

"It is all going," Lachlan says. He sounds calm, almost reverent. "Every cage he built."

To our right, the bedchamber—that suffocating room of velvet and violation—crumbles. The four-poster bed, the altar of my forced marriage, collapses in on itself. The velvet curtains rot in the span of a heartbeat, falling in tatters that turn to ash in the wind. The stone walls crack, spiderwebs of black lightning racing through the mortar, and then they simply let go.

The colors drain away. The vibrant red of the blood on the floor turns to black oil. The blue of Lachlan's tartan fades to slate gray. We are standing in a black-and-white photograph that is being burned from the center out.

The ground beneath us gives a violent lurch.

"Hold onto me!" Lachlan commands.

A chasm opens up three feet away. It is not a hole in the ground; it is a hole in reality. It reveals nothing but absolute, yawning darkness below—no stars, no bottom, just the end of things.

Memories peel away from the air around us like old wallpaper. I see a flash of Isla running through the heather—gone. I see Murray signing a check—gone. I see the knife entering my chest—gone. They unravel, the threads of the narrative snapping and curling back into the void.

The vibration travels up my legs, rattling my bones. The Shadow World is having a seizure. It pulses with a dying rhythm—thump... thump... thump...—and with each beat, more of the world vanishes.

We are standing on an island of dissolving matter in a sea of nothing.

"It's beautiful," I say, the words torn from me by the sheer scale of the destruction. "It's horrific, but it's beautiful."

Lachlan buries his face in my neck. He feels solid, the only real thing left in a universe of ghosts. "It is the cleaning of the wound," he murmurs. "Let it bleed out. Let it all go."

The floor beneath our boots cracks. A fissure runs between my feet, widening rapidly. The darkness below breathes cold air up at us, tugging at the hem of my linen shift.

"We have nowhere to stand," I realize, looking around. The horizon is gone. The ceiling is gone.

"We do not need to stand," Lachlan says. "We only need to fall."

The island crumbles. The last stone gives way.

And the floor drops out from under the world.

My legs betray me. They turn to water, to vapor, to nothing. I do not fall so much as I simply cease to hold myself up.

Lachlan catches me.

We collapse together, a tangle of limbs and exhaustion, sinking not onto stone or earth, but into a suspension that holds us like deep water. The gravity here is soft, apologetic. It pulls us down with a gentle insistence, urging us to rest, to sleep, to stop.

My body feels impossibly heavy, weighted with the fatigue of thirteen lifetimes, yet strangely hollow. It is as if the adrenaline that has fueled me since the dungeon has scooped me out, leaving only a shell of skin and a spark of soul.

"I have ye," Lachlan whispers. His voice is a ghost of a sound, fraying at the edges.

I lift my head from his chest. It takes tremendous effort, like lifting a boulder. I look at him.

He is glowing with a faint, residual light—the embers of the fire we started. His face is pale, the scars smoothed away by the dissolution of the curse, leaving him looking young and impossibly tired. His eyes shine with a fierce, wet relief. Tears track through the grime on his cheeks, silver paths in the gathering gloom.

"We did it," I rasp. My throat feels raw, scoured by the screams.

"Aye," he breathes. "It is done."

His fingers trace the line of my jaw, trembling. The touch is cool, feather-light. He maps my face as if trying to memorize it before the lights go out. I lean into his hand, pressing my cheek against his rough palm, desperate for the friction, for the proof of him.

I slide my hand over his chest. I feel the beat of him—thud... thud... thud. It is slowing. It is syncing with the sluggish rhythm of my own heart. We are winding down, two clockwork toys that have finally run out of spring.

"I'm so tired, Lachlan," I confess. "I can't... I can't keep my eyes open."

"Then close them, mo chridhe," he says softly. "There is nothing left to see here. The monsters are gone."

"But if I close them..." I grip his tartan, the wool feeling smooth now, losing its texture. "Will I find you again?"

"Ye are holding me," he says, pressing his forehead to mine. "Yer woven into me. Darkness cannae separate what is already one thing."

Around us, the last remnants of the Shadow World are vanishing. The gray mist thins to transparency. The few remaining motes of dust flick out like dying sparks. The darkness closes in, not aggressive or biting, but soft and absolute. It is a velvet shroud being drawn over a sleeper.

My limbs grow heavier. The sensation of my own body is fading, becoming distant, like a memory of a sensation. My breath comes in shallow hitches, laboring to pull oxygen from a void that has none.

"Lachlan," I whisper. It is a prayer. A tether.

"Isla," he answers. "Fi. My love."

I force my eyes to stay open for one last second. I need his face to be the last thing recorded on the film of my soul. I see him. He is looking at me with four hundred years of devotion distilled into a single gaze. He is the lighthouse in the black.

"I choose you," I murmur, the words shaping themselves on lips I can no longer feel.

"I have ye," he promises.

The vision blurs. His blue eyes are the last stars in the universe. Then, the darkness takes them, too.

The silence is complete. The weight is gone.

We drift.

CHAPTER 27

A Life Returned

The cold is the first truth.

It is not the numbing, void-like cold of the shadow realm, nor the biting wind of a Boston winter. It is wet, living cold. It seeps into the linen of my shift, soaking the skin of my flank, demanding acknowledgement. I breathe, and the air tastes of chlorophyll and wet stone, rich and cloying in the back of my throat.

I open my eyes.

Green fills them. Blades of grass, individual and distinct, press against my cheek. They are coated in dew that catches the gray morning light, glittering like scattered diamonds. I reach out, my fingers trembling as they dig into the soil. It yields. It smells of worms and rain. It is aggressively, terrifyingly real.

I push myself up. My body feels heavy, a sack of meat and bone that gravity wants to reclaim. The muscles in my arms protest, not with the hollow ache of a spirit, but with the lactic burn of living tissue. I sit back on my heels, gasping as the world spins and settles.

Sutherland Castle looms above me.

But it is not the skeleton I know. It is not the jagged, broken tooth of rock where I led tourists and chased ghosts. It is a beast made whole.

The battlements are sharp, undulled by the centuries. The slate roof is intact, slick with rain, reflecting the leaden sky. There are no gaps in the masonry, no ivy strangling the keep. It stands pristine, a monument to a time that should be dust. It looks aggressive in its perfection, the stone facing smooth and arrogant.

A wave of nausea hits me.

Two minds wrestle for control behind my eyes.

I am Fi MacPherson. I know that carbon dating puts these foundations in the thirteenth century. I know that the roof collapsed in 1702. I know I drove a rental car here three weeks ago.

I am Isla. I know the mason who carved the lintel above the postern gate. I remember the smell of the lye soap used to scrub these very stones. I recall the way the light hits the solar in the mid-afternoon.

The memories layer over each other, a double exposure that makes the horizon twitch. I blink, trying to clear the static. The edges of the castle seem to vibrate, blurring into the gray sky like ink bleeding on wet paper. It is too sharp and yet undefined, a dream constructed with too much detail.

"Where are we?" I whisper.

My voice is solid. It vibrates in a chest that rises and falls with panicked rhythm. I bring a hand to my throat, feeling the pulse hammering there. Thump-thump. Thump-thump. The drumbeat of survival.

Sounds drift across the lawn—ghosts of noise that shouldn't be here. The sharp clack-clack of hooves on cobblestones. The rhythmic shout of a drill sergeant barking orders in broad Scots. The clang of iron on iron from a smithy that hasn't existed for three hundred years.

I turn my head, searching for the source, but the grounds are empty. There are no soldiers. No horses. Only the manicured grass and the looming stone. The sounds are embedded in the atmosphere, a soundtrack playing on a loop for an audience of one.

I stand. My knees shake, threatening to buckle. The wet linen clings to my legs, cold and heavy. I feel naked, exposed under the watching windows of the keep.

Then, movement.

At the main gates, where the great iron-bound doors stand open, a figure detaches itself from the shadow of the archway.

It is a man. He walks with a stride that eats the distance, purposeful and terrifyingly familiar. He is not wearing the spectral gray of the dead. He is vibrant, a slash of color against the stone.

My breath catches, freezing in my lungs.

Lachlan Sutherland runs.

He does not glide. He does not shimmer or fade in the morning mist. He hammers against the earth, his boots tearing up divots of turf, the sound of his impact a heavy, rhythmic thudding that vibrates through the soles of my bare feet.

White plumes of vapor tear from his lips with every breath. He is a furnace in the gray morning. He is a biological fact.

I cannot move. I stand rooted in the wet grass, my hands hovering at my sides, watching the impossible rushing toward me. He wears the plaid of his house—dark green and navy, the colors saturated and rich—wrapped over a linen shirt that is stained with the sweat of his exertion.

He collides with me.

There is no passing through, no icy chill of the void. There is only the hard, bruising shock of matter meeting matter.

His arms wrap around me, lifting me off the ground, crushing the air from my ribs. He is solid rock. He is heat. He smells of horse and leather and the faint, sweet scent of heather smoke.

"Isla," he chokes out, burying his face in the crook of my neck.

His beard scratches my skin—rough, abrasive, wonderful. The sensation is so sharp, so utterly devoid of the numbing indistinctness of the shadow realm, that a sob rips itself from my throat.

I cling to him. My fingers dig into the wool of his plaid, feeling the lanolin and the coarse weave. I slide my hands up to grip the nape of his neck, tangling my fingers in his hair. It is damp, thick, real.

He drops me to my feet but refuses to let go. He pulls back just enough to frame my face in his hands. His palms are calloused, warm and rough against my cheeks. His eyes—that piercing, impossible blue—scan every inch of me, frantic and devouring. He touches my brow, my nose, my lips, as if checking for cracks in the porcelain.

"Yer here," he breathes, his voice rough with grit. "Warm. Yer warm."

I press my palm flat against his chest. beneath the linen and the wool and the muscle, I feel it.

Thud... thud... thud.

A heart. A strong, stubborn, beating heart driving blood through veins that should be dust.

"Are we dead?" I whisper. The words feel jagged in my throat. "Is this... is this the end?"

"We are together," he answers, and the conviction in his tone anchors the spinning world. He pulls me back against him, wrapping his arms around my shoulders, shielding me from the vastness of the sky. "That is all that matters. If it is death, then death is mercy. If it is life..." He shudders against me. "Then it is a miracle."

I bury my face in his chest, inhaling him. The tears come then—hot, scalding things that soak into his shirt. I weep for the dungeon. I weep for the tower. I weep for the four hundred years of cold silence.

Lachlan holds me through the storm. He rocks me slightly, murmuring my name into my hair, his own body trembling with the aftershocks of our war.

I pull away, panic spiking in my gut. My hands fly to his torso, frantically tearing at the folds of his plaid, searching for the wound. I need to see the scar. I need to see the ruin Hamish made of him.

"Show me," I gasp, my fingers fumbling with the fabric.

He lets me. He stands still as I push the heavy wool aside and lift the hem of his shirt.

There is nothing.

The skin over his ribs is smooth, tanned, unbroken. The jagged, puckered ridge of white flesh that marked the killing blow—the mark I felt in the dream-meadow, the mark that defined his ghost—is erased. The history of violence has been rewritten.

I trace the spot where the sword went in. My fingertips brush warm skin, feeling the steady rise and fall of his breathing.

"Gone," I whisper.

"He took nothing with him," Lachlan says softly, covering my hand with his own and pressing it tighter against his side. "And he left nothing behind."

The world seems to exhale around us. The strange, vibrating blur at the edge of my vision steadies. The colors of the grass and the stone deepen, settling into a reality that feels less like a painting and more like a home. The wind picks up, ruffling my hair, carrying the bite of the approaching winter, but it doesn't frighten me. It feels like a promise.

We stand there, two survivors washed up on the shore of a new timeline, trembling in the quiet morning.

"We have a chance," I say, looking up at him. The realization is terrifying. "Lachlan, we have time."

He smiles, and it is the smile of the man who courted me by the river, free of the shadow's weight. "Aye, mo chridhe. We have all the time in the world."

"Come," he says.

He takes my hand. His fingers lace through mine, a simple, intimate geometry that we have been denied for centuries. His grip is firm, dry, real.

We walk toward the castle. The grass gives way to cobblestones, the smooth, river-rounded rocks pressing into the soles of my bare feet. Every step is a reclamation. Every breath is a defiance of the grave.

But as the shadow of the gatehouse falls over us, I falter.

The temperature drops in the shade of the archway. My eyes are drawn upward, against my will, to the tower that looms on the eastern flank. I know the height of it. I know the velocity of a body falling from that parapet. I know the sound bone makes when it meets stone.

I stop. The phantom sensation of the impact jars my spine, a ghost of pain that lingers in the marrow. I can't breathe. The courtyard isn't a home; it's a crime scene.

"Fi."

Lachlan stops. He doesn't pull me. He turns, his body blocking the view of the tower, filling my field of vision with the safety of his presence.

"It is just stone," he says, his voice low and rough, like gravel rolling in the tide. "It has no teeth. Not anymore."

"I died here," I whisper. The words feel like stones in my mouth. "We both died here, over and over."

"And now we live here," he insists. He squeezes my hand, the pressure grounding me, pulling me out of the memory loop. "We washed the blood away, Isla. We burned the hate out of the walls. This is not Hamish's prison. It is our home. No more shadows between us."

I look at him. He is right. The darkness that used to bleed from the mortar is gone. The heavy, suffocating dread that haunted my research trips—the creeping horror that watched from the corners—has evaporated. The castle is just a building. A shell waiting to be filled.

I take a breath. It is shaky, but it fills my lungs. "Okay."

We step across the threshold.

The change is instantaneous. The moment my foot hits the flagstones of the inner ward, the castle seems to wake up. It doesn't groan or shudder; it hums. A subtle vibration runs through the floor, a frequency of welcome.

Torches in iron sconces line the corridor leading to the main keep. They are not lit, yet the hallway feels warm, bathed in a golden ambient light that seems to emanate from the rock itself. The air smells of beeswax and fresh rushes, of baking bread and dried herbs—the scent of Isla's life, stripped of the rot.

We walk deeper. The reality of the place solidifies with every yard we cover. The walls look less like a rendering and more like granite that has withstood the Atlantic gales. The dust motes dancing in the shafts of light are not gray ash, but golden pollen.

It feels ancient, heavy with history, yet newborn. A paradox built for two.

Lachlan pushes open the heavy oak doors to the Great Hall. They swing inward on silent hinges, revealing the cavernous space where we faced the memory of the wedding feast.

But the rotting food is gone. The tattered, bleeding banners are gone. The darkness is banished.

Morning light streams through the high clerestory windows. It cuts through the dusty air in solid, architectural beams, painting the flagstone floor in pools of brilliant white. The dust motes drift lazily, peaceful and slow.

The hall is empty, vast, and silent. But it is a silence of peace, not abandonment. It is a blank page.

Lachlan leads me into the center of the room, into the largest pool of light. He turns to me, and the sun catches the hazel flecks in his blue eyes, turning them to gold. He looks like a king who has finally put down his sword.

"We made it," he whispers, as if he still can't quite believe the silence.

I look down at our joined hands. My pale skin against his weathered, scarred knuckles. We are casting a shadow on the floor—a single, long silhouette that stretches out behind us.

"The curse is broken," I say.

I lift his hand to my lips and kiss the knuckles, tasting the salt of his skin.

"We are just us," he answers.

We stand there in the quiet hall, bathed in the unforgiving, beautiful light of the morning, holding on to the only thing that survived the dark.

Also by Laci Mae Wyld

I Do...Hate You

In the heart of a city ruled by crime, survival means embracing the darkness within.

Meli Vasquez, a fierce and clever young woman, has long been confined to a life of servitude within the walls of a notorious crime family's stronghold. When the ruthless and feared Corbin Argyros, known as "The Executor " for his lethal efficiency, unexpectedly claims her as his bride to fulfill an ancient family decree, Meli is thrust into a world of opulence, danger, and power beyond her wildest dreams.

To Corbin, Meli's defiance is an intriguing challenge, her sharp wit a valuable asset. But to Meli, he is nothing more than a monstrous captor with haunted eyes and hands that stoke a dangerous fire within her. Their fiery clashes soon give way to forbidden passion, blurring the lines between loathing and longing.

In Corbin's brutal world, where compassion is weakness and love is a liability, Meli and Corbin realize that their unlikely partnership may be their most potent weapon yet. As betrayals mount, they must stand together against all who seek to tear them apart.

Content Warning: Contains explicit language and sexual scenes, including light choking, oral sex, manual stimulation, sexual violence, murder, kidnapping, torture, physical and sexual abuse, and themes of parental death.

Mark Me

35-year-old Mica Greer harbors a talent for intricate designs and a shield against emotional entanglements. But when Nyah Summers, with her haunting past and hidden pain, walks into his life, the flames of change flicker to life.

In a bold stand against Nyah's abusive past, Mica's defiance sets off a spark that neither of them can ignore. Drawn together by shared scars and unspoken desires, their connection deepens as they navigate the shadows of their histories.

Offering Nyah refuge within his sanctuary and a role in his creative world, Mica finds himself unraveling the layers of his own defenses. As their bond intensifies from friendship to something more, they must confront the looming threat of Nyah's vindictive ex-lover.

Experience a tale where redemption emerges from chaos, and the brightest flames are forged from the depths of darkness.

Good Girl To Goddess: Dancing with Desire

Cast aside on her birthday for not fitting in a mold, Elara James sheds her timid skin and overnight becomes a bold enchantress. Guided by her loyal confidante, she swaps modest clothing for daring outfits and quiet behavior for a fearless, take-no-prisoners attitude.

For six months, Elara indulges in fleeting affairs and casual flings, vowing to avoid emotional entanglements to protect her heart. One golden rule guides her nights: never stay until dawn.

Then enters Ryker Davis—confident, commanding, and undeniably captivating. In the heat of passion, he awakens her submission to his every whim. But beyond the bedroom, he reveals a tenderness that challenges the barriers guarding her heart.

As her former lover seeks reconciliation and her closest friend leaves town, Elara faces her deepest fears alone. Will she embrace the vulnerability that comes with true desire, or retreat into the safety of emotional distance?

Buried With You

A decade since the night they buried a dark secret in the shadows of the woods, Harper Lane is thrust back into the chilling embrace of Ash Pines, her reluctant return shrouded in impending doom. With her father's life waning and her past haunting her every step, she must face not only the memories she fled but also the man she once abandoned.

Eric Ransom harbours a festering wound from that fateful night—a wound reopened when Harper arrives at his garage, her presence reigniting a dangerous flame long thought extinguished. Amidst whispered threats in the dead of night and ominous messages left at the desolate grave site, they find themselves ensnared in a sinister game of retribution.

As they unravel a sinister web of deceit and betrayal, they realise their victim was no ordinary stranger. With allegiances crumbling and shadows closing in, Harper and Eric must unite to unmask their relentless stalker before they become mere pawns in a deadly chess match.

In a town where alliances shift like whispers in the wind and buried secrets claw their way to the surface, Harper and Eric are faced with an impossible choice—embrace the flames of passion reigniting between them as a beacon of hope or succumb to the darkness that threatens to consume them whole.

Amidst looming threats and betrayals lurking within familiar faces, Harper and Eric must navigate treacherous waters to uncover the truth behind their shared past. Will they emerge unscathed from the shadows of their sins, or will they be swallowed whole by the echoes of the grave that refuse to stay silent?

Vex Me: The Widow Queen

First Book in Vex Me Series: In a world teeming with danger and deceit, Kiera Moore's life takes a treacherous turn when her husband's death leaves her drowning in both grief and debt. Enter the enigmatic figure of Hudson Vex, a man shrouded in mystery and power, who offers Kiera a chilling deal she can't refuse - one night of boundless pleasure in exchange for erasing her late husband's debts and safeguarding her daughter.

As Kiera navigates the treacherous underworld of crime and betrayal, she embraces her transformation into the formidable "Widow Queen," unearthing her own strength and resilience. With Vex by her side, their twisted bond blurs the lines between love and manipulation as they build an empire fuelled by fear and respect.

But when her daughter falls prey to a ruthless cartel, Kiera must unleash her newfound ferocity to save her child, even if it means embracing the darkness within herself. As alliances shift and tensions rise, Kiera and Hudson find themselves entangled in a dangerous dance of passion and manipulation where love and vengeance blur into one.

Can Kiera navigate this treacherous path to reclaim her life, or will she succumb to the seductive allure of power and corruption? Prepare for a gripping tale of obsession, danger, and moral ambiguity in "The Widow Queen," where the line between hero and villain blurs beneath the intoxicating allure of the underworld's most dangerous game.

Fiery Fate (Vex Me: Book 2)

What began as a desperate bid for survival twists into a mesmerising metamorphosis. Immersed in Vex's clandestine world, Kiera unearths a seductive allure in the very violence that shattered her existence. Each brutal lesson and fiery encounter propels the grieving widow towards an unsettling evolution—a queen reborn amidst the chaos.

As an old nemesis resurfaces from Vex's past, Evelyn is forced to confront her escalating duality. With empires crumbling and blood staining her path, she teeters on the precipice between saviour and savage. Her daughter's fate hangs by a thread, and the boundaries between prey and predator blur into oblivion.

In this intoxicating thriller of power and fixation, Kiera will learn that certain debts demand payment in blood—and some reigns can only be forged in flames.

The Heir Will Not Turn (Vex Me: Book 3)

When Sophie is abducted by Falcom, the shadowy puppet masters steering global crime, Kiera and Hudson unleash their full power to rescue her. Their bond—fierce, primal, and unshakeable—drives a perilous chase across continents as they rally allies from the depths of their clandestine Shadow organisation. Clues lead through a web of brutal confrontations, where every victory costs blood and all threats point back to Sophie's fate.

As Falcom tightens its grip, the lovers push past fear toward a final, fortified base where extraction erupts into a desperate war. A heart-stopping gamble ends in a brutal revelation: Sophie's fate hinges on a line between loyalty and danger that could cost them everything. Love for Sophie becomes resolve as Kiera and Hudson vow to crush Falcom, harnessing every ally, every skill, every daring instinct to save the girl who has always been their guiding light—and to claim their own, hard-won happiness in the process.

Awakenings: Legacy of Shadow and Light

From the ashes of tragedy, her fate began to unfold...

Unveiled to a destiny she never fathomed, Suri Taylor emerges from the ruins of her shattered life. Taken captive by the malevolent Lyle Shawcross, she unearths a startling revelation: she is an immortal being bearing dormant powers, safeguarded to shield her from an age-old conflict.

Rescued by enigmatic saviours emanating celestial light, Suri is propelled into a clandestine realm where immortal entities coexist with mortals. As she hones her supernatural gifts under the tutelage of the guardian Drake Tudor, a rare bond sparks between them—a glimmering aura branding them as uniquely united.

Yet Lyle refuses to relinquish his coveted prize without a fight. Embracing her regal lineage and electing her allegiance in the immortal strife, adversaries encroach from every angle. With treachery lurking in the recesses and her extraordinary abilities still unfolding, Suri must discern whom to confide in while navigating her emotions for Drake and bearing the burden of her newfound legacy.

In a realm where luminescent gazes unveil true motives and everlasting existence exacts a dire toll, Suri's emergence may either reconcile ancient rifts or cast both worlds into eternal obscurity.

Content warning: Book contains scenes of sexual abuse and violence

Texting Fate

In the glittering world of Hollywood, he's the enigmatic heartthrob whose every move makes headlines. She's a refreshingly unfiltered woman who just wants to survive an epic Tinder disaster. But when a chance encounter lures them into a whirlwind of mistaken identities and electric chemistry, their lives are about to collide in the most unexpected way.

When a sassy text message meant for a Tinder date gone wrong lands in the hands of A-list actor Charlie Benton, it sparks a digital dance of wit and warmth with a mystery woman known only as Bee. Little do they know that amidst the virtual sparks lies the beginning of an uncharted romance that transcends fame and fortune.

As their playful banter deepens into a magnetic pull, Charlie and Bee find themselves entangled in a hot and steamy connection. But can they navigate the treacherous waters of stardom's spotlight without losing themselves in its glare? With paparazzi lurking and fans clamouring for every detail, their connection is put to the ultimate test.

Amidst the chaos of Hollywood whispers, Charlie and Bee search for authenticity in a world defined by illusions, and they must choose: embrace the unpredictable journey of love despite the odds or retreat to the safety of their separate worlds. Will their hearts find solace in each other's embrace, or will fame's cruel glare shatter their fairy tale dreams?

Haunted Memories of a Broken Girl

Haunted by visions of a violent crime, Kelly's melodic voice offers solace amidst the chaos of her past. Lawyer Michael Lawson is captivated by her singing, his own memories stirred by her haunting presence. When he rescues her from danger, a chilling realisation sets in - Kelly bears an uncanny resemblance to a long-lost childhood friend's deceased wife.

As their connection deepens, Kelly's fragmented past unravels. Each revelation brings them closer to a shocking reality: Kelly is Helayna Cook, the missing daughter of arms tycoon Richard Cook.

Navigating the treacherous waters of truth and deception, their unexpected romance blossoms. But sinister forces lurk in the shadows, determined to keep buried what should never see the light of day. Threats loom and loyalties are tested as Kelly and Michael find themselves ensnared in a dangerous game of obsession and vengeance.

To survive, they must confront the ghosts of their pasts and unearth the secrets shrouding Kelly's mother's untimely demise - before a malevolent force silences them forever.

You Will See Me

When the lifeless body of Louise Mansfield is found on the bustling Chicago River Walk, seasoned detective Samuel Barron is thrust into a macabre investigation that unravels a web of dark secrets and chilling connections. Louise, daughter of the influential Senator James Mansfield, had been striving to escape her turbulent past as an exotic dancer and reconcile with her powerful father before she became the target of a sadistic killer's wrath.

As Samuel delves deeper into the case, he uncovers a sinister pattern linking Louise to five other tormented women, all tied to the charismatic senator. The discovery hints at a twisted serial killer fixated on beautiful victims associated with the prominent politician. The tension escalates when the primary suspect meets a gruesome demise in a manner mirroring the previous murders, pushing Samuel to confront a ruthless and calculating murderer with a disturbing agenda.

The investigation takes an alarming turn when someone they least expected, is driven by a volatile obsession to protect the Senator's reputation, escalating their vendetta by targeting the Mansfield family. In a heart-pounding race against time, Samuel finds himself in a deadly showdown with the killer, unearthing the depths of their malevolent rage. Their harrowing clash culminates in an intense confrontation of wits and wills, revealing a tapestry of hidden truths, envy, and intricate familial bonds.

Haunted by the specter of this chilling case and facing a new wave of brutal crimes, Samuel realises that history has a way of resurfacing when least expected. To thwart the cycle of violence and deceit, he must confront his own demons and navigate through treacherous waters to prevent further tragedy. In this riveting tale of suspense and redemption, Samuel grapples with the enduring legacy of past sins in his relentless quest for justice amid shadows that refuse to fade.

Betrayal of Blood

In a whirlwind of betrayal, Sarsha Mitchell's once-promising future implodes when she catches her fiancé, James, entangled with her very own sister. Reeling from the heartbreak, Sarsha takes flight, leaving the shards of her shattered dreams behind. With her picture-perfect life in ruins, she seeks solace on an impromptu getaway to their abandoned honeymoon destination with her loyal confidante, Jess.

From the sun-kissed shores of Perth to the dazzling allure of the Gold Coast, Sarsha attempts to outrun her anguish amidst carefree escapades and electrifying nights out. Just as the shadows of her past threaten to engulf her present, a chance encounter at a club propels Sarsha into an unexpected charade with a mysterious stranger named Riley.

As sparks ignite between Sarsha and Riley during their fabricated romance, healing begins to seep into her wounded soul. However, upon their return to Melbourne, old wounds are ripped open anew as James refuses to relinquish his hold on her heart while envious desires stir chaos within her own family.

Supported by Riley's unwavering presence and unwavering gallantry, Sarsha finds the courage to confront the toxicity suffusing her familial bonds. Yet just as hope blossoms for a brighter tomorrow, a cruel act of revenge orchestrated by James and Megan threatens to shatter everything they hold dear.

In a race against time and treachery, Sarsha stands vigil by Riley's bedside, clinging to hope amidst the turmoil. Together, they uncover the depths of deceit woven by those she once trusted most. With Riley's love paving the way towards redemption and renewal, Sarsha severs the ties that bind her to darkness and steps boldly into a future brimming with promise

From Hatred to Heat

When fate entwines two souls marked by enmity, can they rewrite their story before the darkness consumes them both?

Within the walls of Hidden Chapters Bookstore, Jetta Kinsley revels in the sanctuary she's created with her partner-in-crime, Brandi. Embracing the solitary bliss of her life, Jetta's world is upended when Brandi's heart veers off course to Owen Cooper, leading Jetta down a path she never wished to tread again. Standing before her is Ethan Cole, the ghost of her past whose cruel grip once shattered her world and scattered the pieces.

Bound by loyalty to their friends, Jetta and Ethan forge a fragile alliance. Buried beneath their animosity smolders an undeniable attraction, stirring emotions neither thought possible. When danger lurks in the shadows of a nightclub, Ethan emerges as Jetta's fierce protector, unveiling a side she never dared to imagine.

From Broken Roads to Healing Hearts

When Natalie's car breaks down on a secluded Tasmanian road, little does she know it will lead her to a ruggedly handsome stranger named Kai and his highland cow farm. Far from the city bustle, Natalie and Kai find themselves tangled in a web of past heartbreaks and hidden scars.

Amidst the picturesque countryside, they form an unexpected bond, discovering solace and passion in each other's arms under the starlit sky. But as secrets unravel and old flames flicker back to life, they must confront their demons together or risk losing everything they've found.

A Dark Descent into Chaos

Caught in the sinister grip of Sydney's underworld, at just 23, she becomes Diego's pawn, a mere facade of a girlfriend to the heartless crime lord. Imprisoned in opulence at Diego's Rose Bay mansion with no way out, Mila endures a life of torment and manipulation. Joe Sullivan is no stranger to shadows and secrets. With a steely gaze that betrays his hidden motives, he infiltrates Diego's inner circle on a covert mission for the authorities. Witnessing Diego's brutal nature firsthand, Joe risks everything to shield Mila from the savagery that lurks within their glamorous facade.

Bound by a dangerous game of deception and desire, Mila and Joe must join forces to uncover the truth amidst a battlefield of power-hungry adversaries. As their partnership deepens, forbidden attraction ignites, threatening to consume them both. With danger closing in and lives hanging in the balance, Joe is determined to protect Mila at any cost, even if it means forsaking everything he holds dear.

In a whirlwind of perilous escapades, high-stakes confrontations, Mila and Joe must navigate a treacherous path towards freedom and justice. But in a world where loyalties shift like shadows and love teeters on the edge of ruin, will they emerge unscathed from the dark empire they're entwined in?

Friend or Foe weaves a tale of passion, loyalty, and sacrifice against the backdrop of Sydney's underworld glamour and danger. In a battle where survival could mean surrendering to love's embrace, will Mila and Joe triumph over the sinister forces that seek to tear them apart?

When We Close Our Eyes

After tragedy strands Casey and Kirk in separate worlds of longing, an unlikely encounter entwines them in a slow dance toward solace. Their love, a tender construction of two battered hearts, finds a tenuous rhythm until a specter from Kirk's past tears through the fragile façade. Obsessed and ruthless, Layla—his ex-wife—emerges from shadow with a plan to reclaim what she believes is hers. As threats mount, Casey and Kirk must fight not only for their love but for their lives, finding strength in their scars and shelter in each other.

Lucky in Love and Bullets

Kitty and Peter are madly in love. Kitty, a successful hair stylist, and Peter, a partner in a prestigious law firm, celebrate a lavish wedding in Hawaii. Their perfect day turns tragic when a gunman appears. Kitty is shot in the head. She regains consciousness in the hospital with no memory of Peter, though she recalls everything else. Kitty struggles to reconnect with Peter, who moves into a separate bedroom. Suspecting he is hiding something, she returns to work and meets Fynn, a handsome new client.

Kitty and Fynn find themselves in dangerous territory with criminals as they try to uncover the truth about why she was shot on her wedding day, with each discovery they see how involved Peter was with the wrong kind of people

Twisted Obsession

In the shadows of a seemingly perfect life, Anya Willows discovers that the past she thought she'd escaped is about to collide with her present in the most terrifying way imaginable. After years of uncertainty, Anya finally finds stability with a loving boyfriend, a loyal best friend, and a newfound relationship with the father she never knew. But when tragedy strikes and her world begins to crumble, Anya finds herself at the centre of a twisted web of obsession, deceit, and murder. As the body count rises and the lines between friend and foe blur, Anya must confront a darkness that has been stalking her since childhood. With each shocking revelation, she's forced to question everything and everyone she thought she knew. Who can she trust when the very foundations of her life prove to be built on lies? In this heart-pounding psychological thriller, love becomes a weapon, trust becomes a liability, and the truth becomes the most dangerous thing of all.

www.ingramcontent.com/pod-product-compliance
Lightning Source LLC
LaVergne TN
LVHW050924080826
845145LV00001B/197

* 9 7 8 1 7 6 4 5 1 6 8 0 8 *